Red Garters, Snow and

Mistletoe

Volume Two

Red Garters, Snow and Mistletoe

Volume Two

By

Melinda Barron, Mia Jae, Demi Alex and
Catrina Calloway

Resplendence Publishing, LLC
http://www.resplendencepublishing.com

Resplendence Publishing, LLC
P.O. Box 992
Edgewater, Florida, 32132

Red Garters, Snow and Mistletoe: Volume Two

Edited by Tiffany Mason, Wendy Williams and Jessica Berry

Cover art by Rika Singh

Print format ISBN: 978-1-60735-092-7

Suggested Retail Price: $15.99

Print release: November 2009

Bound by Tinsel

By Melinda Barron

For CAS, who continues to inspire me in everything I do.

Thanks to Jo for her advice on the legal field. Any mistakes are mine and not hers. Thanks also to Tiff, who suggested the title and, as always, helped me brainstorm ideas.

Table of Contents

Chapter One

"Let's hope this one is better than the last one." Burke Gordon lounged back in his chair, put his feet on the coffee table and loosened his tie. It had been a long day and he wasn't really looking forward to the coming phone call, despite the fact he and his friends were auditioning phone sex operators.

You'd think three men would be thrilled at the idea of listening to a woman moan and groan. Instead they were all praying for this to be over as soon as possible.

"Anything was better than the last one." Caleb Martin held up a sheet of paper. "Her tag line was 'let me make you *cum*.' I think she should change it to 'let me make you *leave*.'"

The third member of their party, Jake Martin, snorted. "In her defense I think she was just trying too hard. I think she could do just fine, if she wasn't so nervous. Maybe we shouldn't let this one know there are three of us in the room."

Burke reached for the tumbler of scotch on the nearby table. "That's the point, isn't it? Amber asked us to find a phone sex operator who could help her play a joke on her husband. If said operator freezes up when she realizes there is more than one person listening to her, then she's not the woman for the job."

There was a round of assent from his friends and Burke took a healthy swig of his drink. It had been a long day, between depositions and making ready for court tomorrow. His assistant had been sick part of the afternoon, too, and he'd had to deal with the records room on gathering a few last minute details, something he hadn't enjoyed very much. Add to that the fact it was the Christmas season and things were definitely on fire. He was a last minute shopper, waiting to buy presents until the weeks before Christmas, which meant he had a little less than a week to find something for his parents, his three sisters, two brothers-in-law and their respective children.

Despite the looming deadline, when he knew he should be at the stores, he sat at Caleb's house, waiting to see if a phone sex operator could get him hard. The last one had come close, until she started giggling. Of course her near victory could come from the fact that he hadn't been laid for eight months, not since he and Bethany had broken up.

Hopefully this one would do a better job and he'd leave here with the memory of her voice in his ear while he jacked off later tonight.

"You take the lead, Caleb," Jake said, pushing up the footrest in his chair. "Make sure you explain to her what we're doing."

"I'm not an idiot." Caleb held up a sheet of paper. "I got this ad out of the same magazine. If this one doesn't work, I'm thinking it's a three strikes and the paper ads are out, then we should try the Internet and see what we get. Do you guys agree with me?"

Burke and Jake both nodded and Caleb picked up the phone. He dialed the number, then put his hand over the mouthpiece. "This one's a call back service, so it may take a while for Ms. Serendipity to get back to us."

"I got nothing better to do," Jake said. "What about you, Burke?"

"Are you kidding me? I haven't bought one present for my family, and I'm due in court tomorrow on the Thompson divorce. What do you think?"

"Man that sucks, getting divorced at Christmas." Jake wrinkled his nose in disgust. "Couldn't you talk your client into postponing it until after New Year's?"

The idea of Max Thompson delaying his divorce made Burke snort. "Since he's planning on getting married New Year's Eve to his new chippy, I would say that's a big fat no."

"What a piece of work," Jake replied. "That sucks."

Burke couldn't agree with him more. But Max Thompson was a major player in San Diego, and he brought lots of money into the firm of White, Watson and Wilson, which Burke hoped would soon be White, Watson, Wilson and Gordon. If he helped Thompson hold on to a great deal of Thompson's money tomorrow, he would be one step closer to partner. And with White and Watson so close to retirement, that meant he was really close to the top, something that thrilled him to no end.

He took another sip of scotch and listened to Caleb provide the operator with a credit card number, birth dates to verify the ages of the men in the room, and finally, a call back number. After he hung up the phone, Caleb picked up his own drink.

"Ms. Serendipity should call us back within the hour."

"You seem rather pleased with yourself," Burke said, finishing off his drink. He went to the bar and refilled his glass. That would be his last one of the night. They had Chinese food on its way, set to be delivered within the hour. He would probably be home around ten, or eleven, far too late for a night before court, but it couldn't be helped.

This was their last "audition." Or at least he hoped it was; he wanted karma to work in their favor tonight and make this sex operator the one who could agree to Amber's gift. Not that Burke thought it was much of a joke. He understood Amber's reasoning, since her husband, Eddie, celebrated his birthday on Christmas it made it hard to find the proper present. She said Eddie had told her not to buy a gift this year but to surprise him with something special.

That "something" was a call from a phone sex operator in the middle of a party, one that Eddie couldn't walk out of for fear of upsetting his bosses, who were also Burke's bosses.

"I want to see his reaction," she'd said when she'd explained the idea. "He told me once that he thought it would be hot to have me get him hard in the middle of a party. But I've tweaked it a little. I want the sex worker to do it while I watch. That will make it perfect."

Burke, Caleb and Jake had been reluctant at first, thinking that the stunt could go wrong, and get Eddie in a heap of trouble. Then they'd decided that, since it would be done at a party and Eddie was a jokester, he would get a kick out of it. They'd agreed to try-out the services, then instruct the woman they picked on what they wanted.

The only problem, according to Burke's viewpoint, was that he hadn't thought finding a decent operator would be so difficult. The first one had turned them down flat, saying that, for all she knew, they could be trying to get someone fired. The second one had thought it would be fun. Then she'd giggled and laughed while trying to give Caleb a virtual blowjob.

Hopefully Ms. Serendipity would be the ultimate and would prove that the third time's a charm.

The doorbell rang and Caleb jumped up, pulling out his wallet. He held out his hand and Burke and Jake placed twenty-dollar bills in his palm before he headed toward the door. He'd just opened it when the phone rang.

"Damn," Jake said, reaching for the receiver. "The number's blocked, so I guess this is our girl. She's quick."

"Hello." Jake nodded, then licked his lips and mouthed the words, "It's her."

"Put her on speaker," Caleb said, setting the bags of food on the coffee table. "That way we can explain things. Burke, take first chair. Consider it practice for tomorrow."

Burke snorted out a laugh. "Like I need practice. But I'll be happy to talk to our new friend."

Jake pressed the speaker button and a deep-throated, very sex voice floated out of the speaker. "Hello, gentlemen. I understand we're a group tonight. How fun to have a little jerk circle. Are you sitting close enough to give each other a helping hand?"

Burke cleared his throat. "We're not helping each other out, Ms. Serendipity." He quickly explained about his friends and the joke, changing their names to Jack and Jill. "Jill asked us to pick out a nice sensual voice for this joke. Are you up for the challenge?"

The sexy laugh made his cock twitch. "Most definitely. I'm up for anything."

The three of them exchanged pleased looks, then Burke hunched forward, putting his elbows on his knees. "Good. For the purpose of this little exercise I'll be X, and my friends will be Y and Z."

"Very creative, Mr. X." Her tone was even and Burke wondered if she was being sarcastic. Then he decided he didn't care when she started talking again. "What would you like me to do? Do you just want to hear my voice? Or do you want blowjobs? Hand jobs? Fucking? Pussy, or back door?"

Burke moaned softly, hoping his friends didn't notice. They exchanged nods, excitement evident on all their faces. Damn, this woman was turning him on already, and she was doing the same to Caleb and Jake. She was perfect. "Are you naked?"

"Would you like me to be?"

"Yes," Caleb said. "This is Y. Get naked, and get on your knees."

"My pleasure, Mr. Y." The rustling of clothes filtered over the phone line and Burke wondered if the woman was really getting undressed. "Mr. Z, are you going to play, too? Or are you a virtual voyeur tonight?"

"Oh I'm going to play," Jake said. "How big are your boobs?"

Burke fought back a laugh. Jake always had been a tit man.

"Big enough to handle your cock." Her voice was low and throaty, and Burke closed his eyes, imagining a large breasted woman tweaking her nipples. "I'll lie down on my back and we'll spread some oil between them, then you can play slip and slide with your dick until your give me the perfect gift."

"Holy fuck," Jake said. "Bring it on, baby."

Definitely bring it on, Burke thought, leaning back. There was a momentary silence, and he was sure she was waiting for instructions besides bring it on. "Go on. Tell us how you're going to handle the three of us at once."

"Well, I have three holes, Mr. X: my warm mouth, my wet pussy, and my tight ass. Shall I assign places, or would you like to do that?"

Burke looked at his friends, who both nodded at him. "You tell us, Ms. Serendipity. And please be very graphic."

There was the slightest of pauses, and then the sexy voice returned. "Very well. Mr. Z, I know you favor breasts, but for a threesome it's not very doable to have you fuck my tits. However, I'm sure your hot, randy cock will fit perfectly in my mouth. I will suck you deep, letting my tongue lap over your balls when you're not in my mouth. I can feel you in there already, pulsing, ready to shoot your load down my throat. Would you like that? I'd swallow it all, and beg for more. Will you give me more? And more? And more?"

"Oh holy fuck." Jake's hands went to his cock. "I'll give you more than you can handle, honey."

Her lilting laugh made Burke's body stiffen even more. Damn this woman was hot. The soft laugh also made his eyebrows knit together just a little. Where had he heard that sound before? Sure, lots of women had low, deep voices. But this one seemed a little familiar.

Her next words pulled him right out of his musings.

"Don't be afraid to handle those lovely tools between your legs, darlings. It's quite normal, and I'm sure your friends are feeling the same need you are, Mr. Z. If your cock's not hard then I'm not doing my job right."

Her voice seemed to purr over the phone lines and Burke wanted to possess magical powers so he could zap the phone and make her appear in the living room, right in front of them. Then he'd get her down on her knees, all right. The only problem was he wasn't thinking about sharing with his two buddies.

"Oh, I'm hard," Jake replied, clearing his throat. His declaration made Burke stop daydreaming about Ms. Serendipity appearing before them. Burke could tell Jake was trying to keep his hands from her suggestion. Hell, he felt the same way.

"So I'm in your mouth. What about X and Y?"

"Well, let's start with Y, the shy, quiet one. You've said so little, Mr. Y, that something tells me you're fascinated by the idea of fucking me while your friends are doing the same thing. You're a less talk, more action sort of man, aren't you?"

"Damn straight." Caleb moved his hips and Burke could see the outline of his cock pressed against his trousers. "I'd like to watch you suck cock."

"Yes, the only bad part about it would be my mouth was full, and I couldn't cry out the pleasure I would feel as you slide your hard, thick prick inside my wet, welcoming walls. Oh, I could feel it now, stretching me, hitting all the right sports, sliding in and out, making my clit seize with pleasure as you stroked it. It feels so fucking good to have you inside me."

Burke concentrated more on Serendipity's than on her words. Her voice was deep and full of need, making him think that she was actually very, very aroused. Did she really want what she was talking about, or was it just an act? If they actually knew her and the three of them offered a night of passion, would she take it, or would she say, "I could never do that. That's just disgusting!'"

Finding a woman who would take on three men might be fascinating, Burke thought. He'd never tried anything like that, but it was a fantasy that stirred his blood.

"What about me?" Burke was surprised by gravelly his voice sounded.

"You? Why Mr. X, I've saved you for last. Where else is there for you to go but in my tight ass?" She licked her lips, the sound very audible over the phone line. "Mr. Y will slow down so you can enter me. I can feel your cock back there now, pressing for entrance against my puckered opening."

She was panting softly now and there was no mistaking the fact she was aroused. Was she playing with her pussy? Burke hoped so. The idea of her sitting there, her fingers dancing over her clit while she described how his prick would slide into her ass made him hotter than he'd been in years."

"Go on." Burke licked his own lips, then looked at Caleb. He'd moved a pillow onto his lap but there was no mistaking the fact he was jacking himself off, his eyes closed, his head leaning back against the chair. He glanced at Jake, who was doing the same thing, minus the pillow, his hand picking up speed with each word Serendipity spoke.

"Do you feel me opening around you, stretching to accommodate your hard dick in my naughtiest of places? Would you like to fuck me in the ass, Mr. X, while Mr. Y is in my pussy and Mr. Z in my mouth?"

"Yes." Burke growled out the word, his hands slowly undoing his belt buckle. He'd never jacked off in front of another man, but right now was the perfect time to start. Besides, they were both doing it and neither of them seemed to notice. His hands slipped inside his pants, his hard cock jumping at the touch.

He thought he might shoot off right on the spot.

"I can feel you inside me, all of you. Sliding in and out, rubbing my most intimate of spots, driving me absolutely insane with need. I want you all, need you all." Her panting had increased, and Burke grasped himself, stroking once, twice, three times. His balls tightened, ready to explode. There was just one thing he needed to ask.

"Can I come inside you? Can we all come inside you?" He grasped himself tighter and pumped.

"Yes, fuck yes, fill me, all of you, give it all to me! Now! I want all three of those hard cocks pounding into me." Cries of masculine fulfillment filled the air and Burke gasped as he realized that he was one of those voices.

He looked down to see the front of one of his best shirts, ruined. "Holy shit."

"No kidding," Caleb agreed. "I didn't expect that."

Burked glanced over at Jake, who sat with his eyes closed, his chest heaving with exertion.

"There's one more thing, Serendipity." Burke leaned toward the phone as if it were an extension of her, as if he could reach out and touch her. "Come for us; bring yourself to orgasm. I want to hear it."

"As you wish." Her breathy voice was full of need, and then the unmistakable sound of a vibrator turning on came over the line. Burke's eyebrows shot up as her soft moans filled the room. All three of them leaned toward the phone, listening intently to her soft cries of pleasure.

"Tell us what you're doing," Burke groaned. "Be graphic."

"I've got a vibrator on my clit, rubbing it gently."

"Describe it for me." Burke cleared his throat, "I mean, for us." He needed to remember there were other men in the room, too.

Her soft moan made his cock twitch, despite the fact he'd just shot off all over himself like a teenage boy.

"It's short, about three inches, just the right length to tickle my clit. It feels so good, moving it around, sending sweet tendrils of pleasure through me." She moaned again, and then there was another unmistakable sound: that of her licking the vibrator. "Tastes so good."

Burke thought he would come on the spot. Damn this woman was hot. "Put it back on your clit, you naughty girl." Burke didn't care that he'd taken over the call, and by his two friends' silences he didn't think they cared, either. They both watched the phone intently, almost as if it was a videoconference and they could see the phone sex operator getting herself off.

"Yes, sir." There was a soft giggle but it was nothing like the one from last night. This woman's sexy giggle sent chills of need snaking through his body. "Are you a Dom?"

"You'll do as I say, do you understand?"

"Yes, sir, Mr. X. Oh, I'm about to come." Her moans increased, and Burke smiled.

"Stop. Don't come yet." He wasn't exactly sure where that came from, since the idea of hearing her climax pressed foremost in his mind. But he wanted to drag this out. He was enjoying it way, *way* too much to let it end so quickly.

"But you said…" Her disappointment was obvious, but she obeyed him.

"Do you have another dildo?"

There was a short pause, and then a barely audible, "Yes."

"Get it. Right now."

He smiled as he heard her moving, and pictured her in the living room of her home. He'd heard that lots of sex operators worked from home. Ms. Serendipity was about to get a totally new experience, or at least he hoped it was.

Chapter Two

"Fallon! Did you just hear what I said?"

Fallon Nichols batted her eyes to try and clear her mind so she could focus on what was happening right now. She wasn't thinking about typing up transcripts, or keeping track of papers. She was thinking about Mr. X, and the fantastic orgasm she'd had last night at his command.

He'd turned the tables on her very neatly. She was the one who was supposed to talk dirty—was supposed to get her clients hard, and get them off. But Mr. X had gotten her wet, then instructed her exactly how long she could keep her dildo inside her, or keep the vibrator pressed against her clit.

After a wonderful half-hour of pleasuring herself, her body had started to rebel. It needed to come, and Fallon…no, not Fallon, Serendipity…had done what any red-blooded heterosexual woman would do. She'd begged Mr. X to let her come.

He'd refused at first, keeping her right on the edge, describing to her all the nasty things he wanted to do to her body. Finally he'd relented, issuing deep, dark commands for her release. When she'd climaxed it had been unlike anything she'd ever felt before. And the three men listening had whistled and clapped as she'd screamed for more, begging for their cocks. The memory of it her behavior, and the fantastic orgasm that still had her tingling, made her blush.

"Are you having a hot flash? You're a little young for that, aren't you? What are you, thirty? Thirty-one?"

"Screw you, Sally."

"You don't have to get huffy, I was just asking because you're all flushed." Sally picked up the folder on Fallon's desk. "Of course I guess that's because you're...you know."

"I'm what?" *Say it, just say it and I'll knock you into next week, I swear.* Sally shrugged and Fallon leaned back in her chair. "Go on, what were you going to say? That I'm fat?"

"Well, you are larger than the rest of us here. And this room can get sort of stuffy."

That little tidbit pushed her over the edge. She was still riding the waves from last night, and the last thing she needed was a stick figure trying to bring her down. "Did you know, Sally, that Marilyn Monroe wore a size twelve, and at times she wore a size sixteen? Do you think she was fat? Do you?"

"Of course not. She was Marilyn Monroe."

Fallon narrowed her eyes at her co-worker. "You're right, she was. And she lived in a time when women weren't afraid to be women, not flag poles who starve themselves to death and then have to buy fake tits."

"Ladies!" They both looked up to where their supervisor, Elaine Phelps, stood. The supervisor did not look happy. "Need I remind you this is a business, and as such has people coming and going? We have clients waiting for files while you two are acting like this is a schoolyard where a fight is about to take place. Get back to work before I suspend you both."

Sally flounced off without another word and Fallon mentally stuck her tongue out at her coworker. The court-reporting firm of Phelps and Jones was generally a great place to work and, despite what Sally said, there were several larger ladies down here. Sally didn't like Fallon because Fallon was better at their job.

More clients asked for her to work their cases and she generally got along with everyone in the office. If Sally knew her secret job as a phone sex entertainer she would broadcast it for all the office to hear, and then Fallon would be fired in record time.

She sat back down at her terminal and worked on the notes she'd been trying to concentrate on when Sally had interrupted her. If she'd screwed something up it would be her ass, and a criminal was liable to go free on a technicality.

Fallon prided herself on not missing one word from a transcript, and she wouldn't stop now, not because of Sally. She meticulously checked her printouts, then went back and rechecked them. Satisfied that everything was in order, she placed the finished product on Elaine's desk. The supervisor checked everything and gave it her final approval before it was given to anyone outside the firm.

A quick check of her watch showed that it was just after five. Quitting time for one job. The second one would start around eight, depending on who was on the schedule for this evening. Mr. X's next appointment, the joke being played on his friend, wasn't for another week, but he'd promised to call her this weekend to make sure everything was set. Fallon hoped he would be as randy then as he was last night.

She went to her desk and pulled out her PDA, the one she used only for her phone sex job. An email popped up on the screen and she checked the names, Chuck and Steve, two of her regulars, were scheduled for eight and nine. Looked like it was going to be a slow night.

Lots of times the two of them didn't even want to jack off. They wanted to talk about sports, or a problem they were facing at the office. When they were discussing issues they had, she knew they were changing things around so she wouldn't find out who they were, but they'd always kept the main part just truthful enough so she could help. She was pretty sure Chuck was a cop, and Steve was a stockbroker.

But she'd never asked either of them their professions, nor would she ever. That was their business and she didn't want to pry into it.

Thinking about that made her wonder what Mr. X did for a living. His authoritative voice and take-charge attitude could put him in several professions: a military office, a cop, or even a lawyer. She thought about last night and decided military was definitely at the top of her list.

She was just about to close out the PDA and collect her things to head home when her email program binged. She opened the file to see a new name on her list.

Mr. X had booked her from ten to one. Three hours didn't come cheap in her business. Her nipples hardened at the thought of another night of phone sex with the sexy Mr. X. She couldn't wait to see what he had in mind for this evening.

Chapter Three

"Sign here." Zoey, the paralegal, pushed a paper in front of Burke and he glanced at it, even though he'd already proofed it once this evening. He still had a few hours before his phone call with Serendipity, and he was excited about hearing her voice again, but that didn't mean he would rush through the paperwork he had to finish tonight.

He signed in all the appropriate places, then took the stack of papers Zoey handed him. He leafed through them and frowned. "Where's the Martin deposition. I wanted to look at that this evening."

"We haven't gotten it back yet," Zoey said, shrugging. "That was the one we had to hire out, remember?"

Oh yes, he remembered. The firm had several court reporters on staff, but when he'd done the Martin deposition everyone had been busy, and they'd had to hire an outside reporter. That had only been two days ago, true, but he'd expected to see the finished product of that meeting tonight.

"Call them, tell them we want it. Now."

"It's after five, Burke." Zoey headed toward the door. Of all the paralegals, she was the mouthiest, and he appreciated the fact she didn't take crap from him, or anyone else. "Besides, according to the contract we have with Phelps and Jones, they have until tomorrow to get us the file. You'll just have to cool your jets and wait for it."

She hurried through the door and Burke laughed. She was right. He would just have to wait. But he didn't know about cooling his heels. He glanced at his watch. Two hours and fifteen minutes to go.

The thought of Serendipity's sexy voice describing how she would suck his prick made him stiffen. He planned to get off at least twice tonight; once while she described sucking his cock, the other while she squirmed as he tied her up, then fucked her tight pussy. Or maybe he'd virtually give it to her up the ass again. She'd enjoyed the thought last night, that was for sure. He'd never heard a woman so thrilled about having a cock in her mouth, pussy and ass at the same time.

Tonight, though, it would be just the two of them. He didn't plan to rush, and the operator had told him that Serendipity only worked until one. He'd booked her tonight and tomorrow night, and then for the Christmas party.

By the time that happened, he planned to know every virtual inch of Serendipity's body. He would know what made her come, and what ideas made her scream the loudest. Then, if he were lucky, he'd convince her to go to her computer and turn on her webcam so he could watch her fuck herself with the dildo.

But he wouldn't try that tonight. It was too soon for that. First they'd play some more; and by the end of their time tonight, she would be panting from exertion, begging him to let her rest. And he would. Until tomorrow night. Then he would wear her out again, and love every minute of it.

* * * *

Fallon felt like she was rushing through her calls. As she'd suspected, neither of them wanted sex. Chuck was upset because his car was on its last legs, and Steve was upset because his mother was trying to fix him up with a woman he didn't care for. They'd spent their hours lamenting their woes and Fallon—rather Serendipity—listened and sympathized with them, all the while watching the clock and wondering when her hours with Mr. X would start.

To make up for the fact that she felt she'd been less than attentive, she docked their call time by half, charging them for thirty minutes instead of an hour. Both of them could use it, she thought, and they were regulars.

"Consider it a Christmas gift," she said as she typed the numbers into her computer and hit enter. Like her PDA, she had a computer she used only for this job. She had another computer she used for work, and a third that she used for play.

Her court reporting computer was never hooked to the Internet. If something happened and someone got hold of confidential files it would be the end of her career. For that very same reason she kept the computer she used for the phone sex records off-line. It was a very cheap model, but it did what it needed to do, which was just fine by her.

The phone rang and her heart raced as she looked at the time. Ten p.m. This would be Mr. X.

Her palms actually felt sweaty as she hit the connect button on her headset.

"Good evening, Mr. X."

"And to you, too, Serendipity. Strip."

Her heart caught in her throat and she tried to think of a proper comeback. She was never tongue tied with clients. That was one of the things she loved about this job. As Fallon, she was always a little nervous around men; could never think of the right thing to say.

But as Serendipity she always had a snappy come back, always knew the right thing to say to let her clients know she was happy they'd called.

"Mr. X, I…"

"Unless you're already, naked you're wasting precious time."

"I'm almost naked."

A deep rumble of pleasure came over the phone line. "Tell me what you're wearing, then."

That was more like it. This was the normal way to start a session. She settled back on the couch, toying with the ties of her short silk robe. "Not much. One little pull on a belt and I'd been totally bare."

"Then do it. Now."

Serendipity made a show of rustling the material of the robe so he would know she was stripping. When she was naked, she lay down on her bed, something she never did for clients. But Mr. X was different. None of the men who called had touched her as he had last night.

"Are you lying down?"

"I am." She laughed softly. "Would you like me to lead for a while? What are you wearing?"

"Later."

"Are you naked?" She wanted to know what he was wearing.

"Tell me about yourself."

Disappointment raced through her as he ignored her question. "Tsk, tsk, that's not allowed." She wished it were, though. She would tell him everything, since he made her wetter than any man ever had.

"You can trust me, Serendipity."

"Why, are you a doctor?" She licked her fingers, making sure she made plenty of noise. "Or do you just like to play doctor? Do I need to put my feet in the stirrups?"

The sound of a zipper going down made her smile. That answered one question. He wasn't naked. Yet.

"I like that idea, you naked on an exam table, your feet high in the air, your legs spread apart. Do you shave?"

Her fingers spread through her bare pussy lips. "Too bumpy. I wax, so it's nice and smooth for you."

"I like that." He was moving and she imagined him taking off his clothes. He was definitely a businessman, either a lawyer or a doctor, she decided. That meant he was probably wearing a suit. She imagined him carefully folding the pants and placing them across a chair. His cock would already be hard and ready for action.

"I'm going to tie you up tonight. Would you like that?"

Excitement raced through her. "Oh yes, I'd love it."

"Good. I'm going to use my tie. Put your hands behind your back."

She followed his instructions, even though he couldn't see her. Her nipples were rock hard and she imagined him watching her, then stroking her thigh before wrapping the tie in a figure eight around her wrists, tying it off so she couldn't get loose. It felt absolutely delicious.

"Good girl. Now kneel on the bed with your ass high in the air."

Serendipity followed his instructions, keeping her hands behind her back even though there was no tie on them. Part of the fantasy was doing exactly as he wanted. She gasped softly as she got into place and his deep moan made her shiver.

"Would you like to know what I'm thinking right now?"

"Sticking your dick inside me?"

"No." He said it so matter-of-factly that she sat up, her mouth hanging open. "You moved out of position, Serendipity. What a naughty girl you are. Get back in place."

"You've either planted a camera in my room or…"

"I'm very good at reading people." There was the sound of ice cubes clinking inside a glass and she licked her lips, imagining him standing naked in front of her, one hand wrapped around a half-full tumbler, the other grasping his cock. "For instance I know you haven't moved yet, although I specifically told you to get back into position."

She moved quickly, eager to obey him.

"Very nice." His voice was like velvet sliding over her bare back. "Now, what I was going to say was I was thinking about leaving you in that position, all tied up. But first I'd attach a spreader bare to your ankles, making it virtually impossible for you to move."

That idea made her juices flow more. Bondage had always been a fantasy of hers, one she'd never indulged in.

"What would you do, Mr. X, while I was tied up?"

There was a pregnant pause and she could hear his breathing, deep and even as he pondered his answer. "Various things. Walk around, get a good, long look at your beautiful body all trussed up for me. I might lie down so that your head was between my legs. Then I could jack off while you watched. Or I might mount you while you're in that position, virtually at my mercy. I could claim your pussy or your ass, depending on what struck my fancy at the moment I climbed on top of you."

"Oh yes." Serendipity's hand slipped down to her pussy, pushing through the wet folds. She moaned as she found her clit, teasing it gently.

"Did I give you permission for that?"

"No, I—" There was sharp sound of leather hitting wood and she jumped. "Oh my lord, what—"

"Someone needs a spanking. A nice hard one to remind her who's in charge."

Chapter Four

"Have you ever been spanked, Serendipity?"

"No." She was sitting back up now, her heart racing. This was a definite twist to the action, one that she hadn't expected. Bondage was one thing, spanking was another. Mr. X had not identified himself as a Dom, but it was obvious to her that, while he may not be a lifestyler, he definitely leaned in that direction.

She wanted to tell him there were ladies who specialized in what he wanted, submissives who worked for the company and knew all the right things to say and do to make a Dom happy. She wasn't one of them.

"Mr. X, I…I'm not submissive."

"I don't want you to be. A little bondage and a little spanking, it's all good. I don't want you to call me Master, or pledge your total obedience to me. I'd just like a little rough play tonight, kick it up a notch or two from last night. If you'd like to stop, though…"

He'd let the question trail off and Serendipity considered her choices. This was being done over the phone, and he had no clue where she lived. For all he knew she could be in Omaha. All that aside, though, this was definitely something she'd never tried before, and while it frightened her a little, it also appealed to her adventurous nature.

"No, I don't want to stop."

"Good." The leather cracked again. "Back in position, and don't forget your hands are tied and there's a spreader bar between your legs."

How could I ever forget that? Serendipity had learned long ago that playing along with the demands, or suggestions, of her phone sex partners helped her get into the mood, and it gave them greater pleasure.

She knelt into position, spreading her legs and clasping her hands behind her back, her face resting against the soft covers.

"Now, the belt was just to get your attention. Do I have it?"

"Yes, Mr. X, you have it." *One hundred percent of it. You had it before then, but you really have it now.*

"Good. Is your pussy wet?"

"Soaking."

"Excellent." The silence stretched out and she imagined him walking around the bed, examining her. "You never did tell me what you do for a living."

"I'm a phone sex artist." She moaned softly. "Right now I'm a frustrated one. Don't you want me to talk about sucking your cock, or feeling your prick buried deep inside me? May I use my vibrator?"

That should get him hot and off the subject of her personal life.

There was another pause. "Are you a lawyer, or a doctor? Maybe a store clerk?"

"We're not allowed to give out personal information." She wiggled her ass, imagining he could see her. "Want to fuck me? My pussy is hot for you, but if you'd like an alternative means of entry, all you need to do is ask."

"A writer maybe? Or are you independently wealthy and just looking for some excitement in your life?"

Damn it! Why wasn't he talking about sex? He'd talked about it all last night, wearing her out. Her clit had throbbed this morning from being used so much the previous evening. It was a delicious ache, one that she'd like to repeat tomorrow morning.

"Mr. X, please. I need you to talk to me."

"I am talking to you, but you're not answering. I may have to treat you as a hostile witness."

Serendipity's shoulders stiffened and then she fought back a laugh. He was a lawyer. What would he say if he found out what she did as a day job?

Chapter Five

Don't let him know you're in the legal field. She repeated the mantra to herself over and over before clearing her throat and saying, "Does that mean the belt's coming back out?"

"Maybe." He gave a satisfied moan and Serendipity felt it deep inside her. "I can imagine your skin is very soft. I'm stroking your backside right now, imagining it just a little red from being spanked. Why won't you answer my question?"

"I'm not allowed to. I could lose my job."

"Fair enough." There was a hissing sound, as if he were sucking in air through clenched teeth. "Look at how swollen that pussy is, all ready to be fucked. If you can't answer my first question, I'll withdraw it and ask this one instead: What state do you live in?"

Before she could reply, he said, "Wait, don't answer. I can tell you. You live in California."

"How did you kn..." She cleared her throat. "We're unable to..."

"Yes, I know. But I live in California, and when I asked for a late time the woman said that was good for 'your time zone.' It could be other Pacific Coast states, but I picked mine, because I'm partial to it.

Damn it! It was an honest mistake for the operator to make, but one that gave out clues to people who listened. Like lawyers. There was no sense denying it, since he wasn't going to drop the subject. But she needed to take control. Soon.

"Yes, I live in California."

"Excellent, again. Are you still in position?"

"Yes, sir."

"Good. Then let's begin."

Begin? Let's move straight to the orgasm! "What would you like me to do?"

"I want to hear your soft, sweet voice talk about sucking my dick. And don't stop until you've heard me come."

It was about damn time! "Look at that wonderful dick. Oh, is it nice and hard just for me?"

"Yeah, baby, it's just for you. I know it's impolite, but stuff your mouth and talk while you eat."

She put her two fingers into her mouth, sucking and talking around them, telling him how good his cock felt, how she loved feeling him swell and pulse as she ran her tongue around him, sliding from tip to balls and back up, bathing him completely before taking him back in her mouth, sucking him as deeply as she could.

Because she knew guys like it, and it stroked their ego, she made gagging noises from time to time, as if he were too big for her mouth, as if his cock had hit the back of her throat.

"Oh yeah, Serendipity, baby, suck me. Fuck you have a great voice. It's like I can feel the warmth of your mouth. Play with your clit, but don't come until I give you permission, and no vibrators tonight. Just your fingers."

A moan of disappointment escaped her mouth before she could stop it. She'd been looking forward to feeling the vibrator, but she would follow his instructions simply because he made her hotter than any of her customers ever had.

She was glad that he ignored her whine as she continued to suck and lick him, describing every inch and perceived vein that she ran across. When she heard his breathing pick up and his whispered, "Fuck yeah, more, more," she knew he was close.

"Come inside me, let me taste all of it, warm and wet and delicious. Oh Mr. X, you have the most fantastic cock. Fill me, let me drink all of it."

"Fuck yeah! Come, baby…with…ahhhhh."

Serendipity pinched her clit, her orgasm exploding, pushed higher by Mr. X's sounds of pure ecstasy. Her body pulsed and her pussy begged to be filled, but she obeyed his orders and left her vibrator in the off position.

"Oh baby, that was fucking incredible. I thought my balls were going to explode"

A feeling of pure satisfaction, unlike any sexual gratification she'd ever felt, raced through her. This man was addicting, and it could turn out to be a bad thing if she wasn't careful. But then again, what was the harm? A cyber relationship could prove to be more fun than she'd ever had with real men, if the last two nights were any indication.

She mentally head slapped herself. Mr. X was a real man. She may not know what he looked like, but she knew he was a lawyer, and that he lived in California. If he were like any lawyer that she knew, he wouldn't settle for a cyber sex buddy for long. He would either (a) grow tired of her, or (b) want to push things to another level.

From the way he was asking about her private life and trying to find out where she lived she voted for option b. What would she tell him if he did that? *"I'm sorry but I just can't?"* Her mind might say it, but her body never would; not after the way he'd made her hum two nights in a row.

"Are you still with me?"

"Yes, Mr. X, I'm still here."

"Your bonds are off now. Lie on your back, legs spread."

The man was insatiable. He'd just had an orgasm and he was ready to play some more. He was going to wear her out.

"Now, you don't have to tell me your name, or what city you live in, but I want to know something about you, Serendipity, something that will make you real."

She laughed softly as she settled herself on the bed. "I hate lima beans."

"So do I." She heard him settle himself on the bed, then sigh. "And I can't stand peas."

"But I love brussel sprouts," she said, knowing that would probably set him off. Most people gave her a horrified look when she said that.

"Excuse me?" She imagined him sitting up in his bed and staring at the phone in utter shock. "I just got a blowjob from a woman who likes brussel sprouts?"

She laughed at his disbelief. "Yes, you did. Yummy!"

"Are you hiding any other horrible secrets, like you're really a man?"

"Only on Tuesdays and Thursdays," Fallon said. Serendipity was gone now, faded into the background.

"Thank God," Mr. X replied. "For a minute there I was really worried it was going to be Mondays, Wednesdays and Fridays."

They both dissolved into laughter and Fallon hugged herself. He could ask her just about anything and she'd tell him, breaking every rule she'd agreed to when she'd taken this job. But frankly, she didn't care. They had another hour and a half, and right now she'd answered impart her innermost secrets to this man.

Chapter Six

Last night she'd done something she'd never done before, and she knew she shouldn't have, but discovering that Mr. X was really Burke Gordon had set her world spinning.

What were the odds that the client that had touched her so perfectly would turn out to be one of the most successful attorneys in San Diego? A million to one, maybe?

The only time anything good ever happened to her, and nothing would ever come of it.

She'd done something she shouldn't do last night, she'd hacked into her own files at the company and discovered his real name. After the initial shock had worn off, she'd spent another two hours surfing the web. He was featured prominently in many different cases in town, and there were a few photos of him at charity events, always with a beautiful woman on his arm.

The pictures showed a fit man in his early thirties, with short dark hair and a smile that made her toes curl. From the looks of his dates, he did the same thing to them. True they weren't stick figures, but they weren't size sixteen court reporters either. She had two more sessions with him; one tonight, and then the Christmas party where she would perform phone sex with his friend. She wasn't looking forward to that.

In fact he'd almost ruined her for her other clients. She'd had two of them call for tonight and she'd pushed them off on other operators, telling her boss that she was tired and needed to take a nap.

Her boss had teased her about "saving" herself for the nine o'clock show and Fallon hadn't disagreed with her. The company frowned on that sort of thing, but she hadn't harped on it. If it happened a few more times, though, Fallon would be called on the carpet and reminded that she needed to keep her identity away from her clients.

Fallon snapped up the phone on the first ring. She checked the ID then hit the connect button on her headset.

"Hello Mr. X. How are you this evening?" She imagined him in his office, sitting back in his chair with his tie undone, a drink in his hand. Then she nixed that idea. It was after nine, and although it wasn't unheard of for a lawyer to work that late she had a feeling he was at home, either lying on his bed or the couch. The picture of him in his work clothes, tie undone and drink in hand, remained, despite the change in location.

"Hello, Serendipity. It's been a hell of a day."

"I'm sorry, can I make it all better?" She murmured deep in her throat, the sound low and seductive. "Perhaps you'd like to feel my mouth on you, or would you prefer something else tonight?"

"Not a bad idea, but before that I want to talk."

"All right." She sat down on the bed, wrapping her robe around her. "About what? The weather? The sad state of the economy? What happened today that troubled you so much?"

"Bad day in cou…at work." He sighed she heard him swallow. Yes, he was definitely drinking. "But I don't want to talk about that. I haven't been able to stop thinking about you."

Shock ran through her body and she cleared her throat. "Well, I have been known to produce fantastic orgasms, which I think I've proven with you a time or two. Men think about sex quite often, so it wouldn't be hard for you to associate my voice with…"

"No, that's not it. I want to know you. Tell me your most secret desire that has nothing to do with sex."

This was different, and it wasn't a good thing. Her clients wanted to talk about themselves, not about her.

Before she could answer he started talking again.

"I know you're not supposed to give out personal information, which is just fine. I just want some insight into the woman who made me shoot off so hard last night, and the night before that, too."

There was a pregnant pause, and then he added, "You're most secret desire."

"Is this one of those 'if you could meet any person in the world who would it be' type questions?"

"Indulge me."

The deep timbre of his voice made her shiver. Right now she would give him just about anything.

"Okay." The word came out of her mouth even as her mind was screaming no. This was a huge mistake, and would probably land her in a world of trouble. "But you have to promise not to laugh at me."

When he laughed, she growled, surprised at the sound. "Sorry about that, but the deal's off."

"No, I was just getting it out of the way now," he said. "I promise not to laugh."

"You've already done that, but since you're paying for it…" She let the words trail off before she took a deep breath. "I have three goals in life. First, I have a list of classic novels I want to read, so that when someone brings them up in a conversation I can say: I've read that."

"Not bad." There was the sound of him taking another drink. "How far along on the list are you?"

"I picked two hundred books, and I've read thirty of them. I just came up with this when I was twenty-four." She wanted to tell him that all her friends had laughed at her, told her that was a stupid goal, but she hadn't care. She loved to read, and she wanted to have this list under her belt.

"What are you reading now?"

She looked toward her bedside table. "*Treasure Island*. Believe it or not, I didn't have to read it in school."

"I love that book." The excitement in his voice made her tingle. "We could get into a great discussion about it, but that would take up all our time. What's next on the goal list?"

"I want to visit every state." She shrugged, even though she knew he couldn't see it. "Right now I've seen eleven of them. To tell the truth, I've added to this goal, in that I have several other places I'd like to visit, too: England, France, Italy, Spain and Egypt."

"I've been to two of those places, England and Italy."

Then take me there, please. She kept those words to herself. "I'm jealous. Was it fun?"

"Beautiful." She wanted him to say it would be much more fun if she'd been with him, but he didn't. "What is the last goal?"

The last one was stupid, and sort of juvenile, so she'd kept it to herself. "That was it, really. I pushed two of them together, the foreign and domestic travel."

"Liar." His voice deepened with authority. "Do I need to take off my belt?"

"Now we're getting somewhere. Do you want to spank me, Mr. X?"

This time he was the one who cleared his throat. "Let's see if I can guess. You want to fall in love."

"No, I've given up on that." The minute the words were out of her mouth she cringed. That opened up a whole kettle of fish that she didn't

"Why?" He sounded genuinely interested, and that made her want to tell him. But she wouldn't.

"I just have. Now, about that spanking…"

"Love is a beautiful thing, you know. Even when it's over, and you get over the pain of it, you remember the good things. All people should experience it at least once."

"Sounds like you're speaking from experience."

Fallon settled down amongst her pillows, wondering why she wasn't putting a stop to this. Phone sex artists were taught to end calls that were going in the wrong direction. The client would be refunded his money if she reported it. But she didn't want to do that. She was enjoying this too much. The sound of his voice was addictive and she wanted to hear it as much as possible.

He was right about the memory thing. When she'd finally got the courage up to refuse his calls she would be able to recall his deep, melodious voice and how it made her feel.

"I was in love once."

His admission made her stomach roil. She wasn't sure why. A man as handsome as him had to have attracted a million women over the years. Of course he would have been in love with at least once of them.

"But it didn't work?"

"No." He didn't sound sad, just matter of fact about it. "She wanted a husband who was a rich lawyer. I was a lawyer, but the money wasn't coming in quick enough for her. She pushed and pushed for me to take bigger cases, make more money. Soon I realized it wasn't me she wanted in her life, it was what I could give her."

"I'm sorry." She wanted to ask him how long ago this had been, since she hadn't seen any mention of a wife in her web searching last night. But that would tell him that she knew who he was, and that she'd been checking up on him. Definitely a bad idea.

"Don't be. It was hard at first, but I learned from it. The next woman I marry will love me, and not my job. Have you ever been married?"

"No." Fallon licked her lips and looked toward the clock. He had thirty minutes left on tonight's session. "We should…"

"Why not?"

How hard was it to say that she'd never found anyone? It wasn't hard, really. She thought it made her sound like a loser. "Life happens."

"Yes, it does." He sighed deeply and she imagined him nestling down into the covers of his bed. "You were going to say something, maybe tell me your third wish?"

"What I was going to say was that the clock is ticking. You sound tired. Shall I lull you to sleep?"

"What do you have in mind?"

"Lie back so I can straddle you."

"Good idea so far. Go on, tell me what comes next."

"Are you naked, Mr. X?"

"Are you, sweet Serendipity?"

"Of course I am, always, for you."

"Hearing that makes my dick nice and hard."

"So I see." Clients liked to think they were in the same room together, she knew, but in this case she wanted to imagine Burke under her, his hands behind his head, letting her have her way with him.

"Your chest is so magnificent, strong muscles and smooth skin. Do you like the way I'm caressing you?"

"Yeah." The word came out strangled and she imagined his hand wrapped around his cock, pumping slowly.

"I'm trailing my fingers over your chest and shoulders, softly caressing you. It feels so nice. I'll keep doing that until you tell me to move lower."

There was a definite hitch in his breathing now and she put in a few moans, and *oohs* and *aahs* as she mentally stroked his chest, his arms and shoulders. It was almost as if she could feel him under her.

"Lower."

The command made her pussy twitch with need and she wanted to ask him if she could use her vibrator, but tonight wasn't about her. It was about him.

"With pleasure." She closed her eyes and imagined her hand wrapped around his cock. "So hard and perfect. May I play?"

"Please do."

"Up and down, slowly moving my hand around. I love this vein, pulsing with your blood, keeping you hard. I'm going to trace it up and down, barely touching it, running the tip of my fingernail over it. Do you like that, Mr. X?"

"More." Oh yes, he was definitely getting there. She could hear the sound of his hand moving up and down his cock, which had obviously been slicked up with lotion, or some sort of lubricant.

"May I taste you?"

"Fuck yeah, do it." Fallon put her three fingers in her mouth and sucked them, knowing the sound of it would increase the pleasure he was feeling. She moved her tongue around, lapping at her salty skin, pretending it was his cock.

"So good," she whispered as she popped them from her mouth. "Your balls are full and ready." She licked her fingers again, letting him imagine her tongue running around his heavy sac, which by now should be full and ready to burst.

She started to lap at the palm of her hand, making noise to simulate her tongue on his cock and balls.

"Oh baby, yeah, do it." He groaned loudly, whispering encouragement to her before his let out a loud, "Fuck yeah, suck me, taste me, take it all."

Fallon didn't answer. Instead she put her fingers back in her mouth and sucked. The sound seemed to drive him harder and his groan deepened before he gave a loud sigh.

"Damn Serendipity, that was fine." He sounded as if he was almost asleep and she took her fingers out of her mouth, letting them drift down to her clit.

"Go to sleep, Mr. X." She stroked herself gently. "I'm lying in your arms, and the heavy movement of your chest feels so wonderful. I'm so glad I could make you feel that way, make you come that hard."

"Oh, baby." Yes, he was definitely almost asleep. "I'll see you in the morning."

Her heart lurched at his words and she pressed the headphone closer to her ear. "Mr. X?"

When there was no answer, she knew he was asleep. *He would see her in the morning?* Damn, this was getting bad. As soon as the Christmas party was over, she needed to end it, tell the operators she'd gotten too close and if Mr. X called and asked for her, they needed to tell him she was unavailable.

It would be the best thing in the long run.

She took off the headset and wiggled down into the bed, letting her fingers touch her clit gently. It took no time at all for her to climax. Her pussy was soaking wet and she imagined Burke Gordon over her, pumping his hard cock into her tightness.

"Burke!" She yelled out his name as she came, then turned and buried her face in the pillow, tears flooding down her face. Damn, life really did suck. Big time. She finally found a man who seemed to appreciate her and he was unattainable. She wanted to curl up into a ball and stay in this one place for the rest of her life.

Chapter Seven

He was such a moron. Burke stared at the information on his desk, wondering why he'd done something that he'd known was wrong. The last two nights with Serendipity had been perfect, and when he'd woken up this morning and realized he'd fallen asleep thinking she was beside him in his bed, he knew he had to do something about it.

He'd called one of the firm's private investigators and put him on the case. "This is personal," Burke had said. "Bill me, and don't say anything to anyone."

O'Brien hadn't asked any questions, and an hour and a half later, Burke's home fax machine had whirled to life, spitting out the name and address of one Fallon Nicholas, a court reporter who lived right here in San Diego.

His cock had hardened when her picture had rolled out of the machine. She was absolutely gorgeous. The photo had been pulled from the Phelps and Jones website, and Burke had gone to the site immediately, verifying what O'Brien had told him.

Fallon Nicholas was thirty-three, which made her a year older than Burke. She was not a pencil thin girl, but a voluptuous woman. She had rich dark hair and hazel eyes that shone with merriment as she smiled for the camera.

Burke fingered the papers once more and an image of her on her knees, her mouth wrapped around his cock popped into his mouth. His dick sprang into action, pressing against his pants. This wouldn't do, wouldn't do at all. He had a meeting with Mr. Watson in thirty minutes, and if he went in there with a hard on, that would be a bad thing.

Things on the Thompson divorce were not going well, and the firm was not happy. But Burke was, as long as he thought about Serendipity...no Fallon. That was who he'd talked to last night. He had to have this woman in his life, and it had to be more than just over the phone.

The decision to call Phelps and Jones was rash, but he had to hear her voice.

The receptionist answered and he asked to speak with Ms. Nichols. Seconds later, her sensuous voice came through the phone and settled right in his balls. "This is Fallon."

"Hello, this is Burke Gordon from White, Watson and Wilson."

There was the slightest pause and then she said, her voice just a little deeper than it had been moments ago. "Yes, sir, what can I do for you?"

Pleasure shot through him. She knew who he was. She knew he was Mr. X.

"Your firm did a deposition for us last week and the file seems to have been misplaced. I was wondering if you could bring it by my office, say at six?"

She was breathing heavily now, almost like she had been the first night, when he'd wanted her more than he'd wanted anything in a long time. That was until the next night. And the next one. There was a definite pattern forming where this woman was concerned.

"I...I wasn't the person assigned to that case, Sally was. I can..."

"I want you, and no other."

"We can't." She whispered the words. "I can't. It's not supposed to…"

"Oh, and Serendipity?"

"Yes?"

He stroked his cock through his pants, afraid he would shoot off in his jeans like a teen-age boy. "Leave your panties in the car."

He hung up before she could answer. The only thing to do now was wait and see if she appeared as he'd asked her to.

* * * *

Fallon stared at the phone in her hand, her heart racing. She cringed at the thought that she'd actually answered to that name on the work phone. What the hell was she doing? And how in the hell had he figured out who she was? It wasn't supposed to happen!

He might like her cyber blowjobs, but when he found out she was a size sixteen, and not a size two, he would run for the hills. There was no way she could go to his office. Why was he doing this? Couldn't he just be satisfied with phone sex?

Obviously not. Maybe she could hire someone to pretend to be her. No, that wouldn't work. The first time he mentioned something about riding her until she screamed in release that person would scream and run.

Besides, she had to be truthful with herself. If he'd searched her out, he obviously already knew she wasn't anything like the beautiful women he was used to being with.

She should call him back right now, tell him there was no way she could come and see him. That would be the best thing to do. She picked up the phone, and then immediately put it back down.

"Leave your panties in the car." His command echoed in her eyes. He planned to have sex with her tonight. No, not with her, with Serendipity. Crap! Why was this happening to her? She needed to talk with the agency about beefing up their security if he could find out the identity of an artist so fast. Had they given it to him, or had he hired someone to find it? She was betting on the latter. Of course she'd found him just as quickly. She tried to justify her hacking by convincing herself that she worked there, and it wasn't so illegal, even though she knew it was.

"What's wrong, did you eat a large pizza for lunch and it's coming back up on you?"

Fallon pushed back and stood up. "Screw you, Sally. Get the hell away from my desk."

"Such language. I'm sure Elaine would be very upset to hear it."

There was a deep sigh and they both turned toward their boss. "I'm tired of hearing you two fight. This is not a schoolyard where you can go at it anytime you want. Straighten up or I'll can you both." She glared at them, then handed Fallon a manila folder. "You're to take this to Burke Gordon at his office. Be there at six on the dot."

That sneaky little bastard. He'd known she would try to weasel out it and he'd fixed it so she couldn't. At least he hadn't said anything to Elaine about Fallon not wearing panties for this errand.

Sally made a grab for the folder but Elaine pulled it away.

"I did that case," Sally whined. "I should be the one to deliver it if he needs another copy."

"He asked for Fallon, and Fallon he will get." The look Elaine gave Sally said it all: one more word and you're gone.

Fallon took the folder and Elaine headed toward her office.

"Trying to steal my clients now? You're not going to get away with it, I'll see to that."

Sally stalked off and Fallon stared at the clock. It was a little after four. She had almost two hours to come up with a way to get out of this meeting. As she thought of escape routes her anger built. How dare he do this?

It was a million to one shot that they'd live in the same city, much less work in the legal field. But for him to take advantage of that work to find her, and to contact her, breached a level of trust they'd built from their first night together. Sure, they'd talk about things she'd never talked about with other clients, but that didn't give him the right to search her out.

Since Burke would have told her last night that he knew she lived in San Diego, she was pretty sure the PI had found her in less than twenty-four hours. Hell, it had probably taken him less than two—or even one hour; a few clicks of the mouse and he'd probably been home free.

"Son of a bitch." She sat down at her desk, then gave an apologetic smile to Lindsey, who sat next to her. "Sorry."

Lindsey gave her a small smile and turned back to her computer. The more she thought about Burke tracking her down, the madder she got. The fact that she'd searched out his identity wasn't the same thing. She'd found out who he was, yes, but she hadn't tried to contact him.

And she never would have. That was going too far. The idea of skipping the meeting flew out of her head. She'd go see him, all right; and she'd give him a piece of her mind.

Chapter Eight

The building was huge. She'd driven by it lots of times but had never been inside. Messengers dropped off depositions and court records; court reporters didn't run this type of errand. She worried about Sally's reaction, and whether or not she would try to cause trouble over this. It wouldn't surprise her if she did.

The two had taken an instant dislike to each other, something that rarely happened to Fallon. She didn't like to think of it happening now, or that it would come up and bite her on the ass where Burke was concerned.

Burke. Somewhere inside this building he sat at his desk, waiting for her to come up. She had to stay strong and let him know this couldn't happen. The only way to do that was to go in with guns blazing, to be madder than hell and let him have it.

Yeah, good thinking Fallon. If you really felt that way why did you go into the bathroom and take your panties off? Her pussy was dripping wet at the prospect of seeing him. And she'd done what he'd asked her to do.

Damn it! She slapped her fist against the steering wheel of her car, then whimpered as pain shot up her arm. Yeah, that was real bright, too.

She snatched up the envelope and headed into the building.

At the front she showed her ID to a security guard, who checked a sheet, and then buzzed her in. She went into the elevator, punching the number nine, and tried not to look nervous as the car made its ascent.

After all, as far as anyone knew she was only here to drop off a deposition. They didn't know she was a phone sex operator who was about to meet the man who'd made her orgasm as if it were the Fourth of July and she were a fireworks display.

The elevator dinged and she stepped off. The receptionist's desk was empty, but per the guard's instructions, she turned to the left and headed down the hallway, her palms sweating as she counted off the doors: one, two, three—four.

The door was open and from her vantage point she could see a long leather sofa sitting against the wall. There was a low table in front of it. She pushed the door open wider and walked inside. His office was bigger than the living room in her apartment. Off to the right was a small table with three chairs. In front of a bank of windows was a huge desk, behind which sat Burke Gordon.

He watched her intently, his eyes alight with interest. "Hello, Fallon. Please close the door."

"I'd rather not." She hurried to the desk and slapped the file down. "I shouldn't be here."

"I think you look absolutely perfect in this office." The look he gave her said he knew what she looked like naked, and she supposed in a way he did. They'd been wonderfully intimate with each other, talking about dreams and wishes, but they'd also been wonderfully nasty with each other, too, discussing sex and listening to each other orgasm. Repeatedly.

"Why did you call for me?"

"Because I wanted to meet you." He stood and strode around the side of the desk.

Fallon backed toward the door, determined not to let him get too near her. She wasn't sure she could resist him if he touched her.

"This breaks every rule. I'm never supposed to meet with clients. It's forbidden."

"No one will find out." He was edging closer to her, as if he were a hunter and he had her in his sights.

"Someone always finds out, Burke." She threw out her arms and laughed. "You're a lawyer; it's why you have this huge fancy office, because someone *always* finds out. And then people get sued, or divorced, or they sue someone."

Fallon stepped into the hallway, continuing to walk backward, increasing her pace so there was distance between them. "Perhaps it's better if you don't call me anymore."

"I doubt that." He licked his lips and she imagined that mouth on her pussy, that tongue circling her clit. Wetness seeped into her folds, making them slick with need. "Are you wearing panties?"

No, damn you! I'm not, you little… "Hush. Someone's going to hear you!"

"Who cares?" This time he was the one who threw his arms out. "We're two single, consenting adults. I don't see what the problem is."

"The problem is I'm here on business." She hissed out the words, wondering where the staircase was. Could she find it and run down? That way she wouldn't need to wait for the elevator.

"Answer my question." His soft demand made her groan softly. "Answer me."

"Why? It's not *me* you want to hear from, it's Serendipity." She stepped closer and lowered her voice. "She's the one who gets you off."

"You're Serendipity."

"No, I'm not. When you imagined me as I was talking about sucking your cock, did you imagine a size sixteen court reporter who lives in a two bedroom apartment and is addicted to chocolate? Or did you picture a busty, beautiful blond who had lots of hair you could pull while you shoved yourself down her throat?"

"You're making me hard."

"Stop it!" She looked around, realizing anyone who was around could probably hear her yelling. "You're not listening to me. I'm. Not. Serendipity."

He was silent for a moment, and then he stroked his chin, looking up in the air. "Does Serendipity make money off her phone calls?"

"You know she does."

"Yes, I do." He fixed a stare on her, one that made her toes tingle. "Does she pay taxes on that income, or do you?"

Her heart dropped to her knees. "Do not argue semantics with me."

"Answer the question." When she didn't say anything, he walked to the receptionist's desk. "Judge, I'd like permission to treat Ms. Nicholas as a hostile witness." He walked back to her slowly. "Do you, or do you not pay taxes on the money Serendipity earns?"

"Of course I do, but…" There had to be a way out of this. She snapped her fingers. "An actor may play a part, but that doesn't make him the character he portrays, does it?"

"No, you're right, it doesn't. But, was it Serendipity who was telling me her goals, or was that you?"

Damn him! "Stop badgering me as if I'm on the witness stand."

"Then admit to me that it was more than just phone calls. You felt a connection the same way I did. That's why when you walked in my office tonight you weren't shocked to hear me ask about your panties, which, I might add, is a question I never got answered."

"And you're not going to." She stood up straight, pretending she had a book on her head, praying it would help her with poise. "I'm leaving. Don't call me anymore."

"You want me as much as I want you. Admit it."

She stopped in front of the elevator and pushed the down button, keeping her back turned to him.

"Fallon, come into my office so we can talk."

She laughed before turning toward him. He'd moved until they were inches apart. "That's rich, you want to talk. That's why you asked me to forget my underwear, so we could talk?"

"Were you wearing undies the last time we talked?" He trailed his finger down her arm and her body felt as if it would explode. "Well, were you?"

"This is some...I don't know, twist of fate. But it won't work. Go back to your office. Jack off, do whatever you want. I'm going home."

"What's wrong, you can suck me off over the phone but I'm not good enough for you to do it in person?"

Rage swept through her, replacing the desire that had been there moments before. She pulled her hand back to slap him just as the elevator dinged. Burke clasped her hand and pulled it down, jerking her against his chest. His mouth came down on hers, swallowing her scream of frustration.

His tongue invaded, sliding into her warmth and making the desire that had just fled return, spreading heat to her nipples and clit and making them throb. She allowed herself to relax just a moment, savoring the taste of him, the feel of his hard body pressed against hers. She wrapped her arms around him, wanting to hold him close just this once.

And then the sound of a woman's voice assaulted her ears. "You little slut."

She turned to find Sally standing in the elevator, eyes flashing in angry triumph. "Just wait until Elaine hears about this. You're going to be unemployed."

Chapter Nine

It was like being called to the principal's office. Fallon sat, hands in her lap, looking at Elaine who was behind her desk, rifling through papers. There was a knock at the door and Sally appeared, a satisfied smirk on her face.

"Come in," Elaine said, indicating the seat next to Fallon.

Sally sat and licked her lips as if she were about to enjoy a huge meal. Fallon wanted to reach across and slap the sneer off her face. But she wouldn't give the other woman the satisfaction of knowing she'd been that riled up.

Elaine continued to search through her papers, and then she took a seat. "Well, I see you two have taken your little feud out of the office and embarrassed the firm.

"She really did," Sally said, shaking her head. "I mean, to see her throwing herself at him like that was…"

"I'm not talking about the kiss," Elaine said, fixing a stare on Sally. "I've talked with Burke Gordon, who told me he initiated the contact, not Fallon."

Fallon's heart soared at her words. Burke had defended her? Had he called her boss, or had Elaine called him to see what had happened? Knowing Elaine's need for keeping things in house, she was sure that Burke had been the one to dial the phone.

Bless his little soul. She wanted to run from the office, race into his arms and be the one to kiss him. She looked over at Sally. The shocked expression on the other woman's face made her laugh. She tried, and failed, to keep it low.

"It's not funny," Elaine said. "None of this is funny. What you do with your private life is your business, Fallon, but it shouldn't have been done on company time, even if you weren't the one to start it. And Sally, I have no idea what you were doing at White, Watson and Wilson, but whatever it was, I did not sanction it."

"But…"

"No buts." Elaine's look silenced the other woman. "I warned you both about your dislike for each other, and now it has spread outside company walls. Do you know how embarrassing it was for me to talk with Burke Gordon? When he called, I was sure he would be laughing at me for my employees engaging in a verbal spar in front of him."

"I'm sorry," Fallon said, remembering how she'd called Sally a witch before Burke stepped in front of her, asking the other woman who she was looking for, and how she'd gotten past the guards.

Sally had hemmed and hawed about how she'd been waiting downstairs for Fallon and wanted to see what was taking so long. Fallon had outed the lie, and Sally had gotten off a few choice words before Burke politely informed her it was time for her to leave, before he called the guards to escort her from the building.

Fallon had been horribly embarrassed, and she'd refused Burke's offer to come back to his office. She'd gone home, her heart hammering as she replayed the night. He'd called her home phone at ten and left a message, asking her to call him back.

Instead she'd taken a long bath, soaking in the hot water and pondering what she would do if she were fired in the morning. She'd slept fitfully, and when the phone had rang at seven, she'd known who it was. She was right.

Burke's deep, calming voice had sang out through the answering machine. "Fallon, please call me back." He gave her his home and cell numbers and the direct line into his office. "Please, don't shut me out. Call me back."

And say what, she'd wondered? I enjoyed phone sex with you, but we don't belong together? Best to end it now, before more people found out and things became more entangled.

Elaine's voice broke into her meanderings. "You're both suspended for the rest of the week without pay."

"You can't do that." Sally jumped up from her chair. "I was only—"

"You will sit before I make your suspension permanent, do I make myself clear?"

Fallon had never heard her boss so angry before. Sally sat, but not before she turned her angry glare on Fallon. The meaning of the look was evident. This is all your fault.

"Your suspension starts today and ends next Monday. You are both valued employees, but I will not tolerate any more foolishness. I hope this drives that home. Now, get your bags and leave. I'll see you at eight Monday morning. You can both go now."

Fallon stood. "Thank you, Elaine. Once again, I'm sorry."

Sally stormed from the office without saying a word.

Fallon followed, and as she neared her desk, she frowned. There was a long, narrow flower box sitting there, tied in red tinsel.

Sally was banging around her desk, making as much noise as possible. She grabbed her purse and stopped at Fallon's desk long enough to give her a one-fingered salute before slamming out the door.

"I don't know what I ever did," Fallon said, her eyes trained on the box. It was obvious who it was from. Did she want to open it in front of everyone?

"She's always needed someone to hate," Margaret said from the desk next to hers. "Sally is a very unhappy person."

There was a silence and Fallon toyed with the tinsel. "Open it," several voices called out.

She giggled, then undid the wrappings, lifting the lid to find a dozen roses, a mixture of white and lavender sitting on a bed of silver tinsel.

"Wow," Margaret said. "You know what those mean, don't you? I mean, red's for love, sure, but white is for weddings, you know, when you're starting something? And lavender is the beginning of love, like falling for someone when you first see them. I'm so impressed. Who are they from?"

Fallon's hands shook as she picked up the card. There was an address in Point Loma with nine p.m. written beneath it.

Margaret's eyebrows shot up. "That's right on the beach. Who are you going to see?"

Fallon wanted to scream that it was Burke Gordon, but then in a few days, when she was back to work, how would she explain that it had probably only been for one night? The reality of it being that Fallon could never live up to the fantasy that Serendipity provided. Why didn't Burke understand that?

She supposed that tonight she would tell him. What would one night hurt? They could enjoy a rousing session between the sheets, and then she could go back to being suspended from her job and talking with customers every night, providing them a fantasy that, for her, would never come true.

Chapter Ten

Fallon hadn't been sure what to wear. Since she'd had the free time, she'd spent it rummaging through her closet, pulling out dresses and pants and sweaters, discarding all of them in a big heap on her bed.

She rarely went out, so she didn't exactly have a lot of fancy clothes. Nothing looked like something she would wear for an outing with Burke Gordon. She finally decided on a full black skirt that she hoped hid her overabundance of hips, and a red blouse made of a nice satiny material. She'd put on the one bra she had that opened in front, and worn thigh-high stockings because they made her feel sexy. She hoped Burke thought the same way.

"Looks a little Christmasy," she said to the mirror as she examined her choice. She'd gone back and forth about whether she should go or not. There was no future in it, but the chance to have sex with a guy like Burke only came around once in life. She needed to grab it while she could.

She'd cancelled all the evening's calls, and her supervisor had complained that this was getting to be the norm for her.

"You're going to lose your regulars," she'd said in a huffy voice. "Does that matter to you?"

No, not right now. "I'm just not in the mood," Fallon had replied. "Tell them I'm on vacation, for a week or so. Then I'll get back to you." *If I feel like doing this again, which something tells me I might not.*

Sure, the money was nice, but after a wonderful experience with a man like Burke, how would she be able to keep on going? She would measure each call with her experience with him, expect each unknown man to take her as high as he had.

Since that wouldn't be happening, it might be best just to let it go. She made enough money at her job to live comfortably; maybe she just needed to leave it at that.

She waffled about her decision as she got into her car, and continued to waver as she drove across town, rolling down the window to inhale the deep, rich smell of the ocean as she drew nearer.

It wasn't hard to find the address he'd given her. As she pulled into the drive, she noted the sports car sitting inside the open garage. The car did nothing more than reinforce the differences between them. This was a two-car garage and she wondered what was hidden behind the closed door.

Another expensive car, or a motorcycle, maybe? Or maybe even a boat? She scratched that idea. If he had a boat, and she had no doubt that he did, it was in a slip somewhere, ready to be taken out at a moment's notice.

"This is a bad idea," she whispered to herself. "Go home and call him, tell him you've changed your mind. End it now."

The rap on the window made her jump. She turned her head to see Burke leaning over. He wore loose tan slacks and a dark blue shirt that was open a few buttons. She suddenly felt very overdressed.

"Open the door, baby. Come inside."

Baby. She sighed, picked up her purse then reached for the flowers she'd brought with her, one of each color rose he'd sent her that morning. She thought it was the best way to thank him, to let him know she'd received them.

She hit the unlock button and he opened the door, offering her hand to help her out. When the door was closed, he lifted her hand to his lips. "You are so gorgeous."

"Thanks." A blush heated her cheeks. She lifted the roses so he could see them. "And thanks again."

"You're welcome, but they pale in comparison."

She wanted to say "Yeah, right," or "Great line," but she just gave him a smile. He didn't let go of her hand as they headed toward the house. She examined it as they walked. It was a white two-story affair with lots of windows. As they stepped inside she marveled at it. The windows were accompanied by lots of chrome and the furniture was very modern, a mixture of black and white.

"This is nice," she said. "Actually, nice doesn't hack it. It's fantastic."

"Thanks. I'd like to take credit for the decorating, but unfortunately I can't. My mother and two sisters did it all."

She murmured in relief, afraid he was going to say his girlfriend had done it. She wasn't sure she wanted to hear that.

He stopped in the main room and took her purse from her hand, tossing it into a chair.

"Thirsty?" The seductive promise of his voice made her knees tremble.

"No."

"Hungry?"

Only for you. "No, no food."

"Good." He grasped her face between his hands and kissed her, pressing his lips against her in a deep, searing passion that made her clit twitch in appreciation. Wetness soaked into her panties as his tongue delved inside her. He tasted of toothpaste, with a slight tang of beer and she smiled.

"You've been drinking."

"A little. I had to try and get hold of myself before I got…well, hold of myself. I've been hard all day, thinking of you. I was hoping the beer would make my cock go down, but, it didn't. Please don't tell me you're going to say no."

"No."

The crestfallen look on his face made her giggle. "No, I meant no, I'm not going to say, no. Oh, I sound like a moron." She put her face in her hands, willing Serendipity to step forward and take control of the situation.

"You're not a moron," he said, gently moving her hands from her face. "Look at me."

She lifted her gaze to his, gasping at the look of utter desire she saw. "I need you, need to be inside you. I haven't been able to stop thinking about you for days. Do you know how hard it is to negotiate a divorce settlement when you're constantly…well, hard?"

"No, I can honestly say that I don't." She leaned toward him and kissed him, letting her lips linger on his before pulling back just a little. "But it wasn't me who made you hard. It was Serendipity. It was her voice, her ideas."

"The voice is yours." He returned the kiss, soft and chaste. "And every last word came from you, from the talk of sucking my dick to the discussion about wishes and dreams. All of it was you."

"No, it wasn't." She was ready to bolt if her emotions got the best of her. Doing without him would be tough once she'd had a taste. He was just too yummy for words.

Burke gave her an evil grin before he kissed her again. "I thought you might say that," he whispered against her lips.

He kissed her deeper, and she cried out in dismay when she heard something click. There was pressure on one wrist, and then suddenly on the other.

He lifted her arms above her head and attached them to a hook. She struggled as he held her close. "Shush, it's all right, just a pair of adult handcuffs." He stroked her sides and kissed her again. "Is the position uncomfortable? Do I need to let out the chain just a little?"

She looked up to see a chain handing from a hook in the ceiling. She swallowed hard, then shook her head. Breathe deeply, she coached herself, relax.

"No, I'm fine."

"Good. I guessed at your height after seeing you last night." His hand drifted down her hips and he wiggled his eyebrows at her. "Yummy."

He flicked his tongue over her lips as his hands drifted to the edge of her skirt, gathering it into his palms and inching it up. "Relax, Fallon, just relax."

"Easy for you to say," she said, her breath seeming to catch in her throat.

In response, he gave her a grin that made her stomach flip.

He lifted her skirt over her lips and put his hands in the waist of her panties. She'd worn the sexiest pair she owned, a red, lacy one that was as close to a thong as she'd ever get. He pulled them, down, leaving them around her ankles.

"Spread your legs, pretty one." She did as he asked, resisting the urge to ask if he was talking about her. When his hand cupped her mons, she moaned deeply.

"Already wet for me. It goes well with the hard cock in my pants."

"I want to see.' She let her gaze drift down. No more waffling. She was going to enjoy this night. Being tied up was a fantasy, and to live it out with Burke would make things perfect.

"Not yet." His hand left her pussy and went to her blouse, unfastening the buttons slowly. She looked over his shoulder, realizing they were standing in front of the outer walls, which were lined with glass.

"Someone could see us."

"Yes, maybe, if they got close enough." Her blouse was open now, but still tucked into her skirt. He put a hand over each breast, palming them through the satin of her bra. "You are so beautiful."

She blushed, then groaned as his hands slipped inside the bra, his fingers seeking her nipples. He found them easily enough, teasing the already rock hard buds until Fallon whimpered and tried to push herself into him.

"Please."

"Not yet. It's early, and we have all night to enjoy each other."

Yes, one night. She closed her eyes and gasped as his mouth claimed a nipple, sucking it in deeply, his tongue flickering over the bud as she wiggled, the hard wall against her back, his hard body against her front.

"Tasty," he said, running his tongue in the valley between her breasts and capturing the other nipple, his teeth nibbling it as she writhed against him. He was going to drive her crazy. She needed him inside her. Now.

One of his hands dropped back between her legs and he expertly parted her lips, found her clit. He flicked his thumb over it.

"You're so beautiful," he murmured in her ear. "In my wildest dreams I never thought something this perfect would happen in this room."

He pinched her clit and she came, rocking against his hand, the feeling spreading over her like shock waves, leaving her limp and thankful for the chain that was holding her up.

"Burke!"

"Yes, Fallon? Is something wrong?" He sounded very pleased with himself.

"Yes." She thought back to their phone sessions. "I need to fuck, need to feel your dick inside my hot, wet pussy."

"Oh, I like that idea. But I'm not quite ready for it." He stepped away from her, walking over to the table. She watched his every move, wondering what he would do next. Her arms were beginning to ache but it was a delicious feeling, even if her position did frighten her just a little.

After all, she didn't know that much about him. What if he were some sort of a sadist, and...her eyes bulged as he picked up a string of red tinsel and began walking back toward her. The garland trailed the floor on either side of him and she tried not to laugh as nerves sliced through her. It looked like it was long enough to...bind her whole body with. Oh good heavens above.

"What are you going to do with that?"

He stopped in front of her and rubbed the tinsel against her nipples, sliding it back and forth. The small strands tickled her already aroused buds and she cried out in pleasure.

"It occurred to me that you might not show up. And then, I was afraid that you would show up and then try to leave. That's why I rigged the device to bind you for a little while."

She smiled up at him. "Okay. But the tinsel?"

"Something else occurred to me. You're the most perfect Christmas present I've ever received. I've looked for a woman like you for years, Fallon."

He wrapped the tinsel around her waist, reaching behind her to trade the ends between his hands, bringing it to the front and letting it drop between her legs. He bent and wrapped her legs with each strand, then lifted the ends back up to her arms, repeating the motion.

"Burke, you don't know me."

"Yes, I do." He took the two ends drop to her side. "Not as well as I'm going to, but I believe in sparks, and there was one between us. Admit it."

She nodded, afraid to let the words come out of her mouth. If she said them they would be real; would mean something.

"I'm wrapping up my present, binding you to me. I'm not letting you go, Fallon."

Her heart went into double time as he kissed her again. "The tinsel is a symbol, of the spark we felt. I wanted to drape you in it so you'd feel it, let it soak into your body, envelop your body. This is what I want, Fallon, you and me, encased together."

She laughed softly. "Seems to me I'm the only one encased."

"Yeah, well, you look so beautiful that way. Plus, you're already wrapped up my heart, and I knew it. Promise me you'll give us a chance. Don't push me away because of differences between us, or because of what you think society will think. I want you in my life, Fallon, for a very long time to come."

Tears welled in her eyes as he kissed her. He wanted her, truly wanted her, and for more than just tonight.

"I promise." The words slipped out of her mouth before she could stop them. He clasped her face and kissed her deeply, his lips claiming her and making her feel as if they would set her on fire.

"You've just made me the happiest man in the world." He stepped back and put his hands inside his pants. Her eyes widened as she watched him fondle himself, then push down the pants. His cock leapt to life, hard and ready for her.

Burke captured her lips and entered her in one swift stroke and made her cry out in surprise and pleasure. He kept one hand on her hips while the other one moved behind her, clasping her ass and holding her close to him.

More...perfect...oh fuck." He grasped both hips and thrust into her, harder and harder. She felt it the moment he swelled, then released inside her, muttering her name repeatedly as his head sank into her shoulder.

Her eyes continued to leak as he once against said, "Fallon, oh baby. So beautiful."

The ache in her arms increased, and as if he could read her mind, he reached up and released her restraints, wrapping his around her as they tumbled to the floor. He kissed her again, then lay back, pulling her into the cradle of his arms.

"Fallon?"

"Yes?" She put her ear on his chest, listening to the sweet thud-thud of his heartbeat.

"Do you remember the goals you told me about?"

She nodded in response, afraid that if she opened her mouth to speak, it would break the spell that seemed to have encased them both.

"You told me two, and I'm going to help with the travel one. But what was the third?"

She sniffled and tried to pull away, but he kept her wrapped in his arms. The tinsel tickled her skin where it was exposed and she kissed his nipple.

"Tell me."

"I don't want to…"

"Tell me, please."

"It was about love," she let the words spill out. "I wanted to find someone to love, something I never thought would happen. Not that I think you have to love me. But I…"

He lifted her chin and kissed her, then gathered her close in his arms. "I like that idea, too, but no more phone sex, unless it's with me. Deal?"

"Deal." She thought she should probably tell him she'd pretty much made that decision. "What about your friends?"

"I already told them they had to find someone else. We can go to the party and watch. It'll be great fun."

They both laughed. "But first, I'm going to take you upstairs and unwrap you. Then I plan on keeping you chained to the bed all night long."

"That sounds perfect, as long as you're there with me."

"Sweetheart, I wouldn't want to be anywhere else." He stood and helped her up and out of her panties, then led her toward the stairs. He had said she was his most perfect present, and right now, she totally agreed with him, in the reverse.

She'd never had a more perfect gift, and she didn't plan to ever return it.

About the Author

Melinda Barron loves to explore Egyptian tombs and temples, discover Mayan ruins, play in castles towers, and explore new cities and countries. She generally does it all from the comfort of her home by opening a book.

Melinda loves to lose herself between the pages of a book. The only thing she loves more is creating stories from the wonderful heroes and heroines that haunt her dreams and crowd her head. She believes love is for everyone, not just those who are a size 2. Her books are full of magic, suspense and love, in all sorts of shapes and sizes.

Mel currently lives in the Texas Panhandle, with two cats, and a file stuffed with new ideas to keep her typing fingers busy, and your heart engaged.

Lust, Lies and Tinsel Ties

By Mia Jae

Table of Contents

Chapter One

The black thong was a perfect fit, if she did say so herself. It cupped her nicely in front, making a perfect vee at her crotch. The tiny straps hugged her hipbone.

Bree Noël Conner smoothed her hands over her hips and tucked the tips of her fingers under the thin string. She'd invested in an airbrushed tan for the occasion and was glad of it. Her skin was bronze and silky, even though it was Christmas Eve. Pasty white and dry wasn't for her, though her complexion was naturally milky. Since moving to Albuquerque, she tried her best to stay sun-kissed and healthy-looking, like everyone else. Besides, she had a skimpy dress to wear tonight and she'd be damned if she was wearing pantyhose.

Even in the middle of winter.

Turning, she glanced over her shoulder in the mirror and smiled. "Nice ass, if I do say so myself." She adjusted the thong and then ran her palms over her backside too.

Wearing only the scrap of fabric, she padded across her bedroom and sat on the bench at the foot of her bed. Warming her favorite cocoa butter lotion in her hands, she skimmed her hands over her legs, lifting first one, then the other, into the air.

"Nice and moist," she whispered. "Perfect."

One at a time, she slipped a foot into a black patent leather boot, complete with five-inch tall, white faux-fur tops and three-inch heels, then laced each boot up her shin, from the top of her foot all the way to the fur at her knees.

Standing, she moved to the mirror again and admired the high-heeled boots, again turning this way and that to get the full effect.

"Nice," she whispered. "Yes." These will do just fine.

Lifting her gaze to her bare chest, she perused each of her girls. Firm, full, and bronzed as well, she noted her erect, upturned nipples.

She liked breasts. On her and on other women. Not that she went around feeling up other women's breasts—it wasn't her gig—she secretly admired other women's from afar. To her own way of thinking, hers were topnotch.

Her last boyfriend thought so, too.

Until she'd screwed up. Again.

Sighing, she was actually glad he was out of her life, and relieved she didn't have a man to answer to right now. Picking up her black strapless bra from the dresser, she clasped it around her waist. Twisting it upward, she shimmied the girls into place. It was a cup size too small.

Damn.

A lazy smiled curled over her lips. She liked the look of her breasts spilling out over the rim of the cups.

Her cell rang; she glanced down at the number, picked it up. "Hey, Ging."

Her best friend's high-pitched voice pinged through from the other side.

Bree grimaced. "I hear you! Yes. I know it's snowing. What?"

Ginger explained once more, "We need to leave now. We'll never get up the mountain if we wait an hour."

Shit. That came through loud and clear. The party was in a home up in the East Mountain area of the Sandias.

They'd had light snow off and on all day. She hadn't realized that it was getting worse.

Teach her to dally in the tub.

But tonight, she had to look nice. She was hoping to come away from this evening with a purse full of pocket change, all for a good cause, of course.

"All right! I'll be downstairs in ten."

She ended the call and tossed the phone on the bed. Her Santa dress hung in the doorway. She grasped the thing—if you could call it a dress, even—and gave it a quick perusal. Pulling it over her head, she wriggled into it. Skin tight, it cinched at her waist and flared out over her hips. She struggled with the zipper at the side, finally managing to pull it all the way up.

"Belt."

Locating the black patent leather belt, she circled her waist and pulled it tight, buckling it snug at her center. Again, she gave herself a once-over in the mirror. The dress barely skimmed her ass. The red velveteen, trimmed in faux fur along the hem, tickled her cheeks. Fur cradled her breasts, as well.

"Nice."

A horn sounded outside.

"Crap."

She clutched at her makeup bag, the elbow-length red satin gloves, and her Santa hat, then tripped down the stairs of her townhouse toward the front door.

* * * *

The roads in the city weren't too bad. Once they left the highway, however, the mountain two-lane was somewhat messy. Bree stared through the swiping blades pushing the dry snow pellets off the windshield. "God, I hope this isn't a mistake."

"Quit worrying."

Bree turned to Ginger, who was leaning forward in her seat, staring out the window.

"This is going to be fine," Ginger said. "The party is over at one and hopefully by the end of the evening, our names will be a little more prominent in higher circles."

"I'm worried about the snow."

"Oh hell." She patted the dash of her Jeep. "Ol' Ginny here will get us back home again just fine. That's why I like a four-wheel drive. Doesn't keep me from getting where I need to go. Besides, it's a dry snow. Not thick and wet like back home."

Bree didn't know about that. Back home in Ohio, when it snowed like this it generally wasn't a big problem. But in Ohio, they had the proper snow removal equipment and had the systems all worked out. Here, big snows rarely came. And even though the weathermen weren't predicting a huge mess, Bree was antsy. Her father was a farmer, after all, and she'd learned to watch the sky and respect the weather.

She didn't like how the sky looked to the north and west.

Again, she looked to Ginger, taking in her party attire. She wore as skimpy an outfit as Bree, the color was tan with white trimming her cuffs and collar; the neckline low cut. Red hearts were centered up the bodice and a red petticoat peeked out from beneath the short skirt. A teeny white apron completed the look. The outfit was topped off with red sparkling Mary Jane's and red and white candy cane striped knee socks.

"So what the hell are you supposed to be?" she asked.

"What? You can't tell?"

She shook her head. "Not sure."

"I'm the Gingerbread girl!" She pointed to her apron, covering her crotch. "See? There is my cookie."

"Ah." She did indeed see Ginger's cookie. "I get it. Ginger the Gingerbread girl. Hell, I hope we don't get stopped on this road due to the weather. We look like hookers."

"We are so not hookers."

"But we sure look like it."

Ginger edged a glance her way. "Bree, we're businesswomen who are volunteering their time tonight for a good cause. Not to mention that it will be a good promo op for our business. That's all. We're not hookers."

"We look like hookers."

"Give it a rest."

Bree wondered how she'd gotten talked into this. She watched the snow out her window and replied, "I'm wearing a dress that barely covers my ass with nothing but a thong underneath. If I don't look like I'm out for sex, then I don't know what…"

"So what's new? You're always out for sex."

Whipping her head around to look at Ginger, she spat back, "And you are Miss Goody Two-Shoes?"

Ginger braked and stopped the car dead in the road. Probably not a good move, given the mush and the ever climbing incline, because the Jeep shimmied a little to the right. "Hell, Bree, what is up with you? So we both like sex. So what? Has nothing to do with what we are doing tonight. Tonight, we are cocktail waitresses at an artsy-fartsy benefit party. Volunteers. Nothing more, nothing less. And we're out for tips, nothing more, nothing less. The proceeds all go to the homeless shelter that we, Conner & Baker Realty, are helping to sponsor. It's a good thing, Bree. For the homeless. For us. So, if you flip your skirt accidentally and show a little cheek, all the better."

Ginger was right. The real estate business they co-owned needed a boost. They were doing okay, but lately, they were just making ends meet. Volunteering for this charity event would make them more prominent in the community, since neither of them was from here.

Besides, she'd never been against showing a little ass cheek.

"I hope like hell no one we know is there." Bree adjusted her bra at her cleavage, and felt a lurch forward as Ginger put her foot on the accelerator. Going nude on the beach at Daytona during Spring Break was one thing. "I mean, how embarrassing? What if we truly ran into a client? It could be the kiss of death…" Baring it to a colleague was quite another.

"Give it a rest, Bree. We need to run into our clients and colleagues. They need to see us giving back to the community we live in."

"They don't need to see the cheeks of my ass."

"Oh hell! When did you become Ms. Prude! It's a flamboyant, funky, charity party with all the artsy community attending so they will get their pictures in the paper. No one will care if you are showing your ass!"

"How can you be so sure?"

"Because, I just know these things."

Not comforting. Ginger's sixth sense about "things" was what led them out to the Southwest in the first place. And so far, that hadn't panned out too well.

Ginger maneuvered a curve and slowed. "Oh. My. God."

Even through the slanting snow, they faced a spectacular view of the land stretching between the east side of the Sandias and toward Santa Fe. A little to their right, sat a very large stucco house, artfully placed into the mountain landscape and facing that same view. There were a couple of cars in the drive, as they were early.

The volunteers were to arrive at seven. The party was due to begin at eight. Bree figured it wouldn't really get started until about ten.

"This is the house," Ginger said.

"Damn."

"Money."

"Yep."

Then Ginger pointed. "And look. There."

A SOLD sign was perched rather cockeyed at the end of the drive. "Dammit," Ginger hissed. "We sure could have used a sale like that."

Bree frowned. "Way things have been going lately, I'd settle for the sale of that casita off Rio Grande."

* * * *

Jake Baldwin peered out the window. Even though it was now dark, the lights from the house reflected off the white, snow-covered hills and valleys below. He sat at the back of the house, away from the party, a bit disgruntled and lost in thought, as usual. His life, for the most part, was all he'd wanted it to be. Successful career, huge home— this new home—in the mountains, a satisfying social life with an eclectic bevy of friends, and...

"Jake?"

Carson.

He stood and turned toward the voice of his lover. The opening of the door threw a triangle of light into the dark room. Carson strode slowly inside, stooping slightly to twist the switch on a lamp, low lighting the room.

Yes, and he had Carson.

And for a long time, that had been enough.

"What are you doing back here?" he asked. "The party is in full swing."

"I know."

"Guests are asking for you."

"I'll be there in time for the auction."

"Good. I have my eye on an item for you," he went on. "I may have bid too high."

He wished he wouldn't do that. "Please, don't go overboard."

Carson eyed him. "I know my limits. And you are still in a funk."

Nodding, he cast his gaze away. "I'm sorry. I know I promised to snap out of it for the party, but it's not working."

They both stood for a moment staring at the floor.

The silence between them was telling. There had been too much of it between them the past few months. Talking didn't seem to be on their common agenda.

He felt the warmth of Carson's palm on his bicep. "Look at me, Jake," he said softly, lifting his chin with the forefinger of the other hand.

Jake hooked his gaze into Carson's and exhaled. "I appreciate your patience with me. I'm just…"

"Sh…" Carson drew closer. "Stop talking and listen to me. We'll get through this. I am a patient man. But you need to decide, Jake, what you want, sooner or later."

He knew that.

Carson was patient when they bought the house together. Jake had pushed it, wanting to be high in the Sandias. Carson would have preferred the city. He thought buying the house would settle him somewhat. Ground him into their life together. Help him forget…

It hadn't.

Carson didn't want to know what was wrong. Had said he didn't need to know the truth. But he knew that it was serious and that Jake had screwed up. He'd even said he had forgiven him, even though he didn't know what for.

Why couldn't he forgive himself?

And why couldn't he just fess up and tell Carson that he'd fucked up?

No. Instead, he'd lied. Told him the moodiness was due to depression. In reality that probably wasn't far from being true. His brain was screwed on crooked, and he couldn't make sense of what was, and wasn't, the right thing to do anymore.

He wanted to be fair. Wanted it like hell. And he didn't want to ask anything of Carson that was outside of his comfort zone. But things changed.

And he knew exactly when.

Since then, nothing sat well. Nothing satisfied.

Decide what I want. Sooner or later.

Thing was, the decision wasn't totally up to him, was it?

"That's the thing, Carson," he whispered, "I know what I want. I'm just not sure you will agree."

Waiting, he stared into the blue of his lover's eyes. Slowly, his partner leaned into him, clutched his bicep a little tighter, and placed a soft kiss on his lips.

"Leave it to me." Carson's soft breath tickled his cheek. "I will make this work."

Jake wasn't sure that he could.

Chapter Two

Glancing at the clock over the bartender's head, Bree sighed and tried not to hobble in her black stiletto patent leather boots. It was damned difficult, though, and she leaned into the bar in an attempt to take the pressure off the balls of her feet. She sat her empty tray down on the counter. "I need a Vodka Collins, a Mojito with light ice, straight bourbon, and something fruity. She doesn't care what it is as long as it has pineapple."

The bartender—his name was Ted, she thought—snickered and started on the drinks. Turning her back to him, she glanced out over the party crowd. Her earlier thoughts that the party wouldn't heat up until ten o'clock were on track. Even though the crowd was smaller than anticipated, and rather sophisticated and artsy, they knew how to throw down a good time.

She was ready to go home.

"How you doing?" Ginger tap-danced her way up to the bar. "Isn't this exciting?" She smiled broadly, tossing her amber locks over her shoulder. Sidling closer, she lowered her voice and said, "How are the tips? I think I've tucked minimum of five hundred in my bra. Hell, we are going to have a pile of money to give to the shelter."

Bree glanced to Ginger's chest. "You look lopsided. Your right tit is lumpy."

Slapping her tray on the bar, she did a quick adjustment. "Look at this place, Bree. My God! I wish we could land a sale like this. They just bought it, I heard. I'm thinking close to a mil. What do you think?"

Bree broke her gaze from Ginger and perused the room. A harmony of party sounds swirled around them—a classy jazz tune laid a nice bass level to the cacophony; people talking and bursts of laughter balanced the treble. The people were a trip. Dressed in all kinds of couture, from vintage eclectic, to Goth Christmas, to diamonds and black tie, there was an air of sophisticated funk about the room.

But Bree was only in tune with the home. Floor to ceiling windows faced the view of the mountains and the twinkling valley lights below. The great room was large; the bar she stood at was a permanent fixture. Solid oak. Wood beams crisscrossed the ceiling; others stood as pillars throughout the room, lending a rustic, Southwest feel. The interior walls were stucco; the floors terra cotta tile. The kitchen behind her was magnificent—she'd stuck her head in there earlier in the evening—complete with state-of-the art stainless everything.

"It's all custom. Fixtures. Woodwork. Don't you love those built-ins over there? And what about that stained glass sky light. Look at that fireplace, Bree. Looks like red rock stone. Fabulous. Four bedrooms and baths. A spa downstairs. Indoor pool. A guest casita outside...."

"One mil, eight hundred thousand." Bree uttered her prediction while Ginger continued to spout the home's assets.

"Actually, we got it for a steal at one-point-two."

Both women turned. Bree gasped at the sight of the man standing immediately behind them, leaning into the bar. The color of his sparkling eyes rivaled the most clear blue turquoise she'd ever seen. His chiseled features forced her to catch a breath. It was difficult to immediately discern whether he was Anglo or Native...probably bi-racial. His complexion was much darker than hers; his semi-short, light brown hair, deliciously unkempt.

What a beautiful man.

And there was something slightly familiar about him.

Looking anywhere but straight into his face, Bree acted nonchalant. "You're right. That price was a steal."

"We know."

The man pushed away from the bar and held out a hand to Bree. "Carson Graham. And you are?"

"The hired help."

Ginger poked her elbow in her side, and Bree jumped. She took Carson's hand and shook it. "I'm Bree, and she's Ginger."

Carson snickered. "Bree?"

"Yeah. Like the cheese."

The right corner of his mouth stayed in smile-mode.

"And she's Ginger, like the cookie."

Carson laughed out loud.

The bartender set the last of her drinks on her tray. Squeezing between Carson and Ginger, she smiled back and said, "And I have drinks to deliver. Nice to meet you."

Her fumbling fingers grasped the tray and in that second, she realized she was trembling. Not since she'd broken up with Sam a couple of months ago, had she realized how much she missed being close to a man.

She loved men.

Men.

Plural.

And that was the trouble. The men she dated always seemed to want some sort of commitment. It was difficult for her to settle. And sooner or later, bored and unsatisfied, she strayed...

Carson stopped her with a hand to her forearm. She rested the tray against the bar and once more, peered into his eyes. "Have we met?" he queried.

Confused, unsure why he seemed so familiar, she shook her head. "Um, earlier tonight? No."

Cocking his head to one side, he narrowed his gaze and studied her. "No. Prior to tonight. I never forget a face." He wriggled his fingers, as if he was itching to touch her. "Or a profile." Then he did just that, touched her. Reaching out, he grazed a soft, fingertip stroke across her cheekbone and then traced the outline of her jaw, as if he were rendering a line drawing of her face. An unexpected shiver crannied through her and sped toward her center. His touch had instantly aroused her and it came from out of nowhere. "I'm an artist," he continued, "and I never forget a contour…"

Bree huffed out a quick breath, trying to quell the short pants that wanted to escape her mouth. "I'm not sure, Carson. I—"

Someone bumped into her from behind, pushing her closer into him. He steadied her against his chest—which did absolutely nothing to quell her arousal, but served to completely stimulate it. She inhaled, deep, and took in the sharp spice of his aftershave, and nearly melted.

Her face was in his neck. "I should deliver those drinks," she whispered.

Steadying her in front of him, Carson stared deep into her eyes, then lifted the tray and put it in her hands. "Go deliver your drinks, Ms. Santa. I'm not going anywhere."

She hesitated, and did a slow turn, as Carson's hands dropped to her hips and his fingertips grazed the hem of her skirt.

And the cheeks of her ass.

The action sent her sex into a decadent pucker of desire.

* * * *

It was another hour before things slowed down enough to where Bree could catch her breath and a couple of sideways glances at Carson. Each time their eyes met, a little thrill raced through her. It was approaching midnight, the appointed time of the charity auction, and the remaining crowd of about forty people were either settling into sofas and overstuffed chairs, drinks in hand, or milling about aimlessly chatting with one another.

Carson Graham, at the moment, was no where to be found.

She snickered to herself. Graham. Like the cracker.

"What's so funny?"

Ted the bartender busied himself cleaning up behind the bar. "Just thought of something," she told him. "No big deal. Hey, you need some help?"

"Yeah." He was loading some dirty glasses into a plastic carrier. "Mind taking some of these back to the kitchen? I need to start a dishwasher load. Somehow I became bartender and chief bottle washer once the weather turned nasty."

"Sure." Bree joined him behind the bar. Much of the hired help had been dismissed an hour or so earlier. She and Ginger had decided to stay on, confident 'ol Ginny would get them back down the mountain.

Ginger moved in, slid an arm around Ted's waist, smiled, and gave him a quick peck on the cheek. Bree raised a brow. Obviously, there was another reason Ginger wanted to stick around.

"What time do you think we can get out of here," she asked, adding glasses to Bree's plastic bin. "I am so ready to go." She kicked off a red Mary Jane and reached down to rub a foot. "What about you, Bree?"

At the moment, Bree was conflicted about leaving sooner rather than later. She scanned the room again. No Carson. She shrugged. "I'm with you, Ginger. I leave when you leave."

"Ted needs a ride," Ginger returned.

"Okay by me." She hefted the bin of glasses, wondering just what kind of ride Ted would get later tonight. She watched as he palmed Ginger's butt through her dress. "I'll get these started." Behind her, she heard a tinkling of glasses and a female voice raise over the crowd, attempting to gain attention. She continued on into the kitchen.

With an oomph, she hoisted the container onto the counter and bent to open the dishwasher. Good. Clean dishes. One by one she emptied the glasses and small plates and stacked them on the counter. Every once in a while she stretched to work the kinks out of her back.

Oh boy, was she ever tired.

* * * *

Had he been on his game tonight, Jake would have been out in the great room, peering up at Grace Walker, the chair of the committee raising money for the homeless shelter downtown off Central, smiling and clapping his hands as she announced the merits of each item up for auction.

Of course, he wasn't on his game, and he didn't give a rat's ass what useless trinkets were up for grabs tonight. The whole notion was silly, anyway. Each of those items was already sold to their owners, the bidding having taken place prior to the party. It was all show, and he wondered why they were even going through the motions since the press didn't show up for the party, anyway, due to the weather.

At best, he felt disconnected to the entire ordeal, but his body sure as hell jerked to attention as soon as he stepped through the back entrance to the kitchen.

His heart pounded in his throat. Thank God there was no one else in the room with whom he had to speak. He wasn't sure he could. All he could do, however, was stand and stare.

The obvious item that caught his attention was the skimpy red Santa dress trimmed in white fur—and the woman wearing it. The boots, why yes, those were quite the thing, as well. Sleek and sexy and screaming "come fuck me" at the top of their lungs. The long mane of almost jet-black hair that swung over her shoulder was the piece of the picture that made his chest clutch in addled surprise. The bronzed and dewy skin of her long legs made him think of only one thing—a perfect passage to the nectar of the gods. Her thighs gave way to a luscious round derrière that peeked out from beneath that fur-lined skirt each time she bent to pull out a dish or put one in.

His gut quivered.

She stood and he got the full profile effect.

"No." The word whooshed out on a breath before he could drag it back.

Bree sensed, more than heard, the one word exclamation of angst that filled the room around her. Slowly, she rotated to her rear, and immediately caught site of the man standing behind her.

Her entire being trilled at the sight of him, and suddenly it all came back in a whoosh...

* * * *

She tapped her pencil on her desktop, keeping rhythm with the nervous kick of her leg beneath it. Leaning toward the two men, she feigned attention on both but was totally fixated on the tall, dark-headed man who sat to her left. And he, it appeared, was giving off come-hither vibes like nobody's business.

"So you're looking for something in the mountains?"

"I'd actually prefer downtown," the sandy-haired one remarked. Drawing her gaze away, she focused on this man for a moment. "A condo would be best," he offered. "Small and efficient. Perhaps an outside deck area but nothing elaborate. Good lighting, natural, at least in one room, for my studio."

"What do you consider small?" she asked.

"Thirty-five hundred square feet, or about."

Handsome, sexy, and rich. Nice combo. And there were two of them.

The way-too-viral man to his left cleared his throat and leaned closer. "That's his preference. Not necessarily mine. If you're asking for our wish lists, yes, I do prefer the mountains. The east side, of course, looking down over the Turquoise Trail. Something sprawling and authentic that reeks of the Southwest. A great view. A pool would be nice. Guest quarters for when the families come to visit, should they visit, and so on."

Bree swallowed and kept tapping her pencil against the Plexiglas desktop. She glanced from one man to another. The dark-headed one—what was his name? Oh yes. Jake. Jake Baldwin—appeared engrossed with her. She licked her lips and found it difficult to sit still in her seat. "So in other words the two of you are at an impasse."

"No," Jake scooted even closer and laid a hand over her tapping pencil and fingers. Her knee stopped jerking. "Where we are at, is that you will find something that comprises both our needs." He grinned, and Bree felt an electric current spark from his eyes and make a beeline straight for her pussy. Dammit. These two men were a couple, and she was getting so turned on by that. What the hell?

But his eyes...the lightest shade of blue, and the contrast of his inky black hair. The combination was spellbinding and, shit, yes, she was captivated.

He continued, "We need for you to be our common ground, Ms. Conner. The bridge between us, so to speak. We trust you."

Between them. She glanced from one highly potent male specimen to another. They both oozed sexuality and pure, unadulterated maleness. They were a couple. Gay, she supposed, or bi-sexual?

Why was she feeling like this?

Not to mention that the heat from his palm, still tented over hers, felt erotic as hell and somehow protective at the same time. She glanced down. Was his thumb caressing hers?

"I see I have my work cut out for me."

He cast a sly smile her way. "That, you do." Then breaking away, he stood. "May I borrow your restroom?"

"Of course." She stood as well. "Down the hall and to the left."

He nodded and headed that way.

Ginger swept in at that moment. "I found those listings," she began, sitting beside the sandy-haired client. "Let's see how you like some of these."

Carson nodded and reached for the files.

Bree glanced down the hall.

No. She shouldn't.

"Excuse me."

Her heels clicked down the ceramic tile hallway. Loud. Her small, private office sat across the hall from the single bathroom. Pausing in the doorway, her hands resting on the casing, she cast a sideways glance. The fine hairs at her neck stood erect.

She swiveled on the ball of her foot.

He stood framed in the opposite doorway, a question on his face that must have rivaled the one on her own. Her heart banged against her chest as she stepped across the hallway.

He pulled her inside with one swift motion. The door clicked shut behind them. He locked it and crowded her up against it.

She moaned as he covered her mouth with his firm, wet lips and kissed her. Hard.

His hands wandered, bunching up the hem of her dress; the heat of his fingers scorched her inner thigh as they inched toward her center.

Breaking away with a gasp, she took his face into her hands and searched his face. In the next instant, she lunged forward and plunged her tongue into his mouth. Passion raced through her, and every nerve ending in her body felt alive with anticipation—and desire—as they sloppily and hungrily tasted each other.

He pushed her skirt up around her waist and curled a finger around her thong, jerking downward. She tugged his shirt out of his trousers.

"Hurry," she whispered.

"Yes." The single word came from deep in his throat and echoed her urgency.

"Fuck me."

"Yes."

Her hands worked over his fly and boxers as she unveiled his glorious cock. She gasped and took it in her palm, curling her fingers around his velvet smoothness, thumbing over his throbbing maleness. "Oh, my god..." He was, indeed, scrumptious. Long and thick, with a massive head that promised pleasure.

He turned her against the door in one rough, insistent move, then raised her hands over her head. One of his large hands held her wrists tight while the other slid down her back, over her ass, and slipped between her thighs.

Slowly, he dragged a finger into her slit and backwards up between her ass cheeks. Then again. Shivering at his touch, she squirmed against his hand. "More," she whimpered.

"Goddamn you are hot and wet. Spread for me."

She arched her back and pushed her ass toward him. His fingers plunged into her. She pushed her shoulders into the door for leverage and groaned.

Heightened passion gripped her as he stroked.

"Fuck me," she begged. "Hurry." They'd already been gone several minutes. Would anyone notice? In her mind's eye, she could see him large and engorged behind her, waiting to plunge himself...

He did as she asked.

The length of his silky cock sank into her; she exhaled in exquisite pleasure. He covered her body with his and pushed slowly in and out, both his hands now above her head, laying flat over her arms and hands, holding her there. She was trapped between the door and the hard plane of his body, impaled by his firm flesh and one helluva decadent cock.

She lost all sense of time and place.

Jake groaned and repeatedly pumped into her, over and over again.

"Oh god, don't stop," she whispered.

"I could fuck your ass forever," he breathed.

"Do it."

His lips were at her ear, his breath moist and warm. "Your pussy is as good as I thought...knew..."

Moaning, and clasping his fingers tightly over hers, he increased his thrusts until she silently panted her own explosive release, mingling her fingers with his grip, and pancaking the side of her face against the door. With a stifled shout, and an overall trembling of his body, he held on to her and lowered his mouth to her shoulder and bit...while he spilled his own release.

Their breathing settled into slow unison. They stayed together against the door for only a moment. Jake pulled out and turned her to face him. Still breathing heavily, she searched his face. Never had she been taken quite so unexpectedly, or spontaneously, by a man who intrigued her as much. His exotic looks and sensuality were her undoing. And at that moment, she wasn't quite sure what to do with any of the thoughts and feelings racing through her head and heart.

He traced a forefinger over her cheekbone and peered deep into her eyes.

"I've not been with a woman in years," he offered. "You... Dammit. You..."

Then he broke away, shaking his head. She watched as he tucked that marvelous cock of his inside his pants and straightened the rest of his clothing. Finally, rubbing his hands over his face, he lifted his gaze to look at her again. "I'm sorry. I should have had more control."

She shook her head, ready to say something—to say, *No, it was me. I should have had more control. You are so damned irresistible*—but he grasped her by the forearms and scooted her out of the way, and left.

* * * *

Six months flew through Bree's psyche with a flash of memory. All of a sudden, she knew why Carson had looked so familiar. She'd not paid him much attention that day, her world totally filled with the man standing before her now. Jake Baldwin. Ginger hadn't questioned later that day when she said they couldn't take the two men on as clients. They had an unspoken rule that when one of them said no, the other listened. It was professional suicide, she knew, but it couldn't happen.

But Jake and Carson had not called back, making it easy.

Now, here they stood, facing each other again.

"So you got your way, huh?" She hooked into his gaze and held.

Shaking himself, Jake took a tentative step forward. "The house, you mean."

"Yes."

"We compromised. Sort of."

"It's a lovely place."

The connection between them was magnetic, and she felt drawn to him like she was the back end of a rubber band. It didn't help that he was slowly walking toward her, increasing the tension.

"What are you doing here?" he asked.

Bree glanced over her shoulder. "Oh. The benefit. Volunteering. The company…"

He nodded. "I see." Then, staring off to the side, added, "I couldn't call back."

"I was glad you didn't."

He jerked back to look at her. "It was…complicated."

Nodding, she agreed. "Yes."

"Bree…"

She closed her eyes at the sound of her name rolling off his tongue. With him out of sight, the distance between them was even more palpable. Her chest quavered with pins and needles, every nerve ending on edge. And then…

He touched her. Gently. Taking her hand in his.

"I have never been so fascinated by a woman..." he whispered. "And I've not been able to get you out of..."

Noise from the living area interrupted their encounter, and Ginger and Ted burst into the kitchen on its heels. They broke away from each other. Jake sidestepped her and moved toward the entrance to the great room. Turning, Bree watched him disappear into the room; then she exhaled, long and hard.

"Goddamn..."

Chapter Three

"Get this auction over and get these people the hell out of here."

Jake made a beeline to Carson and hissed out the words in his ear. Turning, his partner studied his face, narrowed his gaze and dipped his head in agreement. Jake hadn't intended for the words to come out in such a blunt, angry manner, but they had.

"My, what a cheery character you are this Christmas Eve," Carson replied. "You better be careful, Santa may leave you nothing but stones in your stocking." He backed away, swept a hand in front of him and added with sarcasm, "Your wish is my command, sir."

Jake's stomach turned. He was an ass and knew it. Taking a half step forward, he reached out for Carson, who turned abruptly and stalked off.

"Shit." The curse slipped between his teeth.

He watched as Carson threaded through the crowd and toward the front of the room where Grace Walker was holding court with what was left of the partiers. He whispered in her ear, then took the center stage himself while Grace stepped to the side.

"Jake and I certainly want to thank each and every one of you for coming this evening, particularly with this unexpected weather," he began. "Who would have thought? Snow on Christmas Eve in Albuquerque?"

The crowd chuckled, and he continued. "But the evening is long, and I just heard that law enforcement is recommending people get home and stay off the roads. We want you to use your own judgment. Know that we have guest accommodations here for anyone who would rather not travel home this evening. But for those of you who are eager to leave, we have one more item up for auction."

He paused and scanned the room. Jake's gut tightened.

"You may have noticed our lovely cocktail waitresses this evening." He pointed toward the bar at the back of the room; Jake followed his direction and bristled. Bree and her business partner—Ginger? He hadn't really focused much on her—they were busying themselves behind it cleaning up. Both of their heads lifted, and they nodded as the crowd turned their way. Ginger smiled broadly. Bree gave a slight smile and glanced off. "In case you didn't know," Carson went on, "these generous ladies are the owners of Conner & Baker Realty. They volunteered their time this evening. All of the tips they earned," he glanced back over the crowd, "from all of you generous people, will be donated to the homeless shelter. Let's hear it for our sexy servers!"

The crowd clapped madly.

"Come up here! Come!" Carson waved toward the women.

Jake wondered what in hell Carson was up to.

The last thing Bree wanted at the moment was to parade herself in front of all the party-goers *and* Jake Baldwin *and* Carson Graham. Could people tell how distracted and turned on she was by him? Them? Shit, yes, there was Carson too, with whom she'd been making eyes all evening…and who had slipped his finger up her dress earlier, taunting her.

Talk about libido confusion. Seemed like they all had it. At the moment, she didn't trust her sexual psyche.

But here she was, being pushed from behind the bar to the center of attention by a giggling Ginger. "Move it, honey. This is the part we've been waiting for."

Bree stopped and grasped Ginger's arm. "What are you talking about?"

"No time now."

"Yes. Time. Now."

"The crowd is watching."

"I don't give a flying fucking leap! Tell me what is going on."

Ginger huffed, her eyes darting back and forth. Leaning closer, she whispered, "Just shut up and follow my lead. It's for the shelter. We're getting auctioned."

"We?" Panic seized her chest. "Auctioned?"

"Yes."

"The company, right?"

"No. You. Me."

"Fuck."

"That's not part of the deal. Not unless you want it to be." She grinned slyly. "Seriously, we just donate twenty-four hours of our time to whoever buys us. I'm sure it will be shelter-related, or something like that."

"Dammit, Ginger! You knew this ahead of time?"

"Yes. Now, shut up and smile. You're on first."

Ginger Baker, I will make you freakin' pay! If the truth be known, Bree was glad for the anger that raced over her at that moment. It replaced the confused sexual crap that was rolling around in her head seconds earlier.

The crowd cheered and clapped wildly again, and suddenly Bree found herself being catapulted forward into the throng, and before she knew it, was standing on an ottoman and Grace Walker was saying...

"May I have five thousand, please?"

As they used to say back home in Southern Ohio, *What. The. Hell?*

Five thousand!

"I'll give you seven." Bree's head whipped to a voice in the corner. She couldn't see from where it came.

"Eight." She jerked to the left. A woman's voice. Crap.

"Ten thousand." Back to the right. Carson.

Carson?

He grinned at her. Her chest heaved. Oh, fuck...

"Twelve," came the voice from the shadows again.

Sonofabitch!

Grace Walker twittered in delight beside her. Bree scowled and clenched her fists. What in the world was she going to have to do to earn this much money?

"Fifteen thousand." Carson put in.

"Twenty." The woman again.

"Twenty-five," came from the corner.

The crowd jittered, individual heads rotating back and forth, straining to see the man in the shadows who was topping every bid made. After a moment, they all turned their attention back to Carson.

As did Bree. Her guts trembled.

Carson grinned. "Thirty thousand," he said coolly and winked.

The room fell silent. Waiting. Anticipating the countering voice from the back of the room, or from the left. But one never came.

Her chest was tight from holding her breath for too long.

Grace Walker stepped between Carson and Bree, and it seemed the entire room exhaled. As did Bree. Finally. "Thirty thousand dollars! Oh, my! Going once. Twice. Sold!"

The dizzying thought Bree had at that moment, was that her roughly seven hundred dollars in tips seemed mighty paltry. Why in the hell had she spent all night on her feet—in these heels!—to bring in tips if this was going to happen?

I'm killing Ginger...

Grace hugged Bree who stood stiff and unmoving, eyeing Carson, who appeared quite pleased with himself. He stepped up and shook Grace's hand, then reached for Bree's elbow. "Come with me," he whispered.

The crowed oohed and clapped. Bree tried to shut them out.

Behind her, she heard Grace begin the bidding on Ginger. She hoped Ted had deep pockets, if he expected to get any tonight.

Her hand felt small and warm in Carson's as he led her out of the room and into a low-lit hallway. Immediately, she felt flushed. They walked in silence for a few seconds, the only sound was Bree's boot heels making a soft click on the tile floor.

"Where are you taking me," she finally said. Her tummy was filled with a thousand butterflies. What was in store for her?

"Just down here. So we can talk."

They passed a fully decorated Christmas tree, a few artsy structures, and some pottery on their way to…wherever. She supposed they needed to iron out the deals of her twenty-four hour servitude. "Okay, so what is it you have in mind for me, boss man?"

He didn't answer. They turned a corner and faced massive, carved, double oak doors. They swung open with ease as he turned the knobs and led her into the room.

Bedroom. A very large bedroom.

A very large and masculine chamber of love was more like it.

She stopped short. "Um, Carson. I don't think this is what the shelter people had in mind when they thought of this slave auction thing…" Although she had to admit, glancing about, that the room intrigued her.

"No worries, love," he said, "We're just in a holding pattern here for a moment, so to speak."

He led her further into the room.

A huge oak bed, which echoed the carved design of the doors, sat regally in the center of the room. Four oversized posters anchored the piece of furniture, set up on a two-foot tall bed frame, also made of solid oak. The headboard was the crowning jewel, with ornate carved gargoyles, animals and nude figures, cutting deep grooves into the wood.

A red fur bedspread with gaudy six-inch gold fringe was draped over the mattress. Low lights were scattered about the room lending shadows and a golden glow. Candles flickered in the off places where the lamp light didn't reach. The sweet smell of roses and the spicy hint of patchouli met her nose.

Still grasping her hand, the butterflies in her stomach flapping wildly now, Carson led her across the room to the gigantic bed. His large hands went to her waist, and he hoisted her up on it.

"Carson…"

"Just one second, love."

Before she realized it, he'd nestled her back into the fluffy pillows on the bed, and had grasped her left hand firm in his own. In a flash, that wrist was bound with a leather strap and he reached behind her to thread the other end through a large eyebolt embedded in the wood— something that she had not noticed before this—and pulled it taut and secured it with some sort of knot. Still moving swiftly, and reaching over her, he quickly bound her right wrist, as well.

All Bree could do was look up into Carson's eyes in wonder and imagine the puzzled look on her own face.

"Um, Carson. I don't believe this is necessary. I'm not exactly sure what you have in mind for the next twenty four hours, but…. Normally I'm pretty much of a pushover when it comes to sex so, you know, I can be a sure thing. Of course, I know that we've not even talked about that, but…"

"My apologies, sweetheart," he pushed back from the bed, hands on his hips, "but I can't risk you slipping away on me while I tend to something."

"You're asking an awful lot for the thirty grand, aren't you?"

He snickered. "Sorry honey. I'm not asking for anything. I didn't buy you for me."

"What?"

Stepping back from the bed, he said, "Wait here." Then starting for the door, he came up quick, snapping his finger.

"Like I have a choice?"

Turning and tossing back that oh-so-sexy grin of his again, he replied, "No love, you don't. Not for the moment. But remember, I did buy you, and the deal was twenty-four hours to do my bidding."

"I didn't sign any deal." She tugged at the leather strap with her right hand. Hm. Pretty darned secure.

"No, but your lovely business partner did." He glanced at the door. "Remember, it's for the shelter. I'll be right back," he added.

For the shelter.

Somehow, she didn't think Grace Walker had this in mind when she proclaimed her sold for thirty thousand dollars.

Holy shit! He'd paid thirty thousand big ones! For her.

Bree wiggled against the straps and curled her upper body toward the foot of the bed. "Wait!"

But he was gone, although only for a minute. He returned with a handful of tinsel garland, obviously snatched from the Christmas tree down the hall.

"Here love." Working to untangle the tinsel, he wove them into the leather straps at her waist. Then stepping back and admiring his handiwork, he must have decided she needed to look even more festive than she already did, for he draped tinsel over her body, her arms, breasts, thighs…

"I am not a Christmas package, Carson." When would this charade be over?

Leaning forward, he brushed his lips against her cheek and moved to her ear. His body heat radiated, warming her from chest to her toes. The caress was nearly her undoing. Since she couldn't resist much, or push him away, it only excited her more. *Shit.* He lingered, his hot breath on her ear. "Oh, but sweetheart," he sexy-slurred the words, "you are just that. A beautiful Christmas present all wrapped up and waiting."

Her chest lifted and fell and the bed shifted with his weight. The tension between the two of them was palpable. The fine hairs on the side of her cheek were erect and sensing his nearness. Finally, ever so slowly, Carson pulled back far enough to fasten his gaze into hers and hold. She watched the deep blue depths of his eyes flicker and reflect the gold hues of the room.

"Damn…" he said, then abruptly pulled back. His steps toward the door were assured and quick.

"Carson." She let his name slip off her tongue, not sure why or what she wanted from him.

With a sigh, he halted with his hand on the doorknob and dragged his gaze back to her. "Yes, Bree?"

"So are you going to tell me what your bidding is?"

He studied her for a moment, and then calmly replied, "Not yet."

Chapter Four

The wind nipped at his cheeks but Jake didn't care. He needed air. Fucking, frigid air. Standing out on a breezeway, which led from the main house to the casitas, he was sheltered from the fine falling snow, but glad for the sting of cold to numb his brain and still his pounding heart.

The crowd had left, thank God. The last cocktail waitress was auctioned off to her bartender boyfriend, and he'd swooshed them out the door telling them not to worry about cleaning up, given the snow and all. She didn't bring in the dollars that her partner had, but it didn't matter. Damn Carson. He'd forked over thirty thousand dollars of his savings. It was a good cause, of course, but...

What in hell was he going to do with Bree?

Everything that had rolled around inside him for the past few months was coming to a head tonight. He hadn't seen it coming. His entire world could come crashing down around him in one fell swoop. He feared that. He could lose it all.

Carson.

Bree.

Though, he never really had Bree. He simply lusted after her, loathed himself for it and lied about it. But he did have Carson. And he didn't want to give him up. They had been together for eight years. How can one throw away that many years? He couldn't, which was why he felt so conflicted. The sexual encounter with Bree had changed everything, since he and Carson had devoted their lives to each other. That commitment was a life-changing event.

They had both lived bi-sexual lives and were quite open with their sexual and promiscuous selves. Sex was part of their lifestyle. But then, they were young. Carefree.

And stupid.

A little age on both of them caused them to think about their lives and futures. They had been good friends for years then discovered they were more than that—they were in love with each other. Once that realization hit, and they knew they wanted to meld their lives, they made plans and set out to live the dream.

Together.

Eight years ago, they made that commitment. And now, on one Christmas Eve, it was all going to hell.

All due to his indiscretion and lack of self-control.

He wasn't sure what worried him more. Letting the notion and fantasy of Bree go forever? Or losing Carson.

Or perhaps, what truly frightened him was the look in Carson's eyes as he stood in their living room looking up at Bree while he bid on her.

That's when he'd had to walk away. For several seconds, he held the notion that he should buy her, talk to her, figure this out. But he couldn't pull it off. He couldn't bear any of it, any longer.

Was Carson attracted to her?

Was he out to get even? Had he known about Bree all this time?

Behind him, he heard a door open and close.

"So there you are."

Jake closed his eyes at Carson's voice. Perhaps this was it. Was she with him? Slowly, he turned to face the piper. Carson stood alone, framed by the door.

"Needed some air." Lame excuse, he knew. He'd been avoiding this party all evening.

"Come with me." Carson held out his hand. He voice was mellow, his face sporting a serious look.

"We can talk out here."

Shaking his head, Carson returned, "No. I don't want to talk; I want to show you something."

Not in the mood for games. Impatience was eating at him. "If you are going to end our relationship," he told him, "just tell me now, and let's get it over with."

Stepping closer, Carson looked deep into his eyes. "Jake," he said softly, "I don't want to end our relationship. I want to save it. Now please, come with me."

* * * *

Waiting gave Bree time to study the room in which she was being held captive. It also gave her time to think about what might be coming next.

Panning the room, it was obvious the scene was set for seduction. And more. A thought niggled that Carson had planned this...but how could he? He wouldn't have known she would show up tonight. Right?

Oh crap. Was he out for just anyone who would fit the bill? Not her? Was he some perverted sex fiend, and she had willingly fallen into his trap? For that matter, what did she really know about either of them? Jake or Carson?

Not much.

Rich, handsome, and two of them. That's all she knew. And that Jake had a cock made to please.

So, what about this den of seduction? And why her?

Certainly her mind was just spinning scenarios. Jake and Carson were harmless. Right?

But honestly, what seduction would be needed, when one was shackled to a bed, laying in wait? Frightened, intrigued, and confusingly turned-on all at the same time, she waited.

Hell, the waiting alone was practically foreplay.

Her body was growing hot in anticipation. What was in store for her? The yearning... thinking about Carson and Jake...

Carson. Jake.

Shit!

She wanted them both. Now, *that* was a new twist to her sexual repertoire.

Tugging at the leather and tinsel ties that bound her to the bed, she glanced backward at the sturdy headboard and studied the carvings there. The bed was truly a work of art. She found it extremely interesting how a series of antiquated, but quite sturdy, eyehooks dotted the wood.

Had they always been there, or was this a new feature? The way the hooks were embedded, it looked like they had been there for some time.

She arched a brow. All of this brought forth some interesting questions about Carson and Jake's lifestyle. Was she the first woman to be tied to this bed? Or, were the two men regular participants in extra-curricular activities?

With men and women?

Or, was this their bed and theirs alone?

An uneasy, and unexpected, tingling tripped over her tummy.

That's when the double oak doors swung open, again, and in walked the pair.

Jake immediately bolted toward her. "What in hell?" He swung back to look at his partner. "What have you done?"

"Slow down, Jake."

"Let her go." His gaze swept over her. She watched his eyes. Angry. Hungry. And confused.

"I'm fine," she said. "Just a little baffled."

"I needed her to stay put while I went to get you," Carson said. "I couldn't take a chance."

"Ridiculous." Jake swept a hand through his ebony locks. His eyes were crossed with worry while he held her gaze. That one gesture made her groin tighten. Gradually, he dragged his gaze back to Carson. "All right. So what do you want? Tell me. I'm tired of the avoidance and the deception. But I'm a bit bewildered as to why Bree needs to be here to witness this."

Cocking his head, Carson stared at Jake. "Merry Christmas, Jake. I love you."

Bree watched the fixed stare between the two. "I don't understand," Jake said.

Carson glanced back at Bree. She connected with his gaze for a moment before he turned back to Jake. "I know what happened. I suspected the moment you stepped out of that hallway at the realty office those months ago, and I knew for certain when you said you didn't think Conner & Baker were the realtors for us. You've been miserable for months, Jake. I know you like I know the back of my hand. So, I arranged for Conner & Baker to be a part of the event tonight. I bought Bree for you. She's yours. For the night. Merry Christmas."

He glanced between the two.

Bree felt her chest rise and fall in very short pants.

Carson peered into Jake's eyes and Jake stared back. To her, it didn't appear that Carson was mad, just matter of fact. "Figure out what you want, Jake," he added. "Get her out of your system if you can. Then decide. Who do you want? Her? Me? Or…"

He paused, that last word limping out of his mouth, and then slowly rotated his head to hook directly into Bree's stare. Her heart tripped a little in her chest. "Or, something," he added.

What do you mean by that?

Then, she watched as he nodded to Jake and left. A strong click sounded from behind the door. Was it bolted from the *outside*? Could they leave? Slowly, she pivoted her gaze back to Jake.

Jake's heart pounded with wild anticipation looking at Bree lying on the bed. Draped in tinsel, her wrists bound by both silver and leather rested on the pillows beside her head. Either Carson had nestled her there between the oversized, red silk pillows or she'd maneuvered herself to where she leaned against the antique headboard, pretty as a picture.

Her waist-length hair fell over one shoulder. Her Santa hat was tilted precariously off to one side. With her knees bent, she sat almost as if posed. Her long, silky legs, still clad with those decadent black boots, beckoned. Perusing from toe to forehead, he paused slightly at her chest, watching it lift and fall in quick bursts. Finally, he settled on her questioning face.

"I'm sorry," he whispered.

"Come here," she said back.

He didn't know what to do. They were in here for the long haul, he knew that. Carson wouldn't joke about it. Twenty four hours. He'd slid the old board lock into place on the antique doors from the outside.

"So what are you going to do?" she prompted.

"What?"

"With me."

Do? What *was* he going to do? He wasn't a monster. He didn't take on a sex partner who was unwilling, and he was mightily against coercion of any sort. Rushing to her side, he sat on the edge of the bed and reached for the hand closest to him. "First, I'm untying you. Then, we talk."

"Talk?" He glanced down at the scowl on Bree's face.

"Yes. Talk."

Touching her was almost his undoing. Static crackled between them as he reached for her far hand. Making short work of his mission, he loosened the nooses around her wrists, leaving the straps firmly tied to the eyebolts. Releasing her now, he leaned back, his fists resting on the bed on either side of her hips. The magnetism between them was more powerful than he wanted to admit.

She smelled heavenly, almost like a Christmas sugar cookie, but the heady scent of promised sex won out. She oozed nothing close to sweet and innocence. His pulse pounded and his mouth grew dry. Slowly, he pulled his gaze to her face and stayed fixed there for way too long.

With each slow and deliberate breath she took, he was drawn in. Unable to separate himself from what should, or should not be, he lifted a hand to palm her cheek. Her eyes closed and she sighed at his touch. His heartbeat picked up its cadence and he felt lightheaded.

"Bree..." he whispered.

She opened her round, brown eyes and he fell in. Deep.

"Don't think," she breathed back. "Not yet. Perhaps..." he felt himself leaning involuntarily into her, "...later."

If only he could. "I need to say a couple of things. I don't do this. That time in your office...I'd not done that in years. I am...was...totally devoted to Carson. I don't play around and yet, I fucked you in your office restroom like a wolf in heat. I want to apologize..."

"I was there, too," she told him. "Don't blame yourself, Jake. I stepped over that threshold; you didn't haul me in and have your way with me."

"No, but it was a mistake. I should have had more self-control. And ever since that day, I can't get you out of my head..."

"Nor can I, you," she breathed.

If there was one fraction of resolve left inside him, it was gone with that statement.

Lunging forward, he captured her lips with his. Fully on the bed now, he gathered her into his arms as they both scooted away from the pillows. Body to body, pressed together length to length, he took her face in both hands while his lips and tongue tasted and kissed.

And she kissed back.

With each thrust of her tongue, or gentle caress of her dewy lips against his, his body trilled with her nearness and their connectedness.

He could not stop himself. Nothing could make him…

She wiggled in his arms. "Jake, stop."

Except maybe that.

Groaning, he pulled back. "Bree, I'm in such utter contradiction here. I don't know whether to devour you or put you out in the snow."

"I just want to say one more thing."

"What is it?" He traced the outline of her face with his forefinger, waiting out his frustration. What a beautiful woman. And he wanted her so damned bad.

"I won't hold you to anything. I… I am as conflicted as you. I don't want to come between you and Carson. I just need…" Her voice trailed off and she looked to his chest, "Shit, I just need you for *right now*, okay?" she said with a soft voice. "I don't want to think about anything else."

Huffing out a breath of relief, he rolled fully on top of her. "Okay."

"Last time was too quick," she added.

Closing his eyes, and his mind, against anything but the woman in his arms, he replied, "It appears we have twenty-four hours."

She nodded. "And for those twenty-four hours, I belong to you."

Chapter Five

Never had Bree felt so totally free, and at the same time, consumed by another. She didn't care. She wanted to be totally possessed by Jake. And she had an entire night and day, it seemed, to enjoy.

Pushing back any guilt about Carson, and the relationship she could be infringing upon, she studied Jake's face and the puzzle of emotion painted across it. Her own face likely echoed that sentiment.

But Carson had agreed. Or rather, insisted. He wanted closure, one way or another. She did not want to come between them. Would not. If she and Jake had tonight, with Carson's blessing, then so be it. She, too, would get Jake out of her system.

After that, she couldn't say.

His long fingers threaded through the fine hairs at her temples, holding her against the bed. He peered down into her face, the low flicker of candles reflecting both passion and desire in his eyes. God, she wanted him.

"Please, Jake," she whimpered.

He lowered and thrust his tongue deep into her mouth. The act of penetration into that orifice made her curl toward him in want. His tongue grappled with hers, and he tugged at it with his teeth, slowly drawing it deep inside his mouth with a thorough suck.

Their mouths fused, Jake sucked harder, continuing an erotic and sensuous intake of her tongue into the cavern of his mouth. Her arms went around his broad shoulders and her legs around his hips. She clung to him, and he rocked into her pelvis.

Her pussy longed to have him between her thighs. Now, she only needed him naked, with the hot friction of skin against skin.

Whimpering, she clasped at his head, weaving her fingers through his inky locks. She broke away with a gasp; he jerked back, fire licking in his eyes, as he raked his gaze over her face and down her chest.

He grasped the bodice of her dress and ripped. It fell away like so much crepe paper. Tearing the fabric from her body, Jake unwrapped Bree like a Christmas package. Lingering bits of tinsel scattered about the bedcover, and she was left with nothing but her black thong, strapless bra, and boots.

On his knees now, Jake's hungry stare scraped down her body, his breathing labored. His large hands started at her shoulders and worked their way down either side. He palmed her breasts, lifting them out of the bra cups, pinching her nipples between thumb and forefinger. Passion zinged through her at the squeeze. She ached for more.

Reaching behind her, he grasped the clasps at her back and pulled hard. The bra sailed off as he tossed it over the side of the bed. Continuing downward, he smoothed his hands over the indent of her waist and the flare of her hips. He thumbed over her hipbones and twisted the string of the thong on both sides. With a snap, he jerked his hands in opposite directions and broke the string, the thong falling away, as well.

The only thing left was her boots.

Bree's entire being hummed with expectation.

With aggravating slow precision, he unlaced the left boot. The thin patent leather parted, and he peeled the boot off her calf, then down to her ankle, and finally removed it. He did the same with the other leg, each time smoothing his hands over her calves and ankles in appreciation.

Jake lifted a foot close to his face. Bree watched as he closed his eyes and ran the tender sole of the foot over his stubbled beard. The fine prickles heightened the sensitive nerve endings there and caused her to shiver. Never before, had a touch in her arch sent her into waves of sexual desire.

With his thumbs, he applied pressure just under the pads beneath her toes, massaging and fondling. Starting with her smallest toe, he then began sucking each, pulling the digits into his mouth one by one, laving his tongue over them.

He moved to the other foot and did the same.

She had no clue toe sucking could be so sensual.

"You've been on your feet all night," he murmured. "Let me take care of you."

Oh shit, don't say that. I could get too used to it...

"Lay back, Bree. Close your eyes. And let me."

Without protest, she did just that, but not before saying, "Take your clothes off, Jake. Now."

He did, and she marveled at the glorious planes and hollows of his naked body, and the strong upright profile of his cock-to-die-for.

Moving up into the vee of her core, Jake spanned her thighs with his hands. He settled between her legs and opened her pussy wide. With practiced movements, he palmed over the tender junction of leg and hip and massaged her there. Like butter, she melted into the bed and he smiled, knowing he was providing her with much pleasure. Pushing back the tiny crest of dark brown curls that rimmed her labia, he parted her lips to reveal a glistening bud. He leaned in closer and rubbed a finger over her pearl.

Bree jumped and arched upward; his smile deepened.

With a middle finger, he entered her. Then with two. Moaning, she laid back and allowed him access. He probed, she was slick and open. Both hands played, stretching her, kneading her hot, sticky pussy flesh. He relished in the purely decadent feel of his fingers inside her body.

Jake had always been fascinated with the female anatomy. He loved exploring the contours and grottos of delight it offered. Bree's body was a purely sinful expedition. A woman's body, from his perspective, was a thing to pleasure, not necessarily a thing to take pleasure from. He planned to spend his time these next hours pleasuring her as much as humanly possible.

Trailing a finger over her perineum, he flicked at her anus. She reacted with a jerk and catlike moan.

He pushed her legs higher, allowing him full access. Catching sight of the leather straps still firmly attached to the eyebolts, he contemplated how Bree might react to their use. Their previous sexual encounter was fast and hot. Perhaps they should establish a couple of ground rules until he was certain of her threshold of sex play.

"Bree," he said softly. "I never want to hurt you or make you feel uncomfortable, so let's play a little game." He reached for a strap. "Anytime you want me to stop, say the word *red* and I will stop immediately. I promise you. If you want me to keep going, say *green*, and I will continue. Do you understand?"

She nodded. "Yes."

He trailed a strap over her breast. She caught her breath. "You want me to continue?"

"Green."

He stifled a grin. "Move closer to the headboard."

Her eyes wide, she watched as he toyed with the leather noose in his hand. She did as he asked, and scooted back, pushing pillows out of the way.

Lifting first one foot, then the other, he slipped the leather cuffs over her ankles and tightened them. Moving to the headboard, he loosened the knots slightly and increased the tension until Bree's legs were held in the air, her knees slightly bent, her pussy and ass angled up and open to him. She could move a bit, if she needed to. He knew that the straps would actually help her to keep from straining to keep her legs in this position.

And he wanted them up and her body open.

"You okay?"

Her eyes met his. "Green."

Before settling between her thighs again, he opened a bedside table drawer and withdrew a tube of flavored lubricant. He warmed the lube on his fingers before touching her. Soon, he was back to exploring her depths, probing in and out of her vagina, with first one finger, then two, while increasing pressure and providing a determined internal massage.

Jake alternately watched Bree's face, and her pussy, gauging her reactions by her moans, movements and facial tics, along with the puckering and expanding of her vaginal muscles. Her eyes were closed, her head lolled to one side, then the other, as he continued his play. Dragging a middle finger downward, he teased her perineum and circled her anus. For good measure, he applied a little more lube to that area, allowing his middle finger to play and tempt her hole, then slowly slide into her ass. Bree gasped, and he stilled, looking to her face. Her eyes still closed, she whispered, "Green."

Repositioning himself, he leaned on one hip, angling his body slightly to the left. With the middle finger of his right hand up her ass, he inserted his right thumb into her pussy. Pushing her left leg back toward her chest a bit more, her rear raised up further off the bed. He squeezed his thumb and middle finger together, cupping all of her sex in the palm of his big hand. He pushed both digits up as far into her as he could, massaging her from the inside, squeezing and probing.

She shivered and moaned, her lower body on the brink of convulsion.

He leaned closer, his gaze caught on the wet and shimmering pearl between her labia. Unable to resist tasting her any longer, he touched the tip of his tongue to the fleshy gem and flicked her starving clit. He'd neglected that part of her anatomy for too long. Now, it was time.

"Green...green..." Bree moaned, and he increased his tongue's pressure on her clit. His fingers still worked her holes, pinching and prodding, her perineum caught between them.

Laving sloppy kisses over her pussy, his tongue explored while she trembled beneath him. Moving lower, his tongue teased at her opening, rivaling his thumb for attention. He sucked at her labia and tongue-fucked her while his thumb continued to play.

Her pants and whimpers spurned him on. He knew, as they increased in frequency, that she was close to exploding.

At once, she came up off the bed with a powerful orgasm.

Jake held her with fingers and tongue and thumb while she came down. He laid his head in the cradle of her thighs as he removed his fingers and gave her a moment. Her body hummed with pleasure, and his heart swelled knowing that he had given it to her.

"Green," he heard her whisper from above. "Your cock. Now. In my ass."

Without a second's hesitation, Jake rose above her, his body between her knees. He positioned himself, his hands on her thighs, curling her lower body back toward the headboard. He thumbed her asshole, fingering along the rim, wondering if she could take him.

He added some extra lube to his fingers and again, pushed his thumb inside, readying her.

"Yes, Jake. Please..."

"Green?"

"Yes. Green."

With a groan, he pressed the head of his cock against her hole. Damn, she was small and tight. Headiness overtook him as he pushed forward. He felt he might explode before he was inside.

She opened and he eased himself in. Bree groaned and reached for him. Her fingers grasped his wrists and held tight. He pushed forward and lost himself inside her. For several dizzying moments, all he knew was that he was inside her, fucking her, again, and that was all that mattered.

He came with such force that he shouted and shuddered with explosive reaction. He spilled his seed inside her, burying his cock to the hilt, with thrusts that both invigorated and depleted him.

Fumbling with the leather straps around her ankles, he released her. Sated, he collapsed onto her, drew her into his arms and held onto her with everything that was left inside him.

Finally, they slept.

* * * *

The room was dark when Bree woke a couple of hours later. At some point Jake must have left the bed long enough to blow out the candles and extinguish the lamps. He was beside her now, though, his body heat radiating toward her.

She'd been thoroughly fucked a few hours earlier, but even so, all she could think about at this moment in time, was Jake's cock firmly implanted her pussy.

His back was to her. She spooned him from behind and skimmed her hand over his hip, settling at his groin. His engorged cock felt silky and firm in the palm of her hand. She dragged her fingers over him with a feather light touch, her sex building with want as she did so.

Jake shifted and in one motion, grasped her wrists and pulled her on top of him. The action sent her reeling with desire.

"Fuck me," Jake groaned from the pillows. She could barely see in the dark. But she could find him nonetheless, straddling him, and roughly impaling her body on his dick.

"Ahhhh…shit." Jake called out and grappled for her breasts. He caught them both in his hands and squeezed.

Bree rocked and rode, her hair tossed back, her pussy stretched to accommodate him. She milked with her muscles and he cried out her name over and over again. She clasped her hands over his forearms for leverage, while he continued to clutch her breasts.

"Give it to me," she cried out, wanting to feel him come inside her. "I want your cum, baby." Her own passion was building inside her as his head stroked fervently against her G-spot. "Oh, damn…more, baby…goddamn…"

Fast and furious, she stroked him with her body. His hands dropped to her hips, anchoring her against his pelvis. Jake cried out again, and simultaneously in Bree, the dam burst. "Oh, god…" she gasped, her body rolling forward against his chest.

They lay fused, shuddering in release, sighing with pleasure that bordered on pain. His arms went around her and for some crazy and stupid reason, Bree felt like crying.

Chapter Six

Bree slept a deep and satisfied sleep while lying in Jake's arms. Occasionally she found herself nuzzling into him, feeling safe and protected. And wanted. She loved that feeling and was hard-pressed to move from their private cocoon. She'd ventured in and out of sex-induced slumber until finally going fully under.

Now, she was coming awake, and slowly realizing that something was different. Glancing at the heavily draped window across the room, she noticed a sliver of daylight peeking through, and was embarrassed that she had slept so long. Rising up on one elbow, she instantly realized that she was alone.

Jake was gone.

But where?

Her gaze moved to the heavy doors, now standing slightly ajar. So what did this mean? She was free to go? He'd made a decision...and it wasn't her? Did she not satisfy him or had he simply had his fill of her?

She didn't know, and her brain was too groggy to speculate. Needing to pee, she left the warmth of the bed behind and tiptoed to the adjoining bathroom, closing the door behind her with a soft click.

Alone, she questioned her sanity. How could she have done what she did? She never considered herself the kind of person to break up someone else's relationship. It was one thing to cheat on her own relationship. It was quite another to interfere with someone else's. At the moment, she wasn't sure she could live with herself.

Yet, Carson had given his blessing.

Still…

And what *about* Carson? His come-hither innuendos throughout the evening were a puzzle all unto their own. What did he want out of all of this?

After she'd used the toilet, Bree leaned into the sink looking into her eyes. Her face told the tale of a long night. She looked like that phrase her mother used to say, about women who were less than respectable—that they'd been "rode hard and put up wet."

She'd been ridden hard, that was for certain. And gave as good as she got. Put up wet? Yeah, that, too.

Glancing toward the tiled shower stall, she initiated a short conversation with herself and decided that a shower would be both appropriate and desirable about now. She was sticky and smelled like sex. Besides, while cleaning up, she could contemplate her next move while the water beat over her body.

Nothing like stinging pellets to make one come to their senses.

Standing under the stream, her hair twisted into a knot on top of her head to prevent it from getting too wet, it wasn't long before she realized exactly what she had to do. Not certain how she would get home off the mountain, she knew she had to do just that. Ginger, she figured, was long gone. She had no clue what the snowstorm had done to the roads during the night. And crap, even worse, she had no clothes.

But she had to leave. Jake was too irresistible, and Carson was becoming a temptation in his own right. She was wildly attracted to them both, and that could only spell trouble. She'd never had the opportunity to experience a ménage liaison before, even though the thought intrigued her. She wasn't quite sure how she felt about it.

But it didn't matter, did it? It wasn't in the offering.

If she were totally honest with herself, she feared rejection, big time.

And the rules were changing.

Somehow, the door to the bedroom had been opened in the night. Maybe Carson had changed his mind and came after Jake. Perhaps Jake was having second thoughts and had figured out a way to leave. Either way, she was not going to come between them.

Or be there when either returned.

That was that.

She twisted the knob halting the water and stepped out of the shower. A fluffy towel was draped nearby on a hook. Gathering herself up in the thick terry, she rubbed at her body to absorb some of the droplets, then tucked it under her arms and gathered the remainder at her breast. She padded off into the bedroom in search of clothing.

* * * *

"So, did you come to share the sordid details, or what?" Carson sat at the bar in their kitchen, hunched over a cup of coffee, reading a book. He didn't look up as Jake entered. "Finally jimmied that board off the latch, huh? Funny, I didn't realize you'd be so keen to escape."

"We need to talk." Jake felt the urgency. It was time.

Carson turned a page.

"Look, you forced my hand on this issue," Jake finally said.

Carson replied by carefully closing the book and peering across the kitchen to meet his lover's gaze. "Someone needed to force something. You weren't coming clean, nor were you admitting there was an issue. You made no attempt at resolution, or anything." He stood. "Yes, dammit, I forced your hand. I can't go on like this. I want our life back."

Jake wasn't sure they could ever get back what they once had. Not exactly.

"Yes, I lied to you." He stepped closer to Carson, not breaking the gaze. "I lied. I lusted. I loathed myself for it. I fucked her, and it came out of nowhere. It wasn't planned, Carson, it just happened."

"And you've not been able to forget it."

"No."

"You should have told me."

"I… I tried. I couldn't. Carson, I love you. I need and want to be with you."

"But she got in the way."

"And I didn't know what to do about it."

Narrowing his gaze, Carson held his stare for a moment then broke away to look out the kitchen window. "Not telling me was the first mistake. Lying when I asked you if something was wrong was the second one." His voice trailed off. "Jake, before we have any chance of moving on…of figuring this out…I have to know that I can trust you."

Closing his eyes, Jake wondered if the trust was completely broken. He moved closer to Carson, so close behind him that he wanted to run his hands over his shoulders and hold him. He was in as much pain as him, he was certain.

"I want you to trust me," he said. "How do I earn it back? Where do we go from here? What do I have to do?"

Turning, Carson faced him. "You can start by telling me the truth. Right now." He paused, and Jake held his breath. "Answer me this, Jake. Can you let her go? Are you finished with her now?"

Searching deep, Jake knew that his future rested on how he answered that question. He had to be honest, no matter what. He had to earn the trust back.

Even if it meant the end of their relationship.

"No. I can't let her go."

And that was the truth. He was not ready to give up Bree. Didn't know if he ever could.

The tension between them was tensile-strength and about to snap.

Lifting his chin, Carson peered back with penetrating eyes. "Then I have one more question. Are you willing to share her?"

* * * *

"Men," Bree muttered to herself, "do they not own anything halfway decent to wear besides baggie sweats, long shorts, and t-shirts?" Of course, the walk-in Jake and Carson shared was filled with dress and casual clothes, alike, but she wanted something that would half-way fit her and make her not look like a vagabond wandering the street. She had no clue what she would do for shoes, unless she wore the stupid boots.

Not likely.

Still holding the towel at her chest, she rummaged through one of the men's drawers, not coming up with anything to her liking. "Dammit."

"Looking for something?"

She bolted straight up, her towel taking a lunge. Turning, she grasped it closed between her breasts and looked at Jake—tall and dark and handsome—framed in the open double doors.

"I… I thought I'd find something to put on."

"No need." He reached and shut the doors behind him. "No clothing required for the next," his gaze dropped to his wristwatch, "sixteen hours or so. After that, we'll figure out the clothing situation."

"Sorry, Jake, but I don't think that's a good idea. Really, I need to be going. May I just borrow…?" She picked up a t-shirt.

He swept to her side, took the shirt out of her hand, and laid it back on the dresser. "There will be no talk of leaving, Bree. The roads are snow-covered and nasty. We can't risk it. Besides, your twenty-four hours are not up yet."

Panicking a bit, she drew back, drawing the towel closer. "Surely you are not going to hold me to that silly auction thing, are you Jake? Let me call Ginger. I'm sure her jeep…" At once, she wondered where her cell phone was. Had she even had it last night? The last time she remembered seeing it was back in her apartment. That's right; she'd tossed it on her bed.

But no matter. That was the least of her concern at the moment. Avoiding Jake, she moved toward the bed. "I'll call someone."

"Nobody is coming out in this weather, Bree."

She turned boldly to face him, remembering her conviction of a moment earlier. Even if she couldn't leave, she wasn't going to carry this any further. Surely there was another room where she could hang out…far away from this den of seduction. "Jake, we can't go on with this. Just let me be. The last thing I want to do is come between you and Carson. It's best that we let this die."

"So you didn't enjoy our night together?"

Swallowing hard, she looked into his eyes. "I can't deny that I enjoyed every second. And that is the problem. There is no future here, Jake, and I'm not taking this any further. You and Carson have a life together. I need to exit, and we need to forget this ever happened."

"Your words and the look on your face are in utter contradiction, my dear." Stepping forward, he ran a fingertip over her forehead. "So many frown lines and worry wrinkles," he whispered. Drawing closer, his breath was hot on her neck. "Let me erase those, Bree."

She backed away. "You aren't listening to me." Dammit, for once she was going to have resolve. She was going to do the right thing!

"I'm reading your body language. Your words aren't very convincing."

Frustrated, she balled her hands into fists. "Stop doing that! Quit putting things in my head for me to think about. I know what I need to do. I need for you to stop confusing me!"

Jake's shoulders slumped and he exhaled hard. The relaxation of his body made her more at ease. "Please stop," she whispered. "I'm trying to do the right thing. Please let me."

Jake closed his eyes at her words. "I love you, Bree."

Her head shook in denial. "No. Don't do that."

"I do. I can't deny it. Being with you last night made me realize that I cannot live without you. I love you, and I want you."

No. This wasn't happening. She stalked off. "But what about Carson? You can't throw that relationship away!"

"Bree, that's what I want to talk with you about."

"No. You can't love me."

"I do."

"No!"

"Bree, please…" he reached for her and she jerked away.

"I do not fall in love, Jake. I don't. And you *cannot* and *will* not fall in love with me. I screw up every relationship that comes my way. There is no hope for us."

"I can make you happy. This will be different. Please hear what I have to say…"

"No. It's not in me. I can't settle for one man. Never have I been able to do that. I'll break your heart down the road. I guarantee it. We'll be together, and I'll see someone else. It's what I do. One man just isn't enough for me."

Jake quieted her with a hand in the air. She stopped talking and looked into his face. Finally, he said, "Stop for a moment, okay? Quit selling yourself short. Just because you screwed up in the past doesn't mean you will fuck up in the future."

"But…"

"No. I won't listen to another word, Bree. And I'm not letting you go tonight. You're staying here. With me. And by God, you're going to let me have one more chance of convincing you that we belong together. Do you understand?"

A nervous laugh escaped her throat. "So what are you going to do, tie me to that bed for the next sixteen hours until I cry out my love for you in orgasmic pleasure?"

The expression on his face didn't budge. The silence between them spoke volumes.

"Give me one more chance, Bree," he whispered, "to make this work. Give me a few more hours. I love you. I need you. And I guarantee you that by this evening, you will never want to leave."

Swallowing hard, Bree held his gaze. Her head said no. Her pussy was already wet, betraying her. And her heart was definitely on the fence.

Still, she looked him square in the face and said, "All right."

Chapter Seven

Jake drew closer. "Do you trust me?"

Looking up at him with round, soulful eyes, she replied with a simple, "Yes."

"Good." His hands went to the rim of the over-sized towel. Tugging it away from her body, he tossed it aside. "This will work, Bree," he said softly, "but you must trust me. And remember, red and green. It always works."

She nodded and Jake felt his chest swell and his mouth curl into a smile. God, he loved her. And he could only hope that in the end, all would work out.

Carson had surprised him. Totally, utterly from left field, had thrown him for a loop. But it was a good loop, and if they all were fortunate, things would fall together like a charm.

She stood before him, naked and confident, with a possible hint of vulnerability. Hell, they were all vulnerable. When it came to love, anyone can lose.

Or win.

Tonight he hoped they all were winners.

"You are so...beautiful." His words were raspy and broken. "Come here." He offered her his hand and Bree took it. Slowly, they rounded the bed. Jake admired her firm body and rounded contours, and was eager to explore her again.

With his hands to her waist, he lifted her to sit on the edge of the tall bed. At that height, he looked down on her, liking the position of dominance as she stared up at him with innocent—or maybe not so innocent—eyes.

"You understand you were given to me for twenty-four hours, correct?"

She nodded, lowering her gaze.

"You are mine, Bree. You will do as I ask and strive to meet my needs. In turn, I will see that you are well-satisfied. Tonight, you belong to me, my little Christmas slave."

Her eyelids fluttered as she lifted her gaze to meet his. A sliver of a smile met her lips as their gazes fused. His heart melted. "Yes, sir," she whispered.

"Trust me." It wasn't a question.

She nodded.

Stepping to his right, Jake opened a bedside table drawer. "I have a new addition to our repertoire," he told her, and pulled out the black silk blindfold he'd tucked there earlier.

* * * *

Jake had drawn the heavy drapes tight, eliminating any curls of light coming from the outside. Even though it was about mid-morning, the room was dark enough so that candles and soft lamps were needed. Now blindfolded, Bree could barely see a thing, although she remembered exactly how the room looked a moment before.

Leaning back against the nest of red silk pillows, propped against the massive headboard, she savored the slick, cool fabric against her naked back. The temperature in the room was cool, too, and her nipples puckered at the crispness. Her wrists were bound and rested comfortably against the pillows at her shoulders.

Jake had tied the blindfold around her head with a gentle tug. He had lifted her into his arms and had placed her just so, while he bound her with leather and tinsel.

Now, she waited. She'd felt the swish of the satin sheets as Jake moved off the bed. He left her with a soft, "Be patient, love. I will be right back. Shh…" and a gentle touch of his finger to her lips. That was several minutes ago. The longer she lay in wait, the more heightened her sexual being became. Every nerve in her body stood alert.

He came to her without words, at first touching the hard pebble of her breasts with his fingertips. He pinched and twisted, and she gasped with pleasure. That lone touch caused her to squirm a little.

With a finger, he lifted her chin to angle her face up. The kiss he placed on her lips was sweet and sinful. Her breathing deepened as he slowly delved into her mouth with his tongue, and they mingled breath and lips.

She'd played a little with being cuffed and tied up prior to this but for some reason, blindfolding had never occurred to her, or her partners. She wondered why, because just the one kiss from Jake and only the touch of his lips to hers—coupled with not being able to see—had heightened her awareness and her pleasure.

She could get used to this.

Now she felt his hands on her face, cupping her cheeks in his palms. He angled closer and sat on the bed. Leaning his way with the shift, she felt the heat of his body next to hers.

Lost in the single sensation of his lips plying hers, she found herself slinking into the nest of pillows, lying prone on the bed. The headiness of his kiss overtook her, while his hands smoothed down the column of her neck with lazy, feathery strokes. Involuntarily, she jerked at her bonds, wanting to wrap her arms around his neck and pull him closer.

"Later, Bree…" he breathed. "I will let you loose later. Patience, love."

Lying still, she waited, silently agreeing.

"I am going to move slow, Bree. We have hours. I hope you do not object."

"No," she said softly.

"Good."

"Do you like the blindfold?"

"Yes."

"Good. I want you to keep it on."

That was just fine with her. With a light touch, he trailed his fingertips over her chest and circled each nipple. Her breasts swelled as his touch and she arched into his hands. He lifted and palmed their weight, rolled and squeezed her nipples. Leaning into her, he took one hard bud between his teeth and tugged.

Then again. Harder.

Oh, damn…

A sex-charged current zinged from that nipple straight to her clit. Jake continued a slow, deliberate assault with his teeth…sucking, teasing, tugging, tempting…

And nearly sending her over the edge.

So lost in the sensation, she barely registered another shift on the bed, until she felt a cool hand slowly work its way up the inside of her calf…and thigh. It took a couple of seconds for her brain to register that there were still, indeed, two hands at her breasts, but a third was easing toward her pussy.

What?

"Jake!"

"Shh, love…"

She jerked away. "Stop. Stop!" She twisted to the side, moving her legs away from whoever was at her feet. Jake continued toying with her breasts.

Fingers below grazed her pussy.

Again, she twisted, trying very hard to ignore the fabulous sensation being created down there. *What is happening?* "Stop, Jake. Take this blindfold off of me now!"

"Lay back, Bree. Quiet now. I do not want you to talk."

Dammit. "Lay back? Relax? Whose hand is that?" Fingers again, probing... "Stop. Dammit. Stop." *Oh, hell.* "Red. Red!"

Everything did, indeed, stop.

"Shit." She cursed between her teeth, while attempting to shift upward against the headboard. "Take this blindfold off of me, now."

She sat in silence for a moment, then finally, hands went behind her head and the blindfold was off. It took a moment of blinking before she registered who was sitting on the bed before her.

Jake *and* Carson.

"Oh, fuck..."

Both were naked. Both stared at her in wild expectation. Both of them oozed the promise of delicious, decadent sex.

And both were waiting for her to say something.

Thing was, she couldn't think of one thing to say.

Carson inched forward. "Bree..."

"What do the two of you want from me?" There, that would cut to the chase.

Jake moved closer. "We want you, Bree. Both of us."

"Both of you?"

Her gaze shifted from one man to another.

"Yes."

"And you thought blindfolding me and bringing in Carson would make me receptive to that? Have you thought about a simple conversation?"

"We thought you might enjoy this."

Well, damn, they were right. She *was* beginning to enjoy it. "I..." She truly didn't know what to say. "I just need for you two to talk. I don't have words right now."

Resigned, she sank back into the pillows. "Talk," she ordered.

Jake opened his mouth to speak, but Carson interrupted. "Let me," he said, scooting closer to her side. "Honey, I know that you and I haven't had much time, but there is a spark there, you have to agree."

Nodding, she did agree. They'd made eyes all evening and the slip of his finger up her dress last night had thrilled her beyond belief. She'd not been able to set that feeling aside for long.

"You have a sexual potency that is extremely attractive to both of us," he continued. "We both lived bi-sexual lives for a long time until we committed to each other. But you...you have tempted us back to where we feel most comfortable. There has never been another woman we've each felt this attracted to.

"Jake has been struggling for months. I don't want to lose him. I love him. And he loves you. I know you, and I need time, but there is a strong attraction, and I think..."

She searched his eyes and he paused before saying his next words. "I think the three of us will make a lovely couple, er, threesome. Bree, we want you in our lives. Permanently."

So there it was. Dumbfounded, she swallowed and hooked her gaze into Carson's. Slowly, she dragged it away and then connected with Jake.

Both of them?

Would that satisfy her want for variety? Give her what she needed in a relationship?

"You did say earlier, sweetheart, that one man was not enough for you."

That, she did.

She took a moment to think. Reflect. And wonder...

"I have only one request," she told them finally.

"Your wish is our command." Jake reached for her hand and held it.

She nodded. "All right. Put the blindfold back on me and take away the straps. I have a feeling I am going to need both of my hands. But for our first time together, I don't want to see. I just want to feel and meld you together in my head."

And heart.

I just want to feel, experience, and fall in love with you both. I don't want to think about who is who, and who is doing what.

She paused and watched both of their eyes grow round. "Now, please. Green."

* * * *

The last thing she saw was Jake moving toward her with the blindfold. He fastened it snug around her eyes, then moved to rest beside her on the bed. Carson joined them on the opposite side. For a little while, she lay there sandwiched between them, absorbing the heat of their bodies and relishing in the musky smell of *men*, plural, flanking her.

Turning on one side, she nuzzled into the body on her left. Jake, she was certain. Carson spooned her from behind. Hands wandered over her body from both sides and she simply closed her eyes and let the scene play out in her head behind the silky scrap of fabric.

Being the center of attention between two virile males was definitely not a bad thing, she confessed to herself. There was no hint of resistance even, to whether she should or shouldn't do this. It just seemed right. And the more they smoothed their big male hands over her torso and hips and breasts, the more she was just lost, resigned to live in the moment.

They soon felt like one being.

Jake wasn't Jake and Carson wasn't Carson and Bree wasn't even Bree anymore. Their bodies writhed and rubbed and angled over each other, reminding her of kittens at play; their lean lengths stretched and limber, their actions uninhibited, their passions ready to pop.

A hand slipped between her thighs from the rear. Fingers groped and toyed with her ass. She spread her legs and allowed him access. Her pussy was hot, she could tell, and wet. Her thighs sticky with her nectar. A manly groan from behind her came forth and each of their bodies shifted position. Suddenly, Bree was up on her knees, with strong hands firmly placed just above her hips, holding her steady. She had one man behind her and one in front of her.

Her sense of touch, or near touch, was heightened. She could sense their presence.

The one behind smoothed his hands over her ass and settled himself close. With his mouth, he started at her inner thigh and nibbled his way up toward her core. In the meantime, the other man's hands took her face into his palms and angled her toward him. A soft something brushed against her cheek…something smooth as velvet.

"Yes," she told him. "Cock." She wanted his cock. It didn't matter if it was Jake or Carson, she wanted a cock her mouth.

Now.

Soon her desire was granted. A firm head of kid-leather soft flesh pushed against her mouth. She parted her lips and curled them over him, taking his head into her wetness. Bracing herself with one hand against the mattress, she grasped him with the other to steady him as she licked. The length and size made her wonder if it was Jake, but she couldn't be certain, even though she was quite familiar with his organ. Wouldn't it be lovely if they both had cocks to rival a bull in heat?

What a lucky girl she would be.

That would certainly keep her home nights, wouldn't it?

She stroked with her tongue, playing over him like she was licking an ice cream cone and had to catch every drip; she circled him, tasting the salty drops of moisture at his tip, and smiled at the fullness he brought to her mouth.

She pulled him deeper into her throat.

Her mouth filled and stretched by him was heavenly. She anticipated that same sensation in other ways and areas of her body, very soon.

Hands went to her head, holding her still, and the cock in her mouth began a slow and sure piston-like motion in and out. She felt the thrusts of his hips, and sensed him as he drew nearer, and then back again from her face.

Behind her, the kisses on her inner thighs were moving closer to her core. Fingers spread her ass cheeks, exploring. Arching her back, she spread her legs a little to allow him easier access. A finger probed her hole and she moaned. He stroked, in and out, and added another finger to fill her vagina. Still nibbling, he worked his way up her leg and sent brief kisses down her crack. His tongue lightly rimmed her asshole, sending a thrill of delight straight through her.

She sucked cock harder.

Licking with broad strokes now, the tongue at her pussy laved over her perineum then slipped inside her vagina. He lanced into her with parries and thrusts…in and out…in and out… She grew lightheaded with over stimulation. Unexpectedly, her labia was caught between his lips and drawn into his mouth. He covered her opening and sucked hard. It was a different feeling, being pulled into him like that.

Bree shuddered. Hard.

Filled with a cock in front, and being teased and toyed with tongue from behind, made her lose all sense of time and place and inhibition. She was lost. And dammit, didn't care.

"Oh, fuck…"

The sensation of tumbling overtook her and they worked to change positions on the bed. They rolled and she ended up on top of one man, straddling him.

"There," he said. "Ride me."

Eager to please and intrigued to find out what next was in store, she mounted her man's rigid cock and relished in the feel of the over-sized organ in her pussy. "Oh, shit…" she said. "I like that."

"You'll like this, too," came the other voice.

He was patient and that was a good thing. Leaning forward, she braced herself on the broad chest below. The man beneath steadied her with his hands on her forearms. Curling her fingers over his muscled breast, she leisurely moved up and down on his cock. All the while, behind her, her other lover was preparing to fuck her ass.

His fingers where wet, she supposed with lubricant, as he circled and teased at the pucker of her hole.

"Shit," she heard the curse from behind. "I want inside you."

Her body responded to his ministrations. Her hole opened and flowered. He probed deeper with a digit and she felt the pressure from inside her vagina. The man beneath her groaned and she lay flat against his chest, her ass up, her mouth poised at a nipple. A strong urge to suck came over her, and so she did, fiddling with this erect nipple.

Fingers threaded through her hair, then wound themselves tightly in her locks, holding her against him.

The deeper the finger in her ass stroked, the faster she rode cock on the man between her legs.

At once, she stilled, when the head of another dick slid down her crack and slipped over her slick perineum. She waited, expecting him to move back up to enter and fill her ass.

He didn't.

The pushing came lower, where she was already impaled with one huge cock. Thumbs spread her apart. Fingers dipped inside, skimming along the dick that had already claimed her pussy.

"I want in there, too."

The man beneath her growled and cried out, "Yes…"

The cock behind was dancing over and around the one stroking inside her. He guided his dick with a hand and teased his partner's cock, as well as her clit and vagina. Both men jerked their bodies with excited thrusts. Bree grew wild with the need for both of them to be inside her at the same time.

At the same freakin' time.

"Fuck my pussy," she told them. "I want both your cocks up my cunt."

With a deep inhale and a primal groan, she felt the poke. The bucking from beneath grew urgent.

The spot near her pelvic bone that gave her so much pleasure was growing engorged and sensitive. The dick that belonged to the man behind her slipped inside a little. The pressure grew.

And then more.

"Oh, God…" she breathed. "Yes."

Mumbles, groans and small curses answered her.

Cocks rubbed against cocks.

Inside her.

An incredible feeling of fullness, of being stretched as far as she could possibly be stretched, of being filled with the flesh of her lovers, overcame her. She savored the feeling of *her two men* inside her.

Her two men.

Plenty enough for her. Wherever would there be room for more?

Not in this pussy.

They stroked and she rode. Both cocks filled her, claimed her, and won her over.

Tamed her.

She screamed her release, which ripped across her pelvis unexpectedly. Both men held onto her and continued to stroke until first one, then the other, spilled inside her with shouts and shudders that rivaled the other.

Moments later, sandwiched between them—with her sprawled on top one man and the other laying over her—Bree savored the sweet, sticky mess between her legs and the satisfied and semi-flaccid penises mingling next to her pussy. And smiled.

Reaching up, she pulled the blindfold away from her eyes and met Jake's languid grin. Carson gathered her hair back over her shoulder and gave her a soft kiss on the cheek.

"We'll take care of you, Bree. For always. All you have to do is say yes."

It didn't take her long to respond. "Green."

Both men chuckled.

"I love you guys," she said then, in a soft, slumber-like voice. "Merry Christmas."

What she got back were contented sighs as they wrapped her up like a present between them and held her tight.

Epilogue

"So, what's the plan for today?"

Bree looked down at her Blackberry and punched the button to bring up her calendar. "I have a 10 a.m. appointment to show a condo downtown, and then a two o'clock this afternoon out on the west end of town. I'm good for lunch. That what you are thinking?"

"Maybe." Carson poured himself another cup of coffee and took a small sip. "Ah, nothing like caffeine to get the creative juices going."

Bree frowned. "Oh, well that answers that question."

"What?"

She chuckled. "If your muse is nipping at you today, you're not going to leave that studio to come buy me lunch." Picking up her briefcase and purse, she moved toward him. "Let's do a rain check."

"You're sure?" he asked. "I hate to disappoint my baby girl."

She gave him a quick peck on the lips. "You never disappoint me, big boy." Tossing him a saucy smile, she chucked him on the cheek. "I need to get going."

She turned and he spanked her on the ass. Squealing, she headed for the door, just as Jake entered.

"Casual day at the office?"

Shaking his head, he replied, "Actually, I was thinking of working at home today."

"Oh good." Stepping toward him, she brushed a stray hair off his white t-shirt. God, she loved that jet black mane. "Sounds like a plan. You've been working way too late the past few nights, so take it easy, okay? Take a nap or something."

Yawning, Jake put the back of his hand to his mouth. "I like that idea."

"Good. Well, I need to scoot."

"Drive safe, love."

"Of course." She headed for the door then tossed her long mane and a sultry come-hither glance over her shoulder. "You boys be good while I'm gone today, okay? But if you're not, be sure to think of me, you hear?"

She left them with an air kiss, a little finger wave, and what she hoped, was the tempting sashay of her ass.

Oh, they would think of her. She could guarantee it.

About the Author

Mia is a Midwest girl who always had a thing for travel. Growing up in the middle of the country was one thing but for some reason, she always longed to be "on the edge." Living on the edge meant leaving home for sand and surf on both coasts (she's partial to North Carolina and San Diego beaches) and a stint living in New Orleans, pre-Katrina. Living on the fringes of the country seems to nicely parallel how she's lived her life. No regrets. Always looking forward. Take a risk or two. Just like the characters in her books. Bold, sassy, sexy, sophisticated, and erotic... and experiencing life to the fringes.

Website   http://www.miajae.com

Ribbons Not Included

By Demi Alex

You know who you are, my friend.
But do you know how much your support is
appreciated?

Enjoy your story.
Hugs, Demi

Table of Contents

Chapter One

I held my breath and checked my watch. Ten minutes exactly, and the test band was way darker than the guide band.

Yes!

The time was right.

I adjusted my boobs, fit them into the tiny straps of lace, and then checked my ass in the mirror. A quick little slap to bring some color to my lower cheeks and I was ready for Christian.

Stepping outside my comfort zone, I slipped my feet into my highest fuck-me heels and tapped through the bedroom feeling the heat collect between my thighs as the chain around my waist jingled my arrival. I was so damn horny, that I would have had to go it alone if the test hadn't said it was LH Surge time.

It had been nine days since the last time we'd made love. All the books said that doing *it* too often reduced the sperm's ability to reach the egg and successfully fertilize the little sucker. I wasn't willing to risk it. We needed super-sperm, and we needed it now.

Don't get me wrong, Christian was willing to look after my needs, but the guilt in the one way action was eating me up. And besides, the last time we tried that, I couldn't stop myself with just a little taste of him. I ended up pinning him down, straddling his face, and feasting on his heavenly cock till we were both spent.

Just the thought of his lips on me made my pussy ache and my clit throb. I missed him terribly, and I was so happy the time was right.

"Christian, honey, please come?" I called, perched on the sea of pillows I'd placed on the bed before taking my shower. Amused with the double meaning of my question, I smiled and wet my lips. *Please come, haha.*

"Give me a sec. It's fourth and five."

Damn, he was still watching the game. What did he want from me in order to get off the couch and meet me in the bedroom for a bit of our own *sexcersise*?

Truly, I was trying to add zest to our sex life as he'd suggested. But at the moment, I was all done up and ready to fuck his brains out, so I felt like a wanton woman, rejected by the man she loved and needed when he continued watching the game. I struggled to put my pride aside, struggled to concentrate on the big picture. We needed to have sex tonight in order to take our relationship to the next level. And if that meant I needed to shed my inner prude, I would.

I waited, shifted a little to the right so that my left breast spilled to the side. I played with my exposed nipple, preparing for a night of pure delight. In truth, I expected him to stroll in, totally unsuspecting, and pop a boner so freaking stiff at the sight of me playing with myself. It always turned him on to watch.

Time passed and I tried to get in the mood on my own, but self-stimulation wasn't cutting it. I wanted Christian on a much grander scale than what he'd accused me of. I missed him, too. I needed him more, and I'd prove to him how much.

"Come on, honey. I want to show you something." And I did. I never lied. I had spent the afternoon with an artist-extraordinaire tattooing a henna Super Spermy, with Popeye-sized biceps and a Superman cape, wagging his little tail in a swim for his life above the dimple on my lower back. Christian always rubbed his thumb on that dimple when he entered me from behind, telling me how much he loved it.

From behind was good. It shot semen quicker and stronger to the goal. Maybe I'd ride him the second time around?

"Is everything okay?" Christian asked— his ass obviously still plastered to the couch.

"Yes." I sighed and twisted my hair in a wicked spiral around my finger. "Hurry up. I really want to show you something."

"Then bring it in here," he said. "There's only a few minutes left, but we're down by six. We're going to force a fumble now and run it down the field. We're so pumped. We're going to win this one."

Stupid, stupid football. Why had I ever agreed to the new television set, which took up half our living room?

I let out a long breath and got out of bed, recalling our latest argument: the television set and our demure sex life. Well, that was in the past. But, before I seduced him, I had to get rid of evidence that my enthusiasm was any bit 'mechanical' or motivated by anything other than my desire and need to make passionate love to my husband. He had to know how much I wanted him, had to know how much I needed to have him show me how much he loved me—in every physical way possible.

Balancing on the uncomfortable black, strappy stilettos, I tried not to click too much as I returned to the bathroom and stuffed the box from the test into a drawer. I gave myself a quick glance in the mirror and admired the creamy curve of the tops my breasts. If things went as planned, they'd be much fuller soon and that only meant that Christian would want to suck on them more. Christian's mouth was made for my nipples. It wasn't uncommon for me to come from that simple act as I ground up against him.

Game over.

Time to get things heated and melt some of the ice on our winter windows. I wasn't wearing these damn shoes for my health. I was wearing them because Christian liked to throw my legs over his shoulders and feel the heels scrape into his shoulder blades as my body bowed and begged for him to let me come.

But Christian was so into the freaking game that he didn't turn to look at me as I entered the living room. So, I decided on the direct approach. No more waiting around.

I sauntered right in front of him, gave him my best *damn-you've-kept-me-waiting* look and crossed my arms over my chest, aware that my tits were pushed high and my nipples were about to spill over the lace material. I spread my feet, feeding his imagination on how wet my trimmed curls would be when he removed the tiny black strip of lace that led to my belly button.

"I have needs," I said, raising my foot and placing it squarely on his crotch. "And if you don't meet them, I'll have to find some other way." Inserting my finger into my mouth, I swirled my tongue around the tip and eyed him as seductively as possible.

"Move over, Kat. There is less than a minute of game time, *then* I'll meet your needs."

Damn. My pulse raced and my nails dug into my palm. I made the first move and he blew me off. He'd picked the game over me.

Just because we were married, just because our sex life had been good up until we decided to try for the baby, didn't mean he could dismiss me like that. I wasn't something to pass the time with. I mattered.

The baby. Actually, what really mattered was that the timing was right for conception. I didn't have the luxury of being pissed. We'd work out the rest. We always did.

"I want you, *now*," I cooed, batting my eyelashes in a desperate come hither plea.

"In that case, how can I refuse?"

Shit. That was the quickest attitude adjustment ever.

He moved my foot off his crotch and unzipped his fly. Taking his cock into his hand, he proved me that he wasn't looking to put me off any longer. He was more than a little erect and ready to go.

"Sit on the table, baby." Using a very distinct and appealing appendage, he motioned to where he wanted me on the coffee table. "Spread those beautiful legs of yours and unsnap the teddy so that I can see the sexy treat that you've prepared for me."

I did as he requested, and he nodded his approval. He stood and dropped his jeans to the floor. Stepping out of them, he kicked them to the side and kneeled in front of me.

"It's been a long time," he said, cupping my aching center and sliding his thumb between my moist curls to my clit. "You'd better be ready for me because I'm going to explode the moment I'm inside you."

"I'm ready," I replied, reaching for him.

"Don't be a bad girl." He swatted my hand away. "You do as you're told or they'll be consequences to pay."

My pussy clenched in anticipation. He wanted to play the control game—one of the seasonings I enjoyed most in adding some spice to our sex life. I never thought we needed spicing up, but it wasn't a bad idea. His authoritative and commanding demeanor was *hot*. Feeling the wetness spread between my thighs, I lowered my gaze.

"What would you like me to do?" I asked.

"To do, what?" Christian shook his head in disapproval, moving the bustier and arranging my breasts so that they sat on the shelf of the tight garment. Lowering his head, his breath fanned over my nipples. "I'm waiting."

"What would you like me to do?"

He captured my chin and tilted my head up, immobilizing me with a very intimidating gaze. "Finish the question with the proper address, or I'm watching the rest of the game and you can do with the D batteries I picked up this afternoon."

"You're cruel."

"Excuse me?" he said, straightening and pulling away.

No. He couldn't mean it. He wouldn't leave me like this. He couldn't. Not only was I ready and extremely needy, I was fertile. A vibrator was totally inadequate.

"If you regret your carelessness, I am known to be kind and forgiving to newbie subjects. I'll give you one more chance to make things right." He was taking this role-playing real serious. I inhaled deep then gave him what he wanted.

"What would you like me to do, *master*?"

He nodded and sat back. "Place your feet on my shoulders."

I did, showcasing my pussy for his inspection, but letting my knees drop towards the center and feigning modesty. Coolness swept across the heat as he blew his breath on me. His hands cupped my heavy breasts and his thumbs feathered my nipples as he dipped his head and his tongue slipped between my folds.

"You'd best not be teasing me and hiding your pleasure button from me. I don't like that," he said, waiting for me to open wider.

Inching my butt back, I moved my legs and exposed my swollen clit. But that wasn't enough for him. Pushing between my thighs, he swung my legs over his shoulders, hitching my knees so that my heels were against his back, and spread my thighs farther.

"Better," he acknowledged, suckling my nub and scraping his teeth over the sensitive edges.

Heaven.

His mouth, pure perfection.

It wasn't long before, I wanted to come. I needed to come. Every inch of me burned with desire and ached for release. The man drove me mad. But he stopped as my body tensed and my breath grew erratic.

"You are allowed one wish. What would you like?" Christian demanded, playing his master part to a tee. "Be specific, for I will not waste time to decipher code."

"I want to come."

He raised a brow. Not specific enough, I guess.

"I want you to fuck me."

He waited.

"I want your cock to fill me. I want to shout your name, master, as you make my world spin and my body fly."

"Done," he replied, lowering my legs from his shoulders and rising on his knees.

With no effort, he lifted me off the table and placed me on all fours beside him. Then he turned and plunged deep inside me, holding my hips and pumping his cock into me as hard as humanly possible while his balls slammed against my clit.

He hadn't bothered to remove my lingerie, he hadn't bothered with sweet talk or whispering in my ear, he took what he wanted and what I'd offered. Wild and furious, he kept me from sliding away from his impact by pulling my hips back after each thrust. It was primal, raw, and so damn arousing that I *did* want to shout.

Christian was usually gentle and slow, waiting for my buildup and release before he took his pleasure. I typically climaxed two or three times before he groaned out his finale, but this time was different. He set the pace, demanded I keep up, and drove me fucking insane.

"I'm going to come," I cried.

"Not till I give you permission," he warned, dropping over my body and wrapping one arm around me to play with my nipples.

He had a good eight inches on my frame, so it wasn't difficult for him to entrap me beneath him. His cock did the same to my insides, and as he altered the angle and hit the sweet spot inside my channel, my body rattled with uncontrollable delight.

"Please? Now?" I begged.

"No. Hold your pleasure." He thrust so fucking deep and stroked every sensitive area inside me. "You've been bad denying your master."

His hand left my nipples and curled under me, settling against my clit and intensifying my torture. He rolled my sensitive skin between his thumb and forefinger while he continued pumping into me. I was so wet, so hot, that I thought my pussy was on fire. I tried to drop lower in the front, to raise my ass higher and allow some air to cool me off, but rather than relief, I received a sharp sting.

"Did I tell you to drop?" he demanded, smacking my ass again.

"No," I breathed, the sting spreading over my rear. "My pussy has a mind of its own when it comes to your dick. I'm burning up."

Dirty talk wasn't so dirty, after all. I may have been a newbie, but it was a definite turn-on to vocalize the sensations racing through my body.

He released a bit of his seed in me, but stopped with a guttural sound. I knew what he felt like when he came and that wasn't all of it.

"A little relief," he said, sliding his cock out of my trembling folds.

How'd he stop? Where did he learn that? A chill ran up my spine, but disappeared as he reentered my channel and stroked me in long, slow, repeated thrusts. His thumb rubbed my clit, his breath caressed my ear, and I felt his body tense against mine.

"Come," he said, adding more pressure to my clit. "Now."

And I did. It was the hottest, strongest climax in years. My body shook and the light grew dim. Like a pinball machine breaking the top score, sparks ricocheted inside me as my climax intensified. Christian came like a fucking rocket, his juices mixing with mine for an explosive cocktail.

He pulled me up against his chest and held me till my body relaxed. Still buried within me, he lifted me off the floor and sat on the couch with me on top of him facing the gigantic television set.

"Quiet till the game is over," he warned. "As soon as we make this field goal, I'm going to punish you for distracting me and making me miss the touchdown."

All I wanted to do was cuddle against him, but I had to admit, the discomfort from sitting up had its allure. My pulsing clit liked being against his balls, so I reached down to rub them against me. Everything was so sensitive, it almost hurt. His fingers tightened on my waist and he guided me up so that his cock touched my g-spot. Rotating my hips, I met his groin with my wetness and let my second orgasm take me.

"Oh, this is so fucking good," I moaned.

"Mm, they missed," was all he said, and I knew he was trying to act aloof, but he was hard again.

I didn't care that he was watching the game. I wouldn't have cared if one of his other fantasies was happening, either. It was the best sex we'd had in months.

"At least they held on for the last ten seconds," he muttered, turning off the television and tossing the remote onto the side chair. Sitting up, he moved from within me and let me sit on his cock lengthwise. "Now, I need to punish you extra. You came without asking."

I glanced over my shoulder and smiled. "I like it when you're like this."

"That's irrelevant," he replied, maneuvering my shoulders so that I had to look forward again. "You're still going to get punished, and you're going to say thank you when I'm done."

"Thank you, master," I whispered, anticipating the punishment he had in store for me.

"Do the work and ride to your next orgasm." Totally hard again, he slipped deep into my core and spread his hands over my ass. "I'm not handing it to you this time."

I loved this position. I rose and fell, taking him where and how I wanted him; the sensations floating me higher with each movement. I was so susceptible, so ready to explode again that when he stilled my hips and placed his hands over my thighs to prevent me from rising again, I almost objected, but the anticipation of his next demand had me holding my breath.

"Turn around," he commanded.

My heart thundered in my chest, and my clit ached as I swung my legs together so I could turn and face him. Even though I tried to keep him inside as I pirouetted, he pulled out and pressed his length between my butt cheeks.

"I'll take your suggestion into consideration," he said, reaching up and caressing my breasts.

What consideration? I had no clue, but as the color of his irises darkened, a thrill rocked me again.

"Now bend over me so I can taste those rosy tips," he instructed.

Suckling my nipples, he spread my own moistness on my ass. The sensual massage was making me nuts. I wanted him again. I wanted him back inside.

As if reading my mind, he released my nipple and looked me in the eyes. "You take what I give you."

Thankfully, he gave me two fingers and rubbed my clit. I was so close to going over the edge again, but he hadn't said I could. In a vain attempt to hold back my orgasm, I squeezed my legs together. The tension and friction was overwhelming. I had to let go—had to.

I closed my eyes as my climax hit. My head fell back and I struggled to inhale.

His hands secured my hips and held me tight on him. He didn't enter me, didn't try to come himself. He simply steadied me as the world shattered to millions of pieces.

"Open your eyes," he said evenly in a low voice.

I dared to peek.

"What am I going to do with you?" Christian asked, shaking his head.

Chapter Two

"Sweet punishment," I cooed, stretching my leg over Christian's thighs as the sun entered our room and announced the morning. "When do I get to punish you?"

"When I say so," he replied, dropping a kiss on the top of my head and wrapping me into his embrace. "Sleep a little. We have a few hours before the stores open and you'll have the pleasure of shopping for my Christmas present."

Most of my holiday shopping was done. The only gift left was Christian's, and I still wasn't sure what to get him. He never asked for anything specific. Plus, when he did, it always had to do with buying something I'd use—you know, for our mutual pleasure.

"I'm meeting Ally for lunch. Who said I'm going shopping?"

"Fine. Be like that. Don't buy me a present." Pretending to pout, he stuck out his lower lip and I couldn't resist a quick kiss.

"How do you know I didn't buy it already?"

He laughed, patting my shoulder so I could move over. "It isn't under the tree. I checked every box you've decorated so fancy with those pretty ribbons."

"Well," I breathed, tossing my hair over my shoulder and giving him a stern look. "Perhaps you've been a bad boy and won't be getting a present this year? Especially after all the foul language you employed last night."

"I didn't hear you complaining."

"It doesn't matter what I think. Santa makes those decisions." Licking my lips, I raised my palms up and acted all confused.

"Fine. I see what it's like. Use me and dump me like that." Snapping his fingers, he swung his legs over the side of the bed and got out. "Looks like you don't have much use for me in the daylight hours. Double standard for sure." He shrugged his broad shoulders and stood over the bed. "I remember the plans. Have fun with your sister. I'll just stay home alone and watch the tree lights reflect off other people's presents."

I squinted against the early morning sunlight, admiring his perfect physique. Christian carried his six foot three frame with sculpted muscle from head to toe. Toned and perpetually tanned, he certainly resembled a Roman god. No matter if the ground was frozen and carpeted with fresh snow, it steamed below his feet.

"I love you," I said, smiling and reaching for his hand. "Last night was amazing."

He sat back on the bed, looked at our intertwined fingers, and cleared his throat. His thumb caressed the inside of my wrist, and I could see that his mind was occupied with something. I had a haunting inkling on the culprit, but I didn't want to argue again. I didn't want to give him reason if I was mistaken.

"You okay?" I asked.

"I'm great." He nodded and looked up and straight into my eyes. "Want to join me in the shower and conserve water?"

He knew I couldn't. We hadn't showered together since our anniversary. Besides, if we showered together now, it would lead to making love again. Ejaculating too often could reduce the potency of his sperm. Even the repeated sex last night could have done that, but the sex was so amazing and we were so engrossed in each other that I'd forgotten about our baby plans for a few hours.

I shook my head. "Go ahead without me. I'll put on the coffee."

He didn't get up, but he did let go of my hand and fisted his together. "Kat, were you fertile last night?"

Damn, here was the talk I'd tried to avoid. I didn't want to fight. But, I wasn't about to lie, either.

"Yes."

"So, this willingness to try new *things* was solely attributed to an ovulation test?"

"No," I said. "Not solely." Originally it had been, but once I was with him, I had wanted Christian more than I had in months. "Last night was really amazing. I haven't been so excited in ages, and my orgasms were out of this world."

"So, does that mean that you're now willing to stop doing that damn test twenty-four-seven and enjoy our life again?"

"I do enjoy our life," I insisted. "Don't you?"

Christian had suggested we try to be more spontaneous, not limit our lovemaking to the bed, and not keep it only at night. I listened, I tried. It wasn't easy for me to seduce him the way I had. Actually, that wasn't true. Once I had the guts to get things rolling, it was great. I'd enjoyed it to no end and the thrill still raced through me. I could have told him, but I wasn't ready.

Running his palm down his face, then rubbing his shoulder, Christian certainly didn't look encouraging. He didn't say a thing.

"You wanted variation. You said something adventurous, so I did that. Did I do something wrong?" The silence made my stomach roil and the thrill disappear. I crossed my arms over my abdomen. "Talk to me, Christian. Let's not do this again. We *need* to talk."

"You really want me to talk?" He faced me, sharing his dismay and disappointment. "Will you listen?"

I nodded.

"It's not that I don't want a baby," he said, lowering his gaze and taking an audible breath. "It's that I don't want to lose us in the process. Sometimes I feel like nothing more than a stud horse, here to perform when the test says I should."

"But—"

"No buts," he interrupted. "*That* is how I feel. You asked, so listen and don't try to justify what has been going on."

I'd never thought of him that way. Had I?

No. I loved him. He was my world. Each and every time he touched me, I went up in flames. Sharing a total of ten years together had not put a damper on the way I felt about or reacted to him. I was simply working on what we both wanted. He was the one who had originally suggested that the moment was right to start a family.

"The only time you want to be together is when the test says it's okay." His gaze narrowed as he rubbed his fingers over his knuckles. "I don't know what to think anymore? Have we already lost each other? It's not the variety that's the real problem. It's the stud horse issue."

The heaviness on my chest made it impossible to inhale, so I rolled my lips tightly, scraping my teeth over the bottom one till it hurt. My heart broke, and I whimpered in pain.

How could he think those things?

"I love you," I whispered, unable to stop the tears from spilling down my cheeks.

He cupped my chin and wiped his thumb over the moisture. "I love you more," he said, brushing his lips across my mouth. "And there is no way in hell that I'm going to let what we have fizzle out. You need to get used to the idea, and you need to trust me and in our future. Our relationship will grow and become a greater part of us with each day that passes."

Resting my forehead on his shoulder, I agreed. The baby would come when the time was right. Neither one of us had issues in that department. The doctor had confirmed that little detail. We needed to make sure that we were good with each other and that we didn't forget why we were together in the first place. Christian and I were a *WE*.

We loved each other. We'd play hard and laugh each day. We'd grow old together and enjoy the journey. That was our original plan and that was what I had to focus on.

"I'll be done in a few minutes. Meet you in the kitchen." Kissing the top of my head, he rose to his feet.

I sighed my relief that he hadn't removed the lingerie and noticed Super Spermy. It was dark last night and thankfully he hadn't seen it. I'd scrub it off before I made him feel worse. My tramp stamp was a thing of the past.

* * * *

Ally waved across the crowded dining room, beaming with joy. She had news to share and she was bursting to tell me about it. A quick hug and a flurry of kisses later, she took my hand and offered me the chair next to hers.

"I've met the man of my dreams," she blurted out. "He is to die for."

"Hold on, hold on," I said, cautiously broaching the subject. Ally was bouncing back from a divorce and she was susceptible to being taken for a ride. "Start at the beginning and tell me where, who, and how."

Zane had bumped into Ally on the Friday after Thanksgiving at the mall. Being crowded, like it always is on Black Friday, they shared a table at the food court. The rest was history as they say in the land of romance.

"I'm happy for you," I said, squeezing her hand. "When do I get to meet him?"

"He'll be back by Christmas day. Dinner?" Ally said, smiling her secret message.

"Good. What should I cook?"

"Zane is a vegetarian. He doesn't eat meat or chicken. But other than that, he's easy." Sitting on her hands, Ally swayed side to side. She never cooked, other than to burn her scrambled eggs. So it was clear that dinner would either be at my house or out on the town. And since the holiday meant impossibly long table waits, I was cooking.

"You're the best," she added, grinning real big.

"Yeah, yeah," I replied, shrugging my shoulders and mimicking her sway. "I can't wait to meet him. Get back to me with the exact night." I really couldn't wait. I hadn't seen my sister so happy in a long, long time. She practically glowed with excitement.

"Kat?" She placed her hand on mine. "What's up?"

"Nothing."

"Then why haven't you drilled me, yet? You always ask a thousand questions when I meet a man." Her forehead wrinkled in concern as she swept her thumb over my wrist.

"I don't have to ask. Your baby blues are twinkling like nuts." It was obvious how she felt. What I wanted to know was how he felt about her. Ally didn't pick winners in the past, and I didn't want to see her get hurt.

"Okay." She sipped on her straw and eyed me over her glass, assessing the situation in her own logical manner. She may have been a bad judge of character when it came to her men, but nothing got past her when it came to me. "Tell me about that far away look in *your* eyes. Did you have a rough night?"

"Yeah, but not in a bad way." The sigh that escaped my lips was an accident. I didn't mean to concern her more. "The night was great. Didn't get much sleep, though."

"Oh, did you wear the new lingerie?"

I nodded. "New teddy, different location, funky positions, and even some spanking—"

Gagging on her Diet Coke, Ally covered her mouth with her right hand and raised her left palm out to me. "TMI, sis. TMI."

"What?"

I rarely spoke about my sex life, but she'd never had a problem sharing. She couldn't take offense. No way.

"Spanking changes the rules." She covered her ears and shook her head. "I don't need all the details about an old married couple's night activities."

"That's the problem." My voice cracked and I needed a moment to compose myself. "Christian wants to spice things up. He says things are good, but he's scared we're going to settle into a stale routine if we don't vary things a little."

"That isn't a problem." She waved her hand at the air and swatted away my distress. "We buy more lingerie, pick up a good read or two, maybe a video, and if you're willing, go for a waxing. He won't know what hit him."

"There's more," I admitted and her shoulders drooped. "He wanted variety, so I tried. I tried seducing him in the living room—"

"Ew." She shivered and shut her eyes. "Please tell me you didn't do it on the red chair. I love that freaking chair."

"No. Not the chair." I didn't elaborate on where. She didn't need to squirm when she placed a mug on the coffee table. "Anyways, we had an awesome time. The best in months. But this morning, he told me he felt like a stud horse and implied that I was only being physical to conceive. As if I don't care about or love him."

Ally let out a loud breath and rubbed her temples. Her lips twisted in dismay as she looked everywhere but at me. After a long time, she stretched her arms behind her neck, lifted her long brown hair, and met my gaze.

"You're obsessed with getting pregnant," she said.

"No," I objected. "I mean, it's important to me, but I'm not obse—" Damn, I sucked at lying. My cheeks were flaming and I could barely put two words together. "Yeah, I guess I'm obsessed."

Waving off the waiter, she used the menu to shield us from the neighboring table. "Go back a few years and heed your own advice."

The sad thing was that I knew exactly the moment in time she was talking about, and I knew the advice. When she'd confided in me about how miserable she had been with her ex, I'd told her to leave him and live her life. Ally had tried to justify staying with the jerk because she was getting too old to start over. She wanted children before she was too old to enjoy them.

"If a mom and dad aren't happy together, it only hurts the children," she said, reminding me of my closing argument. "Do you love Christian?"

"More than I thought possible," I whispered.

"Then, tell me. What should we do?"

"Make the waxing appointment and go shopping," I said, determined to show my husband how much I really did love him.

Chapter Three

After two days of sexy shopping (or was it shopping for sex?) and many hours spent searching websites on erotic fantasies, I finally finished wrapping all the gifts and placed them under the tree. Christian's present wasn't there, yet. But, the framework was. It was a personal gift that wouldn't do well with ornate wrapping and fancy ribbons. There were no ribbons included, but it would have bells and whistles the other presents couldn't ever have.

I was going out on a limb, practically risking my sanity, but I knew he'd more than like it. After all, all my research said men were visual creatures.

Hiding the camera inside the only gift box without frilly ribbons was a sure way I would differentiate it from the real presents. Hopefully, Christian would be too occupied to notice the discrepancy. The massive amount of candles supplied ample lighting while still filling the room with a sensual glow. And, I'd moved the red chair a little closer to the tree for a better view.

Santa Clause is Coming to Town played on my cell phone, letting me know I had ten minutes till he arrived. Pressing my palm against my tummy, I tried to soothe the fluttering sensation. I hadn't felt like that since the first time I had sex.

Sitting on the edge of the couch, I finished off my Baileys. With my hands leaving a permanent imprint on my midsection, I waited, poured a new drink, finished it, and waited some more.

He was late, and the camera was recording. What if it ran out of juice before we were done? What if he was still mad at me?

We hadn't talked about the baby since the morning after our amazing marathon, but we hadn't made love either. In a massive expression for my conviction to our marriage, I'd thrown away the ovulation test. If we were meant to have a baby, we would. The doctor had said everything was okay and that we should enjoy the process.

But, how the hell was I not supposed to worry? We'd been together for ten years and there had never been a false alarm. We'd been *trying* for months, and still nothing. Covering my face, I allowed myself a single whining sigh. I had to trust in us and what we had, otherwise nothing would be right. Ally was correct; bringing a child into a strained marriage was not healthy. I had to focus on strengthening my relationship with Christian before I considered any thing else.

He was over an hour late, and he wasn't answering his phone. I carefully unwrapped the box with the camera, changed out the battery, angled it so the lens was clear of the cardboard and paper, set it on standby, rewrapped the darn thing, and placed the remote control on the table. Since I blew out the majority of the candles, I programmed the tree lights on a steady illumination rather than flashing, and hoped between the tree lights and the candles in the glass jars there would be enough lighting to capture us on tape.

The news was on, so I pulled a throw over my shoulders and lay on the couch.

When the jingle indicating the end of the program woke me, Christian was sitting in the red chair by the tree, a towel wrapped around his middle, grinning at me.

"You're so beautiful when you sleep," he said, tucking a tendril of hair behind my ear. "When we started living together, I used to watch you for hours."

"No, that's impossible." I sat up and took a watered down sip of Baileys. "How could you have been watching me, if I was watching you?"

His laughter warmed my chilled bones, reminding me how much I loved the man before me. He held out his arms and I walked into them, sitting on his lap. Every Christmas Eve, at midnight, we opened a special present we had for each other. It was just after eleven-thirty, so I still had time to *prepare* his gift.

"I made sugar cookies. Can I get you some?" I snuggled against him and kissed the side of his neck. Freshly shaven, he smelled clean and spicy. Our plans must have coincided, for the twinkle in his eyes was brighter than the tree lights.

"I have all the sugar I need right here," he said, lowering his head and capturing my lips. His tongue gently caressed my mouth, stoking my desire and heating every cell in my body.

"Love the new baby doll," he said, lifting the see-thru fly away material which was separated down my middle. "Very festive."

"It's red. Your favorite color."

His lips trailed down my neck, around my collar bone and directly to my chest. Taking my nipple into his mouth, his tongue twirled over the sheer material, raising my excitement and making my pussy ache for his touch.

But, it was time to make his present. I'd done a lot of research on male sexual fantasies and one thing that topped all the lists was them receiving oral sex. With his face still against my chest, I reached for the remote control and turned the camera on, then looked at it and licked my lips like I was parched.

Christian pulled the satin ribbon holding together my lingerie and the material fell to either side of my breasts, exposing the sheer g-string thong that barely covered my swollen folds. It was real hard trying to choreograph the blow job when my body wanted him so bad. I arched my back and he suckled my nipples. First one, then the other, and eventually palming the sides of my breasts, he brought them together and paid homage to both nipples simultaneously.

These were the moments my large breasts were made for. I loved my D size.

"You have the most delicious tits in the world," he breathed, tonguing the tight space between them. "I would suck on them for hours if I hadn't seen that beautiful bare pussy of yours and now I need to taste it."

Moisture pooled between my thighs, and the sheer material glistened in the candle glow. I was so wet, so ready for him to see my bare pussy swollen for him, but I had to focus.

Damn, I loved sitting on his lap. It gave him great access while I felt the complete length of his shaft against me. His erection pressed into the back of my thigh, and I moved to fit it in the center of my ass. All the time, I concentrated on keeping us in the camera's line of sight. The secret recording made me hornier, and I couldn't wait to see his reaction to it when I played it back for him.

I lifted my butt, moved my hand under his towel, and wrapped my fingers over his cock. "I need to taste this," I whispered.

Groaning his approval, he shifted his hips and pulled the towel from under us. He raised my face and captured my lips with a searing kiss. The baby doll fell to the floor and his hands cupped my naked ass as his finger moved under the thin string between my cheeks.

My body was on fire. I couldn't think of the camera anymore. The only thing on my mind was Christian, his hard body, and the way he made my world spin.

Reaching beneath me, he lifted me to my knees so that I straddled his thighs, and from behind, he slid his hand inside my folds. My breasts in his face and my pussy aching for more of his touch, I arched my back and pulled him closer.

He didn't disappoint, slipping his thumb into my channel and rubbing my clit with his finger. He suckled a nipple and scraped his teeth over it, making me cream all over his hand. I moaned and groaned like a bitch in heat, but I couldn't stop it. The climax claimed me and my head dropped back as he took me higher. The hand supporting my back tugged my hair down, pushing my breast deeper into his mouth, and he sucked harder. My body trembled and my pussy clamped tight with sheer delight. I was in ecstasy.

This wasn't what I had planned. I was supposed to capture his release. I was supposed to make him come on video.

He pulled the elastic from between my ass and fit his hand against my mound. I ground into him as the final effects of my orgasm consumed my body. Accepting his support, I collapsed and I buried my face into his shoulder.

Stroking my hair, Christian held me there till my breathing settled. His erection, still prominent between us, reminded me of my mission. Raising my head, I looked into his dazzling eyes and kissed his lips. Unfolding my sated body, I trailed my mouth over his chest, his sculpted abdomen, and then down his goody line. Taking his scrotum into my hands, I fit my mouth over his cock and ran my tongue under the ridge.

His fingers tangled into my hair and encouraged me to continue. Eventually, my knees hit the floor, and I was snug between his legs, tasting every inch of his glorious length. Returning to the tip, I was rewarded by a solitary drop of salty-sweetness as he shifted in the chair. My eyes were closed, centering on the sense of his cock filling my mouth and reaching the back of my throat. I wanted to make him come, to taste him, to hear his animalistic groan so that I could come again myself.

I slipped a hand between my thighs and rubbed my pulsing nub. This was decadent. Recording us like this was so fucking hot, and it was making me crazy. I rubbed my clit faster, sucked his cock deeper, and I still couldn't get enough.

He was close and so was I.

In a swift move I hadn't anticipated, he stood and held my head as he slipped from my hungry mouth. He bent and blew out the candles on the table, cleared an area and lay down.

"Come here, Kat," he commanded.

I inched up his body and met his mouth for a branding kiss. He was much taller and bigger than I was, so his legs hung over the edge of the table while mine extended from it. I loved having him beneath me. It was secure, warm, and pure heaven when his arms closed around me.

"I love you, sweetheart," he said, placing tiny kisses all over my face. "And, I'm so ecstatic that you're willing to try new things with me."

"Like what new things?" I said, feigning innocence.

"Like waxing that gorgeous pussy of yours. I know you've shaved it before, but you've never let another woman between your legs like that in the past."

"How do you know it was a woman?" I teased and a huge grin framed his handsome face. "Maybe the person who did the waxing did more than that?"

He smacked my ass, the sting registering in my core. "I'm the only one who gets to do. Understand?" *Smack.* "They can watch, they can pant over your glimmering cunt, but they don't get to do." *Smack. Smack. Smack.*

Laughing, I spread my thighs a bit, giving my swollen clit a little relief. "You're the only one that gets to do," I confirmed.

"Good," he said, rubbing the silky smoothness of my panties over my bare pussy and making it pulse with an intense need for so much more of his attention. "And now, I want to be the one who gets to lick your tasty cream."

Damn, the mere thought of his tongue on my pink pussy intensified my arousal. I shivered with pleasure as the moisture slid between my legs and settled on the tiny strip covering my crotch, displaying my excitement on my new lingerie.

Maneuvering me up his body, he removed my panties and forced me to sit up as he brought his mouth to my core. Licking between my swollen folds, he found my clit and lovingly lapped at it till my hands and feet went numb. As if I was a doll, he fit me over his face and tongue fucked me till my body shook.

In a momentary glimpse of sanity, I remembered the camera and swung my legs over his head so that I reversed my position. The tingle of anticipation grew as I lowered myself over him and took his penis into my mouth. Sixty-nine was the things dreams were made of. I hoped he enjoyed watching this as much as I enjoyed creating his gift.

It didn't last too long, for when my body climbed and cried out its pleasure, he let go and joined me. We stayed on the table, spent and content 'till the night's chill replaced the heat on our naked bodies.

"It's after midnight," I finally said. "I want to give you your Christmas Eve present."

Lifting me, he moved off the table and spread the previously shed towel on the carpet for us to sit on. He leaned his back against the couch, sprawled before me naked, displaying all his tempting goods, and had my pussy protesting the distance between us. I looked around the room and fidgeted, wondering what I should do next. Did I have enough time to video a second part?

"Just stay with me for a while, sweetheart. I miss holding you like this."

He pulled me into his embrace and placed my back against his chest. His legs bent on either side of me, creating the perfect cocoon of warmth and comfort. I lay my head on his shoulder and closed my eyes.

"I'm so happy," I whispered. "I never want anything to come between us. I love you so much, Christian. More than you can ever imagine."

"I can imagine, and I am happy to say that you are my fantasy personified." Fitting his finger beneath my chin, he tilted my head and claimed my lips with incredible tenderness. "You are my dream, and you cannot imagine how much I love you."

I turned and snuggled into him. We sat on the floor, before our Christmas tree for a long time, silently savoring the after glow of our lovemaking. It was the beep of the camera, indicating that the battery was done, that spurred us into action.

Tightening his hold on me, he looked around the room. "Did you hear something?"

I nodded and met his gaze. "Yes."

"But you're not worried?"

"Nope." I smiled, anxious to surprise him.

"Okay," he breathed, whistling long and low. "Care to let me in on the secret?"

"Sure," I said, getting to my feet and walking over to the tree. I reached for his box. "Your Christmas Eve present," I said, presenting him with a red package.

"What?" he said, lifting his brow in jest. "No ribbons included?"

"No ribbons for you. You were a naughty boy."

He shook the box, then immediately tried to still it when the camera banged against the packaging. "What's the thumping sound?"

I shrugged and twisted away to hide my amusement. I wasn't about to tell him a thing, and I certainly wasn't going to let him read the expression in my eyes. Unable to wait a moment more, I rolled my hand urging him to hurry.

Tearing the paper, he made a production of lifting the top lid, but I had taped it up a little better than I had wanted. He needed to remove all the paper, and it was then that he noticed the hole on the side. He captured my gaze and when I nodded, he quickly proceeded.

"You're giving me our own camera?"

"Look carefully," I said. "You never know what you'll find in there."

He flipped it over in his hand, pausing and giving me more quizzical looks before changing the setting from record to play. Then he raised it to his eye and looked through the view finder. At last, he flipped open the little side screen and tried to view what was on the memory.

"The battery is dead."

Shit, he really didn't get it. Did I have to spell it out for him?

Kicking the discarded lingerie across the floor, I reached for the other battery pack that was thankfully on the charger and smacked it firmly in his palm. The next minute or two were actually anticlimactic. I longed to see the shock on his face as our images played on the two inch screen. But no, he was taking his freaking time switching out the batteries.

"We could plug it in," I suggested, placing the towel on the couch. I sat on the edge, as if sitting on a bed of nails, and folded my hands between my knees.

"That means my present is on the camcorder's hard drive," he said, looking all smug and grinning wickedly. "Did you guess your present?"

I shook my head. I had no idea. "There isn't anything I need or desire as much as I do you. Finish with your gift, and then we'll go from there."

He flipped the little screen open again, and his mouth dropped as the video played.

"Damn!" he drawled. "I'm hard again."

I laughed, loving the look on his face. He was stunned, awed, and absolutely hard. His cock stood at attention as he tilted the camera to check out the view, pressed rewind and played parts over and over.

I couldn't help myself. I took him in my hand and pumped him while he played the recording. Over the past decade, I'd learned the pace needed to sustain his excitement, but still keep him from coming. As our video images climaxed with me spread over him, my pussy on his face and his cock disappearing into my mouth, I tightened my grasp and increased the speed.

The tip of his penis glistened with pre-come. I ran my finger over it and he groaned, as the video showed me licking my lips in satisfaction.

He slid his hand between my legs and found my moist, warm center.

"Thank goodness," he said, wasting no time pushing me up against the back of the couch and bending me over the soft cushions.

Entering me from behind, he pumped that harder-than-ever cock deep into my greedy channel, causing me to instantly clench around him. My toes hovered over the floor, and his hands supported my breasts from bouncing as he propelled me closer and closer to losing control. He stretched and filled me with pleasure—pleasure that had seemed surreal only days ago.

A few more thrusts and my vision blurred.

"Christian," I moaned, seeing stars explode around me and hearing his euphoric gratification rumble from within his chest as we climaxed in tandem.

"I fucking love my gift," he said, pulling me into his arms and carrying me to bed.

We relaxed for half an hour and then showered together. Surprisingly, there was no sex, just Christian lathering me in my favorite vanilla scented wash and carefully rinsing the soap suds from my body. He pulled on a pair of sweats and told me to dress warmly.

"Where are we going?" I asked.

"I'm switching out your Christmas Eve present for your Christmas Day present." Sheepishly grinning, he waited for me to get dressed and grabbed my hand the moment I pulled the sweater over my head.

Leading me to the apartment's entryway, he grabbed my boots and fit them on my feet. He then pulled my jacket off the hook and wrapped it over my shoulders.

"It's almost three in the morning," I reminded him.

"Is there a rule about accepting a gift at three in the morning?"

I guess there was no rule. I smiled and followed Christian out the door. He was so excited, that I doubted he'd sleep unless he presented me with whatever he'd gotten. His enthusiasm was contagious, and I felt the thrill deep in my core as the elevator descended to the ground floor.

Right before the doors opened, he covered my eyes with his right hand and brought his mouth besides my ear. "Don't peek."

Placing his body behind me, he guided me and took five steps forward, turned right and walked seven more steps.

A jingling of sorts intrigued me and I turned towards the sound. "What is it?"

"Something you've admired since I met you," Christian said, removing his hand.

Before me sat the most beautiful speed yellow 911 Targa 4S Porsche. For years, I'd lusted after this car, but I never actually thought I'd have one. We'd been saving to buy a house, and such a luxury seemed so far fetched.

"I know it isn't a SUV or a family friendly mini-van, but it has four seats," Christian said. "I figured that it could still fit a car-seat if it needed to, and we could save the

SUV for when the kids are older and feel cramped in the back of the Porsche."

"No one could ever feel cramped in this car," I whispered, blinking repeatedly to make sure I wasn't dreaming. "How?"

"How what?"

"How could we afford this?" I turned toward him and saw the pride displayed on his face.

"I landed the marketing campaign for the wine distributorship. This is only part of the advance." The gleam in his eyes shouted his joy. Now they could move ahead full throttle with all their plans. "We're in the clear, Kat. We can have it all."

"I already do," I said, going up on my toes and kissing the man of my dreams with the comfort and desire of true love. "I have you."

"I love you," he said between kisses. "I love you so much. And I promise to keep things interesting and make every day a little better for you."

After a ride on the deserted city streets, we returned home, and I fell asleep in my husband's arms, wondering how I'd ever gotten so lucky and promising myself to make every day as interesting for him.

Chapter Four

It was exactly one hour since he'd stormed out of the apartment. One hour since he'd taken his tight ass out the door and didn't look back, leaving me in a brand new red teddy with my tits spilling over and no one to attend to them.

Well, screw him. I wasn't about to apologize for blowing my top. I wasn't wrong. Just because he was the most wonderful man on the planet half the time, it didn't mean I had to put up with his insults the rest of the time.

I deserved to be pissed. He gave me a freaking coat. Double x-large. It looked like a huge red sail and I didn't want it. But he forced me to put it on. Naked. And then he'd ask for us to go downstairs and make love on the hood of the new Porsche!

No way. It was daylight. People would be coming and going, and we'd be exposed.

"That's the thrill of it. The possibility of being caught," he'd said.

"You're nuts. Just because you gave me a car, doesn't mean I'll act like a whore and do it anywhere and anytime."

"What the hell is wrong with you?" he'd said, pounding his fist into his hand. "You're giving me mixed signals."

"Am not."

"Fine. You're not. You're just an ungrateful and unimaginative woman who can drive me insane with your mood swings."

Ungrateful?

Unimaginative?

Then why had I concocted a whole new role playing scene for our flourishing sex life? And why had he left me all alone on Christmas? I lived with Dr. Jekyll and Mr. Hyde. He was unreasonable, blaming the fight on my mood swings and saying that no reasonable man could live with such a hormonal woman.

I was not hormonal!

Waiting for the popcorn to finish popping, I checked my cell for the millionth time. He hadn't called. No text. No message directly to voicemail.

"If he wants out, I'll give him out," I yelled to no one but the walls. "I hate him."

I kicked my red feathered, kitten-healed slippers under the table and headed into the bedroom. Lifting the window frame, I reached for the nearest thing I could find to toss the three stories down onto the snow covered lawn. My fingers closed over the worn denim of his favorite pair of Levis. He'd placed them on my makeup table just before he'd started laughing at my lack of adventure. Just before he thought I'd swoon over his suggestion to add excitement and strip out of my clothes to parade around town with him in my new red coat.

As if I hadn't shown him my *adventurous* side the past week? Damn, he had me being adventurous on DVD!

I took aim at the gross mixture of snow and mud near the sidewalk and threw like a quarterback in the Super Bowl. The slush splattered as the jeans met their target.

"Ha! You should appreciate that one. Six points for me. Pass complete."

I threw my hands in the air and did a manic end-zone dance all the way to his bureau. Pulling out his Hard Rock Cancun t-shirt, an Aerosmith shirt, and his favorite threadbare sweater from ten Christmases ago, I walked back to the window and dropped them straight down this time. Watching the colorful garments flutter to the white ground sent a thrill of victory to my gut. It unclenched and started to do a dance of its own.

The smell of burnt popcorn reached my nose and my moment of triumph collapsed with the same intensity it had set on. The stench spread, and gray smoke infused every nook in the house. I walked through the rest of the apartment, opening windows as I made my way to the kitchen in order to throw out the offensive snack.

Adrenaline drummed through my body. I felt so tightly strung, that I knew I would snap if I didn't calm down. So, as soon as all the windows were open, and the thirty degree air-out was under way, I made some coffee, passed on the popcorn in favor of some store bought brownies, and plopped down in front of the television set to watch a marathon of holiday movies in my lace teddy, all alone.

I needed the sanity that came with veging for a few hours and staring numbly at the screen. George Clooney had always proved to be good medicine, so he was my first choice. Once George had me back in the mood, I would splurge the twenty bucks needed for my harem of well hung men and bring out my B.O.B. to get off on my own.

I was adventurous. And, I could prove it. I didn't need *him*. For all I cared, Christian could take a hike and not come back.

My clit didn't agree. It gave a protesting throb, missing Christian, as my mind replayed the way he'd woken me up in the morning.

His tongue circled the tip of my nipple, which was jutting through the lace of the bustier. His fingers splayed over the lower part of my ass and moving in a definite path to my wet folds. I was so hot for him that I ached. An erotic haze settled around us. I placed my hands on his shoulders for balance as he dropped his head and moved the lace panty to the side, exposing my bare skin. His thumb settled on my clit and his tongue slid between my aching pussy. I was about to come, one more flick and I would have been over the edge, but the phone rang.

The moment was temporarily lost as his family confirmed the time for breakfast. I was on the phone, as he slyly licked his lips and lowered himself between my legs. I tried to push him away, but he held me tight and refused to let me close my legs. Trying to finish the conversation, I dropped the phone as his tongue caressed my clit and his fingers filled me. Thankfully, he pulled the cord from the jack and disconnected the call.

"Merry Christmas," I'd said as my orgasm hit.

I smiled and had a wonderful day, up until the moment he'd pushed me too far. It was his fault, not mine. So, where did he get the idea that I was hormonal? How dare he accuse me of being hard to live with?

I told him I didn't need his shit, and he flipped. He was the hormonal one, not me. The yelling which followed left my throat sore. It had been brutal, and I didn't want to think of it.

Turning up the volume on the television, I focused on George, but George wasn't helping. The image of Christian's face between my thighs was stuck in my mind. In a frustrated search for some delayed gratification, I rubbed my clit. Round and round, the friction and heat burned, but I couldn't come. I ground my hips up to my hand, tweaked my nipple through the lace, and nothing. Nada. Couldn't do it alone.

Tears filled my eyes, and I grew angrier with each one that spilt. There was no doubt that I was crying over him. I was crying because I wasn't enough. I didn't have the guts to make him happy. Anyway, he was asking for way too much. I couldn't let him *eat* me on the hood of my new car. It just wasn't right. I was not an exhibitionist. Even the way he'd said 'eat' was crude.

Moisture pooled between my thighs. My mind might be a prude, but my body liked it.

Throwing my head back on the couch in frustration, I spied the candles I'd set up for my night of seduction. Unfortunately, burnt popcorn had settled into my skin, in my hair, and on the cushions of the couch. It turned my stomach a little bit more with each breath I took. I'd be stuck with the revolting smell for days. I needed to light those freaking-fourteen-dollar-candles to get rid of the odor that was inhibiting my orgasm and enabling my sour mood.

Striking the matches, I stood and lit each of the candles. Seventy dollars worth of candles for me to enjoy on my own. Then it hit me. Christian's favorite clothes were spared the clinging stench!

Damn, I got the short end of the stick again.

I hurried to the kitchen trash like a crazed woman. Fishing through the coffee grinds and paper towels I'd intentionally stuffed the can with only moments earlier, I pulled out the singed popcorn that was sealed in two plastic supermarket bags and a gallon-sized baggie. Carrying my weapon at arm's length, I hurried back to the bedroom and emptied Christian's t-shirt drawer on the floor. Then I unzipped the baggie, poured out the popcorn, and set it in the center of the pile. I jumped on it and rolled my body from one end to the other, making sure the smell was evenly distributed. I gathered the mess in my arms, walked to the window, and simply dropped it.

There! Now, his clothes stank as bad as mine did and had the added benefit of being wet.

Maybe I was just a little hormonal.

Maybe.

But, who cared?

The shivering got too great for my body to handle and I wondered what would get me first: the icy cold or my nerves? I slammed the window shut. Grabbing the throw at the foot of the bed, I tried to return to George on my forty-two inch plasma, but there was 'some sort of something' at the door. Not a knock, not a pounding... it sounded again. Louder the second time.

"Open the door," a muffled voice called. "Kat, open the door before I kick it in."

It was Christian. But why wasn't he using his key?

I contemplated letting him stay out there, but I simply couldn't do it. Hearing his voice melted my resolve, and I wanted to give him a chance. Still shivering from the cold, I stretched up and slid the chain off its latch. "You'd better not have anyone with you," I warned.

I cracked the door open and leaned to the side to peek at him. There he stood, grinning at me like he'd just gone out to the corner store and forgot his key on a regular night. His damp hair was covered with fresh snow, his cheeks stung with red cold dots, and his stinky clothes were snug in his arms.

At the sight of him, my traitorous heart beat faster and was about to explode when he dropped his bundle and gathered me into his arms, holding me to him like a long lost treasure. I sank into him, inhaling the fresh woodsy scent so different than the one that had engulfed me in the apartment. My hands snaked under his jacket and around his back. My fingers clenched onto his sweater and I buried my sobbing face into his chest.

"I wasn't sure you'd come back," I said.

"I'm here. I could never leave. No matter what," he breathed against the top of my head, rocking me in his embrace. His broad hand cupped the back of my head and held it against the melting snow just beneath his shoulder. I could feel the erratic beat of his heart, and I could hear the air pushing through his lungs. "Let me kiss it and make it all better," he said, using his thumb to raise my chin, and then lowered his head and captured my lips.

I thought I tried to refuse, which looking back on, I must admit wasn't much, I couldn't. I knew the double meaning of those words, but I couldn't push him away again. I couldn't risk losing him. I wrapped my arms around his neck, intertwined my fingers in his hair, and ensured that his lips wouldn't leave mine. I'd make him understand.

Christian's hands sprawled down my back, settling on the curves of my bottom, and he pulled me tightly so that my body was flush with his. He kicked the clothing through the apartment's threshold, and placing my bare feet on his boots, walked me backwards through the tiny hallway.

I needed him. In spite of the cold he brought in from outside, the heat of his body soothed my trembling and chased away the shivers. The taste of bitter ale lingering on his lips urged my mind into a state of instant intoxication. And lastly, it was his groans of strained control that fed my battered ego.

He wanted me.

He needed me more than I needed him because I could stop at any time.

Couldn't I?

Propping me against the wall, he shrugged out of his jacket and let it fall to the floor. He stepped out of his boots and threw them to the rubber mat. Then he shook the melting snow from his hair and turned to me with a sheepish grin. "Sorry, Kat."

I waited, but he didn't elaborate. What the hell was he sorry for?

He unbuckled his belt and pulled it through the loops, then dropped it over his jacket. "Don't look so concerned. I'm not going to punish you for acting out. Not with the belt."

I hated him. Hated his high-handed arrogance, but I couldn't stop myself from gawking at his crotch. I swear, if I didn't know better, I'd think he stuffed his shorts with knee-high socks. I fisted my hands and pushed them against the side of my thighs to prevent myself from reaching for him, but I couldn't stop from wetting my lips and displaying how anxious I was to stroke the soft steel that I adored.

He caught my tongue between his thumb and forefinger, and encircled it slowly, sensually, until a moan slipped between my lips. Then he fit those same fingers inside my bustier and rolled my aching nipple, sending ripples of pleasure to my core.

"What are you sorry for?" I breathed as he lowered his head and scraped his teeth down the side of my neck. Thoughts evaded my mind. All I could do was feel his lips, his tongue, and his teeth brand my neck and mark me as his.

"Please," I whimpered, but I had no clue what I was begging for.

"You don't have to know," he answered my unasked question. "You just have to be good, Kat." He unzipped his pants and released his erection.

The way I gasped at his wide length, you'd think I never saw his cock before. But I had, and at that moment, all I wanted was to straddle his narrow hips and lower myself onto it.

He shook his head. Again an answer to my non-verbal desire.

Lowering his pants, he stepped out of them with that gleam in his eyes that made my stomach flip. He bent and cupped my ass, lifting my toes off the floor with the mere strength of his fingers on my bottom. I wiggled and spread my thighs, clasping my calves around his hips and hoping that his hand would slip— slip right into my pulsing hole.

"You said I was impossible to live with," I complained.

"That is what I'm sorry for," he said, bypassing the thong and sliding along my aching folds. "You're not impossible to live with, rather you're impossible to live without. And, I'm sorry for walking out on your sexy little arrangement. We could do that soon. But now, you need to trust me. I know what is going to make you nuts. I'm going to make your eyes glaze over and your mouth scream my name while you beg me for more."

"Bastard," I said, lowering myself onto his hand and grinding my hips so that my clit rubbed against the heel of his palm.

"I'm a bastard." He pushed a long, thick finger into me and reached for my special spot. "Tell me how you don't ever want to see me again." He found the mark, and I groaned as my inner muscles clamped on his finger and pulled it deeper.

"Tell me," he repeated. "I like it when you're pissed and demanding, baby. I want a reason to tame you. To bend you to my way, so that you beg me to take you any way I want." He smirked, waiting for me to come back with something smart so he could reprimand me. "Come on, baby. You know you're frustrated. I see where the mascara trickled down your face."

I bit my lower lip, shook my head side to side, and climbed further up his body. Digging my nails into his shoulder, I felt him shudder. He was going to break first. His finger was deep inside me and his palm pressed on my silky smooth mound. It would drive him nuts that I wasn't letting him run his tongue over my naked pussy.

I wasn't going to tell him a thing he wanted to hear. I wasn't going to give him the words that would make him more excited than I was. I wanted him to finger me till the lights went out. The pleasure was going to be all mine. He didn't deserve it.

I thrust my breasts in his face. My nipples strained for his attention, but he didn't notice. He raised his chin in defiance and his stubble chafed my heavy flesh.

"You're so hot, so ready," he whispered. "One finger won't be enough."

I was determined to make it enough. I arched my back and cupped my breasts. Playing with my nipples, I moved my hips in the same rhythm against his hand and looked directly into his eyes. My clit was getting the attention it needed, and I'd take an orgasm any way I could. Just to rouse him further, I opened my mouth as if to speak, but ran the tip of my tongue over my lips instead. His cock jerked.

"Mmmm," was all I said.

Pay back is a bitch. And maybe I wasn't playing by his rules, but his body liked it. His nipples puckered under his shirt, and judging be the reaction of his glistening cock, he more than liked it. He wanted to stake his claim, to prove he could make me do what he wanted in the place and time of his choosing. The intensity of his gaze burned, and I could no longer feel the cold air blowing through the apartment.

"Give me a reason," he growled.

Again, I shook my head.

He pulled his finger out, grasped my hips, forcing my legs to unwrap from him, and lowered my feet to the floor. "You're being a bad girl, Kat. Bad girls don't come unless—"

"Bastard!" I yelled. "I hate you."

"There is a fine line between hate and love," he breathed, tearing the teddy in half and running his hand down my middle, making remarks about the smoothness of my skin and the appeal of my fresh wax.

"You stay pink for days. I like that." He placed me on the table and spread my thighs wide. "It's like kissing a sweet treat that I'm not worthy of," he said, lowering his head and tasting the evidence of what he was doing to me. He flicked his tongue up my trembling folds and suckled my nub till my hips rose to meet him.

"You're not worthy," I confirmed. "I can't stand you."

He laughed as I conceded and played by his rules. I'd given in first.

"Now, do we really need this?" He pulled on the strings of lingerie tucked between my legs.

I shook my head.

"Good. I have no craving for the taste of lace." He tugged at the lace strap, scraping over my sensitive folds and managing to smack my ass as he pulled it up.

Dipping his head, he gave me what I deserved and devoured me like a starved man eating a fresh piece of fruit. Using first one, then two fingers, he fucked me, sucking my clit until sparks shot from my core to every cell of my body. Then he pulled me down the table to the very edge, removed his fingers and plunged his cock into my desperate pussy. I locked my ankles behind his ass and begged for more.

"Will you do it?" he asked, pulling out and holding the smooth tip of his cock at my entrance.

"I can't," I cried, feeling the tears scorching my cheeks.

"Why?" Christian dipped into me and pulled right back out. His thumb encircled my clit with enough pressure to keep me on the edge, but not allowing my release. "It's dark out now."

"I'm too shy," I admitted in defeat.

He pumped into me again. Once, twice, three times, and then a long, heavenly grind had me willing to do anything for my climax. His eyes glittered with the knowledge, and I finally nodded my acceptance.

"Please, Christian, please."

"I'll get your coat," he said, smiling ear to ear.

When he turned his back, my hand settled between my legs, and I played with myself, envisioning what was about to happen. Butterflies danced in my stomach, and I hoped for what I'd always feared, but I couldn't admit to it.

Christian was back in less than a minute. He wrapped my coat around my naked body and carried me out the door.

"I've had wet dreams about tasting your delicious honey as you're body is spread on the hood of that car," he said, pushing the elevator button with his elbow.

His hand burrowed under my coat and between my legs. Spreading my folds, he pushed his thumb into me as his fingers rounded my ass and held my weight. I clung to his neck and buried my head in his shoulder.

I refused to look up. What if the door opened and someone was there? What if they saw?

At the very thought, my climax hit and the world started to spin. "More, Christian, I want more," I called out.

He righted me against the stainless steel wall and thrust his cock into me in a swift move as my body drowned in wave after wave of sweet release. As I came up for air, I realized that the elevator had long reached its destination, and Christian still pumped into me, making me claw at his bare ass to take more of him as the doors opened and closed again.

Bare ass! Shit. He was nude from the waist down!

We were fucking in a public elevator, an elevator in which the doors opened to the night air.

The thrill of getting caught pulsed straight to my clit. I opened my eyes to look up at the mirrored ceiling and was mesmerized, watching his tight ass thrust me up against the wall. My fingers entwined in the tail of his shirt and pulled him closer.

He banged me with such force that the whole elevator shook. The railing pushed against my bottom, and I squirmed an inch higher to rest on it. His hand snaked between us and his thumb flicked my clit as my next climax set. It was surreal. The earth spun, and as he exploded deep inside me, my world shattered in a colorful prism of erotic bliss and the most extreme orgasm of my life took over my body.

Christian kept me from falling, literally screwing me upright. I concentrated on breathing, and when my heartbeat returned to steady, I dared to lift my head from his neck and look into his face.

"I love you, Kat."

"There is a fine line between love and hate." I reversed his saying, kissing the lips I was so addicted to. "I love you with all I have. And now, I'll love you anywhere I can."

The call button sounded and the doors opened. Christian buried his hard cock into my wet pussy and rolled his hips. I wrapped my new coat around us both, and smiled at the thoughtfulness of his gift as the door opened.

"Merry Christmas, folks," said the young man from 5B, helping his very pregnant wife onto the lift.

"Merry Christmas," Christian said, looking past me at the couple's reflection and smiling.

We rode the elevator back down to the underground parking. No doubt the red coat looked great on the yellow hood of the sports car.

We weren't actually caught feasting the hood that Christmas night, but we could always hope for next time.

And oh, Christian was right. I was hormonal. September, little Sammy arrived and curtailed our signature late night trysts in the neighborhood parking lots. We put the red coat in the back of the closet for a while, but that doesn't mean it isn't dry cleaned and ready for action at any time.

About the Author

Demi Alex is a hopeless romantic who sits at her neighborhood café and fabricates stories of magical interludes between her fellow java worshipers. Writing since elementary school, she's been published since junior high, but her stories have taken on a much spicier and more mature tone in the past years.

Needing to taste the flavors life has to offer, Demi attended college in New York. Long before graduating, she developed a passion for 'people watching'. Lunchtimes on St. Patrick's steps and afternoons in the Village led to mornings and nights at the computer typing away like mad to put on paper the stories that played in her head about the colorful people she'd seen and placed into hypothetical relationship in the depths of her mind.

Traveling as often as work would allow her, Demi has since added to the topographies in her writing and does personal research of all her settings in order to make her stories speak to her readers. Her characters can be found in any town or city, but their attitude is what sets them apart. They let loose and experience what is thrown at them!

Demi invites all readers to send her scenarios on a 'what if' they had made a different choice and decision at a certain time. "If you write to me about that specific choice, and I can give you an alternate ending, I'll name the character in the story according to your wish."

If you dare, take a chance and email her: readdemialex@yahoo.com. You can find Demi on www.myspace.com/DemiAlexLetsLoose.

The Elves and I

By Catrina Calloway

Table of Contents

Chapter One

"This is ridiculous!" Marni Sands hissed through clenched teeth.

Her lawyer whispered from the corner of her mouth, "Sit there and be quiet."

"Just who does that judge think he is?"

The attorney rolled her eyes. "He's the one who's going to decide your fate for the next ninety days."

BANG!

Marni jumped when Judge Nicholas Saint pounded the gavel.

"Counselor, this is the last time I'm going to tell you—control your client."

He scanned the documents in front of him. "Speeding in our traffic circle, eh, Ms. Sands?" He narrowed his eyes. "Driving while intoxicated?"

"I was framed!" Marni shot to her feet. "My butler and maid planted those two opened vodka bottles on the floor in back of my Mercedes. They'd do anything to get me in trouble because I fired their sorry asses for stealing."

Behind her, the two arresting officers snickered—loudly. Marni placed her hands behind her back and lifted one of her middle fingers. She wished she could personally tell the two arrogant assholes to fuck-off.

"Ms. Sands, do you expect me to believe such a load of nonsense?"

"Your honor, may I speak?" Marni's lawyer ventured.

"Go ahead, counselor." The judge leaned back in his chair, folding his hands across his ample belly.

She rose and placed a hand on Marni's shoulder, shoving her down into her chair.

"My client is a law-abiding citizen, and a respected member of her community. She's also been forced to live in the limelight because of her family's wealth and reputation."

"I'm well aware of that, *counselor.*"

"Yes, well, my point is that my client's notoriety attracts the paparazzi. Ms. Sands was forced to speed through your town's traffic circle by the photographers pursuing her and—"

"Why didn't she call the police?"

"Unfortunately, my client could not reach her cell phone."

The judge stroked his long, white beard. "Doesn't she have that new-fangled, what the heck is it called?" He glanced at one of the bailiffs. "My brother San, he's got one in his sleigh—you get your phone calls through it, and navigation—"

"It's called 'My Gig' your honor." The bailiff replied.

"Right. My Gig." Judge Saint leaned forward, resting his robed forearms on top of the bench. "Does your client have one of those?"

She sighed. "Yes, she does."

"Then she should have used it to call the police for help. Instead, she chose to speed through our traffic circle. The officers say she was doing sixty in a twenty-five mile an hour zone. And..." He held up his index finger. "She refused to take a sobriety test."

"Because I didn't have anything to drink!" Marni objected. Panic well inside her. It was time to pull out the big guns if she didn't want to spend the holidays in jail. "Your honor, may I approach the bench?" She used her silkiest tone.

He crooked his index finger. "Come forward."

"I don't think this is a good idea." Her attorney whispered. "You know how these small towns are. Just plead guilty, pay the fine and we'll get you out of here."

"No."

She brushed past her lawyer and stood in front of Judge Saint.

"You've got exactly…" He pulled a gold watch from his pocket; it dangled on a long chain. "Two minutes, starting now."

She licked her lips, tossing back her blonde hair over one shoulder.

Marni lowered her voice. "How about we work this out, *together,* in your chambers?" She batted her eyes, pushing out her new, "C" cup, surgically altered breasts. "I'm sure we could come up with a sizable donation, which I'd be willing to make to the town of River's End, *if* you catch my meaning."

Marni knew how to work her angles. She had quite a few judges in her pocket—this one would be no different.

Seconds went by. It became so quiet, Marni thought she could hear a pin drop in the courtroom.

"Ms. Sands," the judge finally said. "I'm older than dirt. I've seen it all and heard it all, but you take the proverbial cake." He rapped the gavel on the bench.

She jumped out of her skin for the second time that evening.

"I'd throw you in jail if I thought it would help, but I can see that you've got a lot to learn. I'm suspending your driver's license and I hereby sentence you to thirty days of community service in Christmas Town."

She scowled. "Christmas Town? What the hel—I mean, heck—is Christmas Town? Is that like the outlets?"

"It is *not* a shopping mall." The look he gave her could freeze water. "It's a small, self-contained community within our little town of River's End."

"What am I supposed to do there?"

"You'll just have to wait and see, now won't you?"

* * * *

Snow crystals landed on her cheeks and nose as the two bailiffs escorted Marni outside. Her breath formed a puffy white haze each time she exhaled.

CRUNCH!

She stepped in snow that had hardened from the frigid temperature. "I can't walk in this. It'll ruin my leather boots."

The two bailiffs smirked. "Should we carry you, *Madame?*"

"These boots cost more than you two make in a month."

They ignored her snide comment and said, "Here's your ride now."

Marni watched a large, old-fashioned sleigh driven by eight reindeer slide to a halt in front of them. The reindeer stomped their hooves, bending their heads to sniff at the snow.

A young man and woman emerged from the sleigh dressed in bright green elf costumes.

"What the hell is going on?" Marni fumed. "Is this some sort of joke?" Her eyes widened. "Oh no, please don't tell me I'm on that show 'Gotcha!'—the one where they have the hidden cameras?"

"Hi Bill, hi Dan!" The young woman addressed the bailiffs.

She wore her auburn hair tucked beneath a three-pointed hat with a large plume. Her bright green dress cinched her waist, its full skirt swirling around her legs.

Bill spoke. "How's it going, Celyn? I see Santa let you drive tonight."

Marni rolled her eyes. "Oh, for heaven's sake. This is *insane.*"

The lead reindeer turned his head and Marni stared in shock. The damn thing's nose glowed bright red.

She quickly turned around.

I must be seeing things…

"Where's your buddy, Celyn? Did Santa let you drive by yourself?" one of the bailiffs asked.

Celyn beamed, her freckled face splitting into a wide smile. "Aardel's here, but I would have been all right alone. It was a smooth landing."

The other 'elf' jumped down from the sleigh. Although short, he had a muscular body. He walked over to shake hands with the bailiffs.

"Happy holidays, guys," he said with a grin. "How are your families?"

One of the bailiffs puffed out his chest. "Sally's expecting our third."

Aardel whistled. "Congratulations." He pumped the man's hand again.

Celyn stuck her nose in the air. "My driving was just fine, Aardel. I didn't need *you.*"

Marni saw something flash in Aardel's sherry-colored eyes. He tapped Celyn on the nose with his index finger. "I didn't want you driving at night alone. Maneuvering around those shooting stars can be tricky."

"I've handled Santa's sleigh before!" She stamped her booted foot in the snow.

Marni was fascinated. She'd never seen such authentic costumes or make-up. The suede lining the toes of their boots turned upward, forming a perfect curl. Their pointy ears and slanty little brows gave their faces a pixie look one would expect from…well, elves.

Aardel took Celyn's hand. "You did a fine job tonight. I was proud of you."

Celyn blushed to the roots of her red-gold hair. For a few seconds, her eyes locked with Aardel's

"Well, here's your charge." The bailiffs handed Marni over to them. "See you around Aardel! 'Bye, Celyn."

They walked back inside the building with a small wave.

Marni ran after them. She pulled on the closed door. It wouldn't budge.

"Ms. Sands, we've got to leave now. Santa's waiting."

Marni rapped her forehead against the door. "This can't be happening. *This can't be happening.*" She chanted.

"Ms. Sands?" Celyn called out. "Are you okay?"

She turned to face them. "Go away."

"The sled won't move unless you're on it." Aardel stated.

She gave the young man a dark look.

"Santa's orders." He shrugged.

"You expect me to believe this bullshit?"

Aardel clapped his hands over Celyn's ears. "Ms. Sands! Watch your language. Santa wouldn't—"

"How much?" Marni dug through her bag.

Celyn frowned. "How much what?"

"How much money will it take to make you leave me the hell alone?"

Aardel clapped his hands over Celyn's ears again.

Marni withdrew her checkbook. "Will a thousand dollars each cover it?" She started to write.

Celyn laid a hand across hers. "Santa wouldn't dream of making people pay for a ride on his sleigh."

Aardel nodded. "She's right. Santa's not like that."

"Would you knock off the Santa shi—stuff?"

Celyn's eyes filled with tears. "You don't believe in Santa Claus?"

"For Pete's sake!" Marni shoved her checkbook into her bag. "Don't cry."

"Ms. Sands, this isn't a joke," Aardel said. "We're here to take you to Christmas Town. Santa is waiting. We need to leave now before the weather gets worse."

"Fine. Go." Marni waggled her fingers at the sleigh.

"Like we said, we can't leave without you."

Celyn reached for her hands. "You'll enjoy the ride. We promise."

"I've been on a sleigh ride before, plenty of times."

"Not like this." Celyn grinned.

* * * *

WHOOSH!

Marni's eyes widened, her mouth falling open while Celyn guided the sleigh into the wintry night sky. The stars twinkled and the moon hung full and golden as they rose higher. A shooting star passed by, then another, leaving a trail of glittering light in their wake.

"Go Dancer, go Prancer, go Donner and go Blitzen!" Celyn shouted above the wind. "Good job, Rudolf. Santa's going to be so proud when I tell him how you led us."

Marni gazed at the front dash of the sleigh where an intricate navigation system guided them through the night.

My brother, San...he's got one on his sleigh...

"Well, I'll be a...that judge wasn't kidding."

"Pardon me?" Aardel asked.

"Nothing." She shook her head. "This ride is pure magic."

He grinned. "Elves never lie."

"Yeah, right." She snorted. "Everyone lies, honey. *Everyone.*"

"Elves always tell the truth."

No one she knew *ever* told the truth—especially to her.

Marni looked down. An ominous, gray castle loomed in the distance.

"Is that Christmas Town?"

"Gosh, no!" Celyn replied. "That's where the evil elf, Glint lives. He'd do anything to destroy Christmas Town and the Holiday Spirit. You must never, ever go there, Ms. Sands. Glint is a bad elf."

"Ooooooookay. If you say so."

Marni wondered if her drinking had finally caught up with her.

She sucked in a breath as another magnificent shooting star flew by, its fiery tail bursting into thousands of shimmery sparks all around them.

A few minutes later, another castle came into view, a magnificent red and green fortress with gold spires that rose high into the sky.

"Is that Christmas Town?"

Her heart beat wildly and her excitement built, which amazed her even further. She couldn't remember the last time she'd been excited or thrilled about anything.

"Isn't it beautiful?" Aardel looked out over the town with a smile.

"It is." Marni agreed without hesitation.

White lights twinkled from every window. Huge gold and silver ornaments dangled from the branches of pine trees surrounding the castle.

"Those ornaments are made of real silver and gold." Celyn told her.

Marni whistled. "Damn things must be worth a fortune."

"That's how Santa pays for what we need throughout the year. He sells off a few of the ornaments each Christmas." Celyn told her.

Aardel placed a hand on Celyn's shoulder. "You shouldn't be telling everyone Santa's business."

She shrugged him off. "You're not the boss of me."

He shook his head and sighed, his eyes filled with longing.

Marni's mouth curved into a smile. Their banter was cute, and she thought it clearly displayed that Aardel had the hots for Celyn.

That made her smile—again. Amazing. Here she was, grinning like a loon, and she didn't even need a drink to accomplish it. Lately, booze was the only thing that made her happy.

She heard the swish of curved metal blades as Celyn landed the sleigh.

"Well done!" Aardel placed an arm around Celyn's shoulders.

The young woman beamed, her smile reaching from ear-to-ear.

Aardel kissed Celyn's cheek, and her lovely mouth formed a perfect 'O.' He jumped off the sleigh, his arms extended so he could help Celyn. She slid against him, their eyes locking for a few seconds.

Then she pulled away, her pink cheeks turning bright red. "Th-thank you."

"My pleasure." Aardel murmured.

He then turned to escort Marni from the sleigh. They all walked together, the snow crunching beneath their feet.

At the entrance to the castle, two tall, life-like wooden soldiers stood guard.

Marni poked one in his chest. He winked.

"Holy shi—I mean—wow."

"Santa's got a hundred of them." Celyn whispered. "Aren't they handsome? When they all march together, I get such chills. Brrrrrr." Celyn shivered.

Marni angled her head. "What's that old saying? 'There's something about a man in uniform.'"

BANG!

Marni jumped when Aardel used the large, gold knocker on the door.

"Next time, warn me." She grumbled.

"Sorry." He shrugged. "But we have to be announced."

The large door swung open and a female elf greeted them. "Aardel, Celyn...we're glad you're back. Everyone's waiting."

She ushered them inside.

Warmth surrounded Marni, along with the smell of fresh-baked cookies and cinnamon.

A petite, older woman with short, white curly hair walked over to them. Her long green and red checked gown stopped just short of her ankles, revealing a pair of black high-button shoes with laces and thin, six-inch heels.

Marni shook her head, thinking she imagined it, but when the older woman turned, she caught a glimpse of black fishnet stockings.

The woman's soft voice floated by Marni's ears.

"I'm glad you finally made it. Word is we're getting a blizzard."

Celyn took Marni by the hand. "Elise, I'd like you to meet Marni Sands."

"Well my dear, I can only say we've been waiting for you with great anticipation."

"You have?" Marni raised a brow.

"Of course. Nicholas said to expect you."

"Nicholas?"

The woman smiled. "Nicholas Saint. My husband's brother."

"The judge! He looked like Santa Claus."

"That's because Nicholas and Santa are twins."

Marni rolled her eyes. *This is getting very weird.*

She noticed that the older woman didn't have one wrinkle on her smooth, peaches and cream skin, yet something about her spoke of times long past. Maybe it was the dress—it had a bustle on the back. Or maybe the shoes or...

The fishnet stockings? Women didn't wear sexy stockings in olden times...or shoes with six-inch heels...

Elise's voice cut through Marni's musings. "Mister Claus and I were looking forward to your arrival."

"Okay, while this whole thing seems nuts, if you want me to go along with the charade, fine. I'll play."

It became very quiet. All eyes were on Marni.

"Whatever do you mean, dear?"

Marni folded her arms beneath her breasts. "Either you all take the holiday season waaay too seriously, or someone slipped something into my drink and this is all one, big fantasy."

The older snapped her white brows together. Pushing her gold, horn-rimmed glasses up her nose, she replied, "You were drugged? By whom?"

"Oh!" Marni threw her hands up in the air. "Just forget it. I already said I'd play along."

The older woman clapped her hands. "Splendid. Mister Claus will be so pleased." She lowered her voice. "And we always want to please *him*." She wagged her index finger at Marni. "You must always be a good girl, never naughty." Her cheeks turned pink. "Or Mr. Claus won't be happy."

"Whatever you say, honey."

"That's Claus, dear. Missus Claus. But you can call me Elise—everyone does. Now let's go into the great hall. Santa is waiting there, and so is the elf council."

Marni did as the older woman bade, wondering if she'd completely lost her mind.

Chapter Two

The great hall teemed with elves. Some lounged in groups, while others lingered by a long table bearing trays of cookies. A fire glowed in a big hearth. Torches burned bright, providing the room with additional warmth and light.

A male elf announced their arrival.

"Missus Claus to see you, sir."

Santa's face lit with a smile. "Hello, my dear. What an assortment of goodies we have—you must have been a good girl and worked very hard."

Elise walked up to Santa and he patted his thighs. She crawled into his lap, nestling her head against his chest. Santa wrapped his arms around her, kissing the white curls on the top of her head.

Envy tore at Marni's heart. Strangely, she longed to cuddle on Santa's lap, too.

"Celyn and Aardel have finally returned, Santa," Elise said. "They've come home with a guest."

Her eyes locked with Santa's while he sat on his golden throne. Bright, white light surrounded him, his aura of love and holiday cheer a powerful presence.

Three tall, male elves flanked him—two on his left, one on his right.

"Ho, ho, *hooooooooooooo.*" He crooked a finger at Marni. "Come closer my dear, come meet Santa."

Next, I'm going to hear the Easter Bunny is alive and well, too.

She refused to believe that she actually stood in the presence of the great, jolly Santa Claus.

Marni gazed at the three tall, handsome elves.

Her pulse raced.

Men! They're men, not elves, damn it! They're wearing costumes. It's all just pretend.

Her eyes settled on the one with the tawny hair and lean, fit body. He folded his arms across his chest and bowed. She could see the play of muscle on his upper arms, beneath the sleeves of his tunic. He rose to his full height and grinned, his blue eyes locking with hers.

"This is Kip." Santa nodded in the tall elf's direction. "He is part of my council."

She swallowed fear and something else...desire.

Kip stepped forward, reaching for her hand. He turned it over, placing a soft kiss on the pad beneath her thumb. His lips lingered for a few seconds, sending shockwaves of sexual need through Marni's body. He released her hand, giving it a gentle squeeze before letting go.

"We're pleased to have you as our guest, love."

His British accent captivated her.

Desire flowed freely through her veins. It mixed with her blood, heating it.

"How did you get the name 'Kip'?"

"I'm named for Kippering, a smoked fish delicacy enjoyed by my native Brits." He sighed, his voice filled with longing. "I sorely miss that treat." His eyes settled on her mouth. "But I see another standing before me."

Careful, Marni. He's a man—and all men are shits.

"This is Noel. He's part of my council, too." Santa's voice rang out.

Another tall elf stepped down from his place near Santa's throne. Marni's eyes flew to the large bulge between his legs, visible beneath his dark green woolen tights. She sucked in a breath when he took her hand, running his thumb across the back of it. She wondered what his hands—particularly his thumb, would feel like if he touched her between her legs.

"A pleasure to meet you, lass."

Her knees turned to rubber when his brogue floated by her ears.

Her traitorous hormones played with her body while she imagined what it would be like to take *both* elves to bed.

Shame on you, Marni!

The final elf standing on Santa's right made her pulse kick up yet another notch. His deep chocolate brown tunic matched his dark eyes and hair. She couldn't stop staring at the expanse of his wide chest and powerful shoulders.

"My second in command." Santa told Marni. "May I present Eldan?"

He stepped forward. Kip and Noel bowed slightly, giving him a wide berth.

Marni's feet stayed rooted to the floor. She felt her body grow smaller with each step he took toward her.

"Ms. Sands." He murmured in a deep, sensual voice.

He didn't take her hand. He didn't tell her it was a pleasure to meet her.

He didn't bow.

Marni felt compelled to bow before *him*.

She gazed at his strong jaw, at the sharp angles and planes of his chiseled face, where she noticed the shadow of a beard. The only thing that softened his countenance was the dimple set dead center in his chin.

She tried to smile, but her trembling lips refuse to obey her command.

Eldan reached out, running a thumb across her mouth.

She gasped, the contact of his thumb against her lips sending a shockwave of need to the little nubbin of flesh nestled between her legs. It quivered just like her lips.

He swept his hand out.

"This is Santa's kingdom. All are welcome and safe here."

But not from you.

* * * *

Eldan took Marni by the hand, leading her out of the great hall. She practically had to run to keep up with his long, powerful strides.

She glanced at Eldan's handsome, serious face, wondering if it would crack if he attempted even the slightest grin.

"You seem a little...dour for an elf. I thought elves were happy little campers."

"I'm very content."

Okay, not much of a talker.

They passed table after table of potted plants bearing bright red and pink blooms.

"What are those flowers?"

"They're called amaryllis. They bloom year-round here in Christmas Town."

"I don't think I've ever since such gorgeous flowers."

He stopped walking and folded his arms across his chest. "Maybe it's because you never bother to notice the beauty around you. You're too busy worrying about petty things."

"Are you trying to say I've never stopped to smell the roses?" Her voice dripped acid. "Is this supposed to be elf psycho-babble?"

"Just an observation."

"You elves *observe* a lot, don't you?"

The look he gave her could have melted chocolate. "A lot more than you think."

"That's a good thing." She ran a finger down his chest.

He captured her hand in his.

"I'm not like the men you've known in the past; don't think you can fool me."

She pulled her hand away, his touch sending a little zing down her spine.

"You use sarcasm to keep people away."

"You're still here."

"That should tell you a lot."

They walked on in silence.

"Where are we going?"

"Wardrobe."

She frowned. "Wardrobe?"

"You need to get into the proper clothing."

Marni stopped and licked her lips, sliding her tongue across them.

"Don't you like what I'm wearing now?"

She lifted her skirt, revealing her thighs. Marni hated wearing underwear. This time, she was particularly glad she didn't have a shred of lace on underneath her skirt.

Eldan's dark eyes lit with a spark of need, their centers glowing.

She tossed her hair over one shoulder, raising her skirt higher to reveal her naked pussy.

"Like what you see, Eldan?"

"Very much." He murmured.

He stepped forward, accepting the invitation. Usually, men just drooled then touched her clit awkwardly, making a mess of the entire sex thing.

Not Eldan.

He stroked each thigh, sliding the tips of his fingers upwards, skimming the smooth-shaven skin lining her pussy.

She could sense his desire, watching his eyes dilate with passion.

"All you have to do is get me the hell out of here and I'm yours," she told him.

His jaw tightened. He dropped his hand.

Marni felt bereft at the loss of contact.

"Nicholas warned me about you." Eldan folded his arms across his powerful chest. "I'm not taking any of your crap." He dropped his arms and pointed his index finger at her pussy. "I'm not interested."

Her eyes flew to the bulge between his legs.

"Ohhhhhhhhhhh, I beg to differ." She grinned.

"When I want a woman," he shoved her skirt down to cover her, "I let her know in my own way. Besides, Santa's got a list of all the naughty things you've done."

She laughed, the sound brittle. "Yeah, right."

"Only you know just how naughty you've been."

"Okay, then." She lifted her chin. "Tell me one bad thing I've done that only *I* would know about."

He stroked his hand across his jaw. "You fired your butler and maid."

She slashed a hand through the air. "You could have found that out from the judge. I told him that in court."

"Yes, but you said in court you fired them for stealing, which we both know isn't the case. You fired them because you couldn't stand to see them happy. You were jealous of your butler. You had the hots for him, but he didn't give a damn about you. When you caught him making love to your maid, you—"

"Enough." Her voice vibrated with anger.

A corner of his mouth lifted.

"Don't look so damned satisfied."

She blew out a breath, wondering what else he knew.

"Now, are you going to behave and put on elf attire?"

"What happens if I don't?"

Seconds went by. He didn't say a word. Marni bit her lower lip, wondering if she hadn't just screwed herself royally.

Then again, she always managed to fuck up everything she touched.

"You have a choice," Eldan said. "You can either get into an elf costume by yourself or…"

She wanted to push the 'elf' to his limit, curious to see what he would do. Usually, men simply did as she bade.

Not Eldan.

"Or what?" She raised a brow, but it quivered.

"I'll get you into the damn clothes myself."

He pushed open a door. Marni peeked inside to see a room filled with racks of tunics, tights, dresses, boots and those silly three-cornered hats.

"That might be fun." She made her voice sound light.

A low grow escaped his throat. He lunged, but she skipped away, sailing through the door. She shut it, locking it behind her.

"If you're not downstairs in the Toy Shop, dressed in proper elf attire in fifteen minutes, there will be consequences."

Marni didn't answer.

"Did you hear me? Fifteen minutes."

Seconds went by, then she heard his retreating footsteps.

She leaned her back against the door, shutting her eyes, the idea of defying the commanding Eldan making her clit beat in time with the holiday music piped into the small room.

She reached under her skirt, placing her fingers against her wet pussy. She rubbed her clit, the tip of her middle finger sliding across the little bud, her mind filled with Eldan. She imagined it was *his* hand between her legs.

She came, but still felt frustrated.

Eldan played with her head as well as her body.

He was so damned sure of himself, so damned masterful, so...

She glanced at the elf clothing, an idea blooming in her head like the amaryllis flowers in the hallway.

Chapter Three

Fifteen minutes later, Marni walked into the Toy Shop.

Hundreds of elves sat on benches around long, wooden tables. Heads bent, intent on their tasks, they worked diligently, their nimble fingers fashioning an array of toys.

Celyn lifted her head, spotting Marni from across the room. Her eyes widened.

Kip walked over and took her hand. "You look wonderful, love." Marni stepped away so he could admire her. "Green is your color."

Noel joined them and made a spinning motion with his index finger. "Turn around, let me see."

They both whistled their approval while Marni pivoted.

Noel's warm breath tickled her lobe. "That outfit is terrific, lass, but you're playing with fire."

She followed the direction of his gaze. Eldan stood in the center of the room, his dark eyes smoldering. His eyes roamed over her body, his hand clenched at his side.

Marni lifted her chin. She wouldn't cower.

Instead of donning an elf dress like the one Celyn and the other females wore, Marni had chosen a pair of lacy green tights, boots and a short tunic designed for a male elf. Most of the tunics were too large for her, but she discovered one intended for a teenager. It stretched across her breasts, outlining their rounded glory. The belt around her waist highlighted her curved hips, her bottom and her long legs.

She refused to wear one of those ridiculous three-cornered hats the other elves wore, so she fashioned her own out of a piece of green felt she'd found in the dressing room. The small cap with its jaunty white feather hugged the crown of her head.

The feather flopped over, covering her face, tickling her nose.

"The darn thing won't stay put," she complained to Kip and Noel.

She stuck her lower lip out, blowing hard, forcing the feather upwards.

Kip laughed. "You are a delight." He ran a finger down her chin.

She shuddered pleasurably.

"Let me adjust that." Noel bent the feather. "There now." He stepped back to admire her. "Kip's right: you are a delightful holiday treat."

Kip leaned over and kissed her ear. "I think I'd like to take a bite of you right now, love." He nipped her ear lightly with his teeth.

A shiver of longing snaked down her spine.

Her eyes strayed to Eldan. He stood at his full height, arms across his chest.

"Time to pay the piper, lass." Noel gave her a nudge. "Go on now. Don't be afraid. Eldan's bark is much worse than his bite."

She walked toward Eldan, feeling every eye in the room on her back.

"I'm going to get an outfit like Marni's!" Celyn whispered to another female elf.

Aardel's eyes widened. "You will *not*."

"Will, too." She lifted her chin, aiming it at Aardel.

Celyn flashed a beautiful smile at Kip. He just rolled his eyes and shook his head, ignoring her.

Aardel's face fell. He walked away from Celyn, taking a seat at another table.

A strange feeling came over Marni—compassion. She suddenly felt very bad for Aardel.

She continued her march to Eldan like a condemned prisoner making her way to her execution.

One of the female elves reached out, squeezing her hand. "Way to go, Marni."

"You look great." Another little female elf beamed in her direction.

Soon, all the female elves chattered.

"I love your hat."

"Terrific outfit."

"I want to look like *her*."

The male elves all sat there, drooling.

Except for Eldan.

She didn't think he had an ounce of drool in him.

Finally, she stood before him, placed her hands at her waist and jutted her right leg to the side. The curled tip of her boot bumped his.

"Nice hat." He nodded.

Her mouth curved into a smile. "Is that all you have to say?"

"Apparently, you have trouble following directions."

She raised her chin. "I changed into elf attire as ordered." She gave him a brisk salute.

A corner of his mouth lifted. "I'll concede the point. This time."

"That's the best smile you can manage? I thought this was the land of holiday cheer?"

He was so close she could smell him. Woodsy. Musky...

Male.

He pointed to an empty seat at a lone table.

"Sit."

She did as he bade, flopping down onto the bench.

He bent and reached around her, placing a wooden block on the table in front of her.

"Time to work." He whispered next to her ear.

"Wh-what am I supposed to do?"

"Paint the letters on the sides of the block."

She shrugged. "Easy enough."

She reached for a clean brush, dipping it in some blue paint, brushing it across the letter 'A.'

Marni continued to paint, her strokes quick, the color smearing on the letters.

He placed a hand over hers. "It isn't a race. The block has to be made with love and care."

Eldan's hands strayed down to the waistband of her tights. He slipped his fingers inside.

"Now, be a good girl and paint the right way."

Marni dipped the brush in some water, but her hand shook.

While she painted the toy, *he* toyed with her clit, sliding the tips of his fingers across it.

"I-I...oh my *God.*"

He chuckled next to her ear, the sound warm, rich and wicked.

"You've got fifty blocks to finish by tonight."

He removed his hand.

Her clit throbbed, her thighs quivered. Eldan had brought her to the brink of satisfaction, and left her dangling.

"Bastard," she hissed.

She picked up the brush, chipping a nail in the process. Her temper flared.

"Now look what you made me do!" she wailed. "My nails are ruined."

The other elves laughed.

Marni rose from the bench. With a glower, she reached over, grabbed the container filled with dirty water, and tossed it at Eldan, soaking his tunic.

He looked down at the front of his shirt. The he lifted his eyes. They flashed with anger. A muscle quivered in his jaw.

"Apologize." He commanded.

"Go to hell! This is stupid!"

She tossed the block across the room. Several elves ducked.

"Children don't play with blocks." Marni looked over at another elf as he finished painting a wooden locomotive. "And they don't play with wooden trains, either." She swept the blocks from the table. "This is bullshit. I'm getting out of here."

She was angry for allowing Eldan to take control. Furious at him for playing with her body. Enraged that he had left her panting for more.

No one did that to Marni Sands.

He was just like her ex-husbands. They never knew how to satisfy her—physically or mentally.

She wouldn't take it anymore.

She looked over at Kip and Noel for support.

They stood with their arms folded across their chests, their jaws set in firm lines.

In the next instant, Marni's feet left the ground. Eldan tucked her against his side, carrying her to a vacant chair. She kicked her feet and screamed.

"Put me down!"

"Oh, I will." He growled. "I most certainly will."

He sat in the chair, tossing her facedown across his lap.

Her thin tights were no barrier for Eldan's wide palm. He smacked her bottom, his hand raining fire on Marni's flesh. The more she kicked and struggled, the more he spanked her.

The elves cheered.

Her bottom stung, but her pride hurt more when she heard Kip and Noel urge Eldan on.

She sunk her teeth into his muscled thigh. He didn't flinch; he just continued to spank her.

SWAT!

Marni beat on his leg, her fists connecting with hard muscle and bone.

SWAT! SWAT! SWAT!

"I'm in charge of you, Marni."

"Go to hell!"

SWAT!

"I won't let you ruin the good work that goes on in Santa's Toy Shop."

"Go fuck yourself!"

SWAT! SWAT! SWAT!

"Such a beautiful body, one I can't resist, but you have a filthy mouth and a terrible disposition. You push people away with your bad attitude."

SWAT! SWAT! SWAT!

Tears filled her eyes. She wasn't sure if it was because her ass hurt like hell or because he was right.

He stopped spanking her, lifting her from his lap.

She stood on shaky legs.

He didn't bother to help steady her.

Marni ran from the Toy Shop, shame washing over her.

She hadn't cried since she was a child.

Not since the fateful day life played on her the dirtiest trick of all: stealing the love of her life.

* * * *

That evening, she sulked in her room, smoking cigarette after cigarette. She reached for the flask she kept hidden in a secret part of her handbag, carefully sipping the few precious drops of vodka that remained.

"Fucking elves." She spoke aloud, her words slurred.

She lifted the flask and took another drink.

She paced back and forth, not even attempting to sit down.

A knock at the door interrupted her sulk a few moments later.

Marni squashed the cigarette butt in an ashtray, slipping it under the bed, wincing when her backside brushed the heels of her boots.

Anger returned.

No one ever spanked her—and in public! Oh, if she got her hands on Eldan, she'd...

Probably *beg* him to do it again. He wasn't so immune to her after all.

She had a body he couldn't resist.

She rose to her feet and stashed the flask in a drawer in the bedside table.

"Who is it?" She waved at the lingering smoke in the air.

"It's Celyn. Can I come in?"

"J-just a second."

She blew at the offending smoke. When she was satisfied the air had cleared, she opened the door.

Celyn walked in.

"I just wanted to see how you are."

Marni folded her arms beneath her breasts and leaned against the doorjamb, her sore backside connecting with the wood.

"Ow!" She screwed up her face, dropping her hands.

She used one to soothe her stinging bottom.

"I brought you this." Celyn held up an ice pack. "And this." She thrust a pillow into Marni's hands.

Marni felt touched by Celyn's concern.

"Thanks."

Celyn snapped her brows together, glancing around the room. Marni followed the direction of her gaze—right to the ashtray peeking out from underneath the bed skirt.

Celyn's eyes widened. "You're smoking? That's not allowed in Christmas Town."

She wanted to reply, 'Fuck Christmas Town', but thought better of it, remembering how Aardel covered Celyn's ears when she used bad language.

These elves were a sensitive bunch.

Celyn walked over to the bed and got on her knees, retrieving the ashtray from its hiding spot.

Marni scowled. "I suppose you're going to rat me out."

"Nope." Celyn grinned. "We female elves had a meeting—we decided you're tops."

"Y-you did?"

Celyn nodded. "It took guts to do what you did this afternoon, to dress the way you did."

Marni noticed Celyn's hat. "I see you've made your own with the green felt."

"We also decided we want you to design new elf wardrobes for all of us."

"Really?"

"Really."

Marni plopped down on the bed. "Ow! Shit." She hopped off the bed, rubbing her bottom. She looked at Celyn. "Cursing is another one of my bad habits."

Celyn bit down on her lower lip. "Can I ask you something?"

"Shoot."

"Can I try one of your cigarettes?"

"No way. It's a dirty, nasty habit."

Celyn angled her chin. "But you do it."

"That doesn't make it right, Celyn. I know you're young, and sometimes, youth makes us—"

"I'm not a baby." Celyn lifted her nose in the air. "Even if Aardel thinks I am."

Marni's lips curved into her first smile in hours. "I think Aardel likes you."

"He's such a geek. Besides, I like Kip."

"Kip?" Marni frowned. "Isn't he a little old for you?"

Celyn clapped her hands together. "He's so dreamy. I love his accent." She flopped down on Marni's bed, drawing her legs up. She hugged her knees. "Kip isn't nerdy like Aardel."

"If I were you, I'd watch who you call a 'nerd.' It's the quiet ones that get you."

Celyn glanced at the half-opened drawer in Marni's nightstand.

"What's in there?"

She got up off the bed and opened the drawer, reaching for the flask.

"It's uh..." *Crap!* "...medicine."

Celyn's eyes filled with tears. "You're ill? That's terrible! I'm going to go and tell the Claus' right now." She started to walk away.

Marni grabbed her arm. "That was a lie, Celyn, please don't tell them anything. I've got Vodka in that flask and—"

"Can I have some?"

"No."

Celyn angled her head. "I just may have to tell everyone you're smoking and how that's going against the rules here in Christmas Town."

"I thought you weren't going to rat me out."

"Maybe I changed my mind."

If word got out that she was smoking, Eldan would tell Judge Saint and he'd surely throw her in jail.

"You can have one sip, but that's it."

Marni passed her the flask. Celyn took a deep drink of the vodka, licking her lips.

"It has no taste."

"Or smell." Marni replied.

"Then no one knows you've been drinking! That's wonderful."

"It sucks, to be quite honest. You can't hide your bad, nasty habits from anyone for very long, particularly booze."

Celyn passed her the flask. "It's no big deal. I don't really like it."

"That's a *good* thing." Marni lowered her voice. "Tell me something."

"What?"

"Mr. and Mrs. Claus, they don't seem, well...old. I mean, they don't seem like what I imagined them to be."

"So?"

"I saw how she sits on his lap, and how he looks at her. And I swear she was wearing fishnet stockings under her dress."

Celyn giggled. "I'll tell you about them, in fact, I'll *show* you."

"Show me?"

"Come on." Celyn whispered. "I think this is the room with the little peephole. She walked around, running her hands over the walls. Her face lit with a smile. "Bingo. I found it."

Just then, a low moan came from the room next door.

Celyn glanced at the clock on the nightstand. "It's time."

"For what?"

"You wanted to know about Elise and uh... *Pappa* Claus, as she calls him. I'm going to show you."

Marni held up both hands. "No, oh no...I'm not into that kinky voyeur stuff. I'm...oh hell." She grinned. "Go ahead, show me."

"Just look through that little peephole. You'll see *everything.*"

"You're positive they won't know I'm watching?"

Celyn grinned. "They enjoy it more when someone does."

Chapter Four

That same evening, Eldan paced the confines of his room, his mind filled with Marni.

She had the female elves rioting and demanding that Mrs. Claus fashion new outfits—clothes they wanted only Marni to design. All the male elves were half in love with her.

Well, who wouldn't be? With a beautiful body like that? And the face of an angel...it was just too bad she was ugly inside.

He couldn't change that with a spanking. Only one thing could turn a rotten human being into a wonderful elf.

He refused to think about it, knowing the effect it would have on his dick.

A loud knock on his door shattered his lustful thoughts.

"Enter."

Kip and Noel strode in.

"It's not like you to miss dinner, Eldan." Kip held out a plate filled with cookies.

"I wasn't hungry."

Kip flopped down into a chair. He swung one long leg over the arm. "When you don't eat, I know you're upset."

"I am upset!" Eldan sighed. "And it's all because of Marni. Santa and Elise think Marni is here in Christmas Town because she wants to be here." "Elise can't stop talking about the new outfits she is going to sew for the female elves, based on Marni's designs, and now I've heard through our little elf 'grapevine' that Marni's got some new fangled ideas on how to make toys—she spoke to Santa about it at dinner."

Kip raised a brow. "What's wrong with that?"

"Kip, she's here because Judge Saint decreed it—she was arrested for speeding and drunk driving."

Kip whistled. "I had no idea."

"She's one messed-up human being." Eldan replied. "I won't burst Santa or Elise's cheery little bubble by telling them that."

"They're such optimists." Noel replied. "They believe in goodness, in holiday spirit."

"Well, I won't allow them to be hurt, and I won't let a spoiled, selfish human ruin the year-round holiday spirit of Christmas Town, either."

Kip munched a cookie. "Then what do you propose we do? Turn Marni into a happy little elf?"

"I think the lass wants to be good little elf," Noel chimed in. "She just doesn't want to admit it."

Eldan slashed a hand through the air. "She's a spoiled, childish woman—a bold, brazen little troublemaker. She thinks everyone's going to kow-tow to her."

Kip piped in. "Except for you."

"Yeah, except for me."

Eldan wished someone would tell that to his swelling cock. He'd had a hard-on for Marni since she arrived. He'd read about her antics, her sexual escapades. She was the darling of the paparazzi—a wealthy, media sensation who's money allowed her to do whatever she desired, but her list of naughty deeds didn't stop his attraction for her.

In fact, it challenged him.

Noel spoke, cutting through his musings. "Look man, she deserved that spanking. If you weren't here to do it, one of us would have. We're behind you all the way." He grinned. "Pun intended."

Kip popped another cookie into his mouth.

Eldan frowned. "Where'd you get those? I thought we were all out of cookies."

"Mrs. Claus has been on a cookie-baking binge. I can't seem to get enough of these." Kip licked his fingers. "Marni is going to need a lot of loving to turn her into an elf."

"She's got to truly *want* to become an elf." Eldan replied. "She doesn't have one shred of kindness in her, not one elf-like quality."

Noel grabbed a cookie. He chewed it thoughtfully.

"She's got a lot of demons riding her back. All her 'swagger' is just for show." He grinned. "Donning that sexy little elf costume was just to get our attention."

"She got mine." Kip leaped into the air, clicking the curled toes of his boots together. He landed on the ground. "I don't mind taking charge of Marni. I think it'll be fun."

"You think *everything's* fun." Eldan growled.

His right hand tingled. If Marni were here now he'd paddle her again. She was one human female who probably needed a paddling every day of her miserable life. He showed her who was in charge: him. He'd spanked the arrogance from her—at least temporarily. That was evident by the shocked look on her face earlier, and the wash of tears lining her beautiful, high cheekbones.

"Eldan, you're at odds with yourself."

He glanced at Kip. "What's that supposed to mean?"

"You'd much rather make love to her than spank her."

Elf psychobabble...

He tried to shove thoughts of Marni aside, but his stiff dick wouldn't allow it.

Kip winked at Noel.

"Poor girl must be hurting. I think Noel and I will have to tend to her luscious little bum. Just think: we'll have to remove her lacy tights—slowly."

Eldan shifted his stance.

"We'll have to soothe the sting from her tender skin." Noel sighed. "Sliding our hands over her tight, firm backside."

Eldan swallowed—hard.

"That beautiful, tear-stained face. I'll have to kiss it, and every other part of her."

"I imagine her breasts will need kissing."

"Her belly button, too."

Noel drew his brows together, a thoughtful look on his face. "I wonder if it is an 'inny' or an 'outy.'"

"But the job of soothing Marni would be easier if there were three of us." Kip grinned.

"Enough!"

They both looked at Eldan.

"Something wrong?" Kip asked.

Eldan swore it was the most innocent look Kip had ever mastered.

Noel angled his head. "Eldan, you look positively...pained."

The only pain Eldan felt was in his cock. It got so hard, he swore it would bust through the woolen tights covering it.

"No more talk of making love to Marni." He growled.

Kip laid a hand over his heart. "We didn't mention one word about making love to beautiful, sexy, *gorgeous*, Marni, we only—"

"Shut up.

Kip tipped his head back and laughed. Then his eyes met Eldan's.

"Soooooooooooo, you *would* rather make love to her than spank her."

"I never said *I didn't* want to make love to her."

"Eldan, it is the only thing that will turn a human into an elf."

The room got very quiet.

"She's our charge, Eldan. It's up to us to help her reform, especially if we don't want to let on to Santa and Missus Claus about the real reason Marni is here."

Eldan sighed. "We owe them too much to burst their bubble of happiness."

"Remember, a human must be turned into an elf by Christmas in order for Santa to make it official."

"That doesn't leave us much time." Kip stroked his chin.

"Humility, forgiveness—those are two elf traits Marni *must* demonstrate before we can make love to her."

"She must desire us as much as we desire her." Kip grinned. "I personally volunteer for that job."

Eldan shook his head. "Are you ever serious?"

"Only on Thursdays."

Eldan rolled his eyes.

"She must become humble and forgiving." Noel added. "Eldan's right about that."

"That's not happening in *our* elf lifetime." Eldan grumbled.

Noel smiled. "Miracles do happen, my friend. Especially during the holidays."

Chapter Five

The next morning, Marni went in search of a cup of coffee. She needed a shot of caffeine—badly. And sweets—she was dying for a taste of something sugary.

After what she'd seen last night, maybe she needed a shot of booze, too. The thing was, lately, booze made her see the strangest things... like what she saw through that peephole in her room last night...

Yeah, it was definitely time to give up drinking.

The odor of cinnamon and fresh-baked cookies wafted by her nose, making her mouth water. She stopped at the entrance to a large kitchen. Mrs. Claus worked inside, removing some cookies from a pan. Santa stood behind her, his arms around her waist. He kissed the back of her neck, raising her skirt to run his hands across her bottom.

Okay, so maybe I wasn't imagining it...

Marni grinned, catching sight of Elise's red, lacy thong. Mister and Missus Claus definitely weren't an old, staid couple.

They were young at heart.

Marni wished she could feel that way, too. Sometimes, she felt exactly what Judge Saint said *he* was—older than dirt.

She was suddenly very tired of feeling that way.

But what could she do to turn back the hands of time? Could she really change anything now?

She cleared her throat, announcing her arrival.

Santa stepped away, pushing his wife's skirt down.

"Ho, ho, *hooooooooo*. Good morning, Marni. Did you sleep well?"

"Yes, thank you, Santa, I did."

He walked over to her, stroking his long, white beard.

"I've discussed your toy ideas with Eldan."

She raised a brow. "Y-you have?"

"I had no idea you owned Sands Toy and Game."

"I inherited the company from my father when he passed away."

"Yes, I was sorry to hear about that. He was a good man who helped me out plenty of times."

Her mouth hung open. She snapped it closed. "Y-you knew my father?"

"Of course. There were several years when we ran short and your father generously donated several thousand toys to my bag."

"I don't believe it."

Santa angled his head. "Why is that?"

He was a cheap, miserly bastard who detested everyone...he had no holiday spirit.

"Never judge a toy by the packaging, Marni. You must open it, and play with it, to get the real joy. Now, your ideas on toy production are sound. I told Eldan to confer with you this morning."

Eldan wouldn't give me the time of day. Not after the way I acted.

"Eldan, Kip, Noel and the rest of the elves are expecting you—I told them you'd do a presentation of your ideas at ten a.m. sharp."

Marni's eyes widened. "A-a presentation?"

"I have a feeling you know toys like the back of your hand." He patted hers. "Now, I've got some work to do. Christmas will be here before you know it, and I've got to be ready."

He walked out of the kitchen, his jolly laugh echoing down the hall.

Marni shook her head. "Is he always this happy?"

"Always." Elise beamed. "Now, how about some cookies and tea?"

"Tea?" Marni screwed up her face. "I was hoping you had coffee."

"Oh dear me, no. We have green tea or white tea."

"I'll take white tea." Marni flopped into a chair.

"My dear, I'm so glad you volunteered to come to Christmas Town. We appreciate all your help and ideas."

Marni's heart beat a staccato rhythm in her chest.

Elves don't lie...

I'm not a damned elf! There are no such things as elves. What do I care if she thinks that I'm here voluntarily? Let her believe what she wants.

But elves don't lie...

Marni took a deep breath. "Elise, I think you've got the wrong impression."

"Oh, no dear, I couldn't possibly. I'm never wrong about people."

"Yeah, well, there's a first time for everything."

She raised one white brow while she put a plate of cookies and a small pot of tea in front of Marni. "Why do you say that?"

Marni reached out and grabbed Elise's hand. "I'm here because Judge Saint ordered me to do community service. I was arrested for speeding and drunk driving."

Elise gave her a long, level look. "The reason you came to Christmas Town doesn't matter. It's what you do with the time you're given here that counts."

Marni chewed and swallowed a cookie, but it tasted like sand. Tears clogged her throat.

"I've seen what you're capable of. You fit right in with all of our female elves here—and you've made them so happy with your new wardrobe ideas." She beamed at Marni. "And you've made me and Santa very happy." She winked. "I've noticed how Eldan, Kip and Noel look at you. You've made them, happy, too. They didn't have it easy when they first came here. They share a special bond because all three came to us when their parents died in a tragic accident during the holidays. The boys were holy terrors when they arrived." Elise grinned. "Three little 'curtain climbers'. But soon, with love, they grew into the fine, strong elves they are today." She took a seat next to Marni. "And they adore you. I can tell."

Marni squirmed in her chair, shifting her right butt cheek, then her left. Her ass still stung.

Elise patted her hand. "Sometimes, when we're naughty, we need to be punished. But it doesn't make us bad people."

"I don't think Eldan sees it that way."

"He did what was best for you, Marni. Eldan looks out for everyone here at Christmas Town. So do Kip and Noel. Especially now that Santa and I are getting on in years." She rose from the table. "Why don't you go speak to Eldan?"

"I doubt very much that he wants to speak to me."

"Elves never carry a grudge."

Marni sighed. "Is that more elf legend?"

"It's fact. Now go and do what you feel in your heart." Elise patted her chest.

Marni got up from her seat.

She wasn't sure she had a heart, never mind feelings, but she would give it a shot.

* * * *

Sometime later, Marni stood in front of the elves, all eyes on her.

"What I want each of you to understand is that you have unique talents. We have to put those abilities to good use and not waste them."

One of the elves piped up. "Why change what we've done these last few hundred years?"

Marni bit back a smile. "May I ask you something?"

The elf nodded, folding his arms across his chest.

"First, what's your name?"

"Pepper." He grinned.

Marni scratched her head. "That's an elf name?"

"My full name is Pepper Minstix."

The other elves giggled.

"Silence!" Eldan's voice boomed. The walls shook. "Ms. Sands is making a special presentation on behalf of Santa Claus. We owe her our attention and respect."

She blew out a breath, wondering how she would manage to get through this without throwing up.

"Pepper, haven't there been years when you've felt rushed to meet the holiday deadline? Years when there hasn't been enough toys, and Santa had to scramble to fill all the orders of every little good girl and boy?"

Pepper scratched his head. "Well, sure, but—"

"All I'm asking is for you to try my production line idea. Instead of picking one toy and creating it from start to finish, you work on one specific aspect. Like you." She pointed at Celyn. "You're very talented."

"Me?" Celyn looked around. "What am I good at?"

"Adding hair to the dolls' heads and styling it. I saw you do it. You fashioned curls and waves on some of those dolls that would make the world's greatest hairdresser jealous."

Celyn beamed.

"So, you should do the hair and Pepper can dress the dolls."

"Only the male dolls!" One of the elves called out.

There was a round of giggles.

Marni laughed, too. "Yes, perhaps Pepper should only dress the male dolls, but if we take it one step further, we can set aside a group of you to work on dolls only. Then another group of elves can work on toy trains, a group can work on toy cars, etc. The work will go much faster with each of you specializing in one toy, and one part of that toy's completion."

"Will the toys still be made with love?" Eldan's voice rang out.

The room became quiet. Marni licked her dry lips.

"Always." She replied, her voice steady. She wouldn't let Eldan rattle her.

"This will guarantee we meet our deadline?" Kip asked.

"Yes."

Noel spoke. "More toys in less time, is that what you're saying, lass?"

"Precisely."

Eldan rose to his feet. "Now, if you all will be so kind as to visit the tables where you can sign up for the special group you want to work with. We have them all labeled—dolls, trains, cars, blocks, etc. Then we'll see you all back here bright and early tomorrow morning, when we begin our new assembly line production."

Marni blew out a relieved breath.

She watched the elves linger by the tables, chattering about the 'new way' of making toys, signing up for the different groups.

Marni felt something besides relief—pride. She'd actually contributed something worthwhile.

She couldn't remember the last time she felt pride in something she'd done.

"Marni." Celyn tugged on her sleeve. "We've got to get going."

Marni followed Celyn out of the Toy Shop. "Where?"

"This is the day we visit the sick children who are in the River's End hospital during the holidays."

Marni stopped dead in her tracks.

"I-I can't."

Celyn angled her head. "Why not?"

"I've uh, I've got to get started on this 'assembly-line' thing, I've..."

"Celyn, will you excuse Marni for a minute?"

Eldan stood directly behind Marni. Strange, but she felt his presence even before he spoke.

"Sure." Celyn curtsied then walked away.

Eldan took Marni's hand.

"We'll have more privacy in here."

He opened two large gold doors that led into a solarium where tiered fountains spilled water from one level to another. A giant Christmas tree made of individual red poinsettia plants stood in the center of the room. White doves flew overhead, landing on the tree, the sound of gentle, running water filling the room.

Eldan shut the door then turned and faced her.

"I wanted to say..." They both spoke at once.

Marni's heart raced, Eldan's presence made her feel like she was five.

"I should go first," she said, "before I lose my nerve."

He nodded.

"I'm sorry, Eldan. I'm sorry for the way I behaved. Sorry for the trouble I've caused you."

He held up a hand.

She stepped away. "You're not going to use that on me again, are you?"

That made him laugh, but he sobered quickly.

"It pained me to have to punish you."

"Yeah, well—" She rubbed her backside. "You weren't the one getting spanked."

He grinned.

"Wow, you really *can* smile." She walked up to him, dipping her finger in the cleft of his chin.

He stepped away. "You shouldn't do that. Not unless you mean it."

"You think I'm not sincere?"

"You've known many men—men who haven't given a damn about you, except for your money. Here, we care about one and other. Truly care. If you're not ready for that, then I'm not the man for you."

She swallowed back tears—and his rejection.

"Can't we be friends?"

He looked like he wanted to say something, but then simply nodded his head.

She bit her lower lip. "Celyn mentioned something about going to a hospital."

"A group of us go each holiday season to the River's End Hospital to bring cheer and happiness to some very ill children."

Her heart raced. "That's really *not* my forte, if you know what I mean. I'd rather—"

"Sit in your room and smoke? Nurse your emotional pain with liquor?"

Her eyes widened. She'd kill Celyn for ratting her out, she'd—

"Don't look so surprised. It's all on Santa's naughty list."

She blew out a relieved breath, but fear returned quickly.

She hated hospitals. Hated their smell. The stark white rooms, the...despair.

"Come." He held out his hand. "Give it a try. Help children who can't help themselves."

She walked with Eldan, holding onto his hand as if it was a lifeline.

I can do this...I can do this...

"It will be all right, Marni. You'll see."

Elves don't lie.

Right.

Now, if she could only tell that to her sweating palms and knocking knees.

Chapter Six

"...and so, the little dog brought good cheer and happiness to everyone, reminding them of the real meaning of Christmas."

Celyn closed the book, placing it on the table next to a little boy lying in bed. She stroked his hair, giving him a sip of water from a cup.

"Did you like that story, James?"

Marni clenched her hands in her lap. Her stomach roiled, the smell of antiseptic filling her nose. Machines hummed and clicked, people strode in the corridor outside where holiday decorations lined the stark, white walls.

PING!

Doctor Sloane, paging Doctor Sloane...

The boy yawned. "I like when you read to me, Celyn." He shut his eyes, his breathing deep and even. "I like it a lot," he murmured, his voice sleepy.

"Let's go." Celyn whispered. "I think he'll doze for awhile. We've got another child to visit."

Outside in the hall, Marni slapped a hand across her mouth. Tears filled her eyes. She gagged, nausea rising in her throat.

Celyn grabbed her arm. "What's wrong?"

"I-I have to get out of here."

"Why?"

"I-I don't feel good."

Celyn patted her arm. "I'll find a doctor."

"No!" Marni shouted. "No." She shook her head. "Drive me back to Christmas Town. Please."

"But—"

"Celyn, *please.*"

Celyn led Marni down the hall and out of the hospital. They boarded Santa's sleigh.

"Hold on, Marni. I'll have you back at Christmas Town in no time."

Celyn cracked the whip in the air. The reindeer moved, their hooves sliding across the snowy pavement. Soon, they lifted high into the sky.

A few minutes later, the sleigh touched down at Christmas Town.

"Marni! What are you doing back so soon?"

She ran past Elise and Santa.

Elise looked at Celyn. "What's wrong?"

"She doesn't feel well. She said she needed to come back to Christmas Town."

"Oh my. Santa!" Elise called. "Please drive back to the hospital—go get Eldan, Kip and Noel."

"Why?"

I have a feeling they're the only ones who can help our Marni."

* * * *

The setting sun cast a warm glow in the solarium. Marni watched it, her heart aching. She couldn't get that little boy's pale face or his bald little head out of her mind.

He has a rare form of leukemia...

The doctor's pronouncement rang in her ears.

Her head pounded, her stomach cramped. She hadn't felt this sick in years.

Huddled in the corner of the solarium, she drew her legs up to her chest and wrapped her arms across her shins, squeezing them tight. She bowed her head, laying her cheek against her knees, wishing she could blot out the painful memories tearing her heart into pieces

She heard a creak then the door opened.

"Marni, lass, are you in here?"

Her heart pounded. She swore it beat through her chest.

Footsteps echoed in the room.

"Ah lass, there you are."

Noel squatted on his haunches, taking one of her hands in his. "You're freezing." He rubbed her hand. "It's warm as toast in here, and yet, you're cold."

She shivered violently. Glancing upward, she saw Kip's face through a watery veil of tears.

His usual, playful tone vanished. "Celyn told us you were upset."

"Oh God, please, just get me out of here." She scrambled to her feet, but fell against the hard wall of Noel's chest. He steadied her.

"You're not well enough to go anywhere." He held her against his chest. "It will be all right, lass, if you'd just let go of all those painful memories."

She beat her fist against him.

Her eyes flew to his. They were filled with sadness, mirroring her pain.

Marni tore away from him, only to collide with Kip.

"Whatever it is that's upsetting you, we can make it better."

She lashed out, hitting Kip in the chest. "You can't make anything better!"

She buried her face in her hands.

Kip eased her into his arms, stroking her hair.

"Have a good cry." He whispered.

She looked past Kip's shoulder to see Eldan. His tall frame filled the high back of a large, ornate gold chair decorated with an intricate pattern of cherubs dancing in the clouds.

For a second, she thought one cherub's face resembled Trevor's.

It can't be!

"Come." He held out his hand.

She needed a drink...and a cigarette.

Marni walked over to him on shaky legs. She crawled into his lap, settling her head against his chest.

Kip and Noel followed. They sat at her feet, reaching up to stroke her hair, her back.

She buried her face in Eldan's chest, her voice muffled.

"D-did you ever love someone so much, that you'd do anything for them?"

He grasped her chin with his thumb and index finger. Lifting it, he replied, "Yes."

"That's how I felt about Trevor."

Kip ran a hand across her shoulder, kneading her tense muscles. "Who was Trevor?"

She sucked in a breath. "My brother. He was six years younger than me."

Tears welled in her eyes.

Eldan lifted the hem of his tunic, using it to wipe the moisture from her cheeks.

"Did something happen to him, lass?" Noel laid a hand on her knee. He gave it a gentle shake. "You can tell us."

"He died." Her voice broke. "He had cancer. He suffered so much, and then, he died, wh-when he was only six years old."

She settled against Eldan's shoulder, absorbing his strength.

"I felt so helpless when Trevor got sick. When he died, I felt so alone. Our mother died a few years before— we hardly got a chance to know her. And I was left alone with a father who hated me. My father wished that I died, not Trevor. "

"He loved you." Eldan told her. "He was hurting, he couldn't have wished that."

"He hated me. And that's why I hate *everyone*." She scrubbed her hands across her face. "But I can't stand feeling this way anymore."

"Let it go, Marni. Try to forgive your father." Kip told her.

"Forgive him? How can I do that?"

"By putting yourself in his shoes. He lost his son."

"And he lost his daughter by treating me like shit. All he ever gave me was money. Our fortune was supposed to solve everything in his eyes."

Eldan grasped her shoulders. "Then his pain doubled when he lost you. Maybe he realized he couldn't get you back, so he gave you a gift, instead."

"Money." She snorted. "That's what he gave me."

"He gave you a head for business and a sense for what people are truly worth. Money can't buy that, or replace it."

It was the first time she had ever spoken about her misery over Trevor's death and her father's rejection. For many years, she could only remember Trevor as he was when he was ill, fighting for his little life. Now, in her mind's eye, she saw him, happy, smiling...just like he was before he got sick.

She cuddled against Eldan, her bottom nestled on his muscled thighs. Night settled over Christmas Town. The glittering ornaments and twinkling lights made her feel at peace.

Eldan lifted her in his arms and kissed her forehead.

He strode out of the solarium with her tucked against his chest, while Kip and Noel followed behind.

For the first time in years, Marni felt cherished.

Money couldn't buy *that*, either.

* * * *

Eldan carried Marni to her room and laid her on the bed as if she was made of the finest crystal.

The need to mate with her was strong. He had to fight the urge to strip them both of their clothing. His dick swelled. All he wanted to do was pump into her, make her his.

Sadness washed over him. She had come so far, yet...

She had to surrender—not only her painful memories, but she also had to relinquish her desire to control everyone around her.

He started to walk away when she grabbed his hand.

"Stay."

Kip and Noel stood in the doorway.

"I want you all to stay."

Noel shook his head. "I think it's better, lass, if we leave and let you get some rest."

She rolled to her side, nestling her head in the palm of her hand.

"It's the strangest thing. I was so tired before, but now, I feel energized."

"It's because you finally let go of what ailed you." Kip tapped the side of his head. "Up here."

Noel patted his heart. "And here."

She licked her lips. "There it is again—that weird feeling."

"What?" Eldan frowned.

He glanced at the tip of her pink tongue, but quickly looked away, the sight making his woolen tights painfully tight.

"I want something..."

"Sweet?"

She looked at Noel. "How did you know?"

"Ah lass, ya have a hankering for cookies, is that it?"

"Yes. Cookies." She sat cross-legged on the bed. "Maybe Elise made some."

"Marni, do you have any idea why you crave sweets so much?"

She glanced at Eldan. "I really haven't given it much thought."

Kip nodded towards the mirror hanging above her dresser. "Take a look at yourself."

"Huh?"

"In the mirror."

She rose from the bed and walked over to the mirror.

"My ears!" She gasped, grabbing each one. "They look pointy." She peered closer. "My eyebrows have this odd slant."

Eldan held his breath, wondering if vanity would win out or she'd accept the change in herself. He thought she looked beautiful.

So did his cock. He had to fight the urge to sink himself inside her warm, moist channel.

Marni smiled. "Am I an elf?"

"Almost." Eldan murmured.

"What else has to happen?"

Eldan glanced at Kip and Noel. They nodded.

"You have to make love with an elf."

"I see...more of that old elf folklore, is that it?"

"It's fact, lass. If you truly want to become an elf—"

"A good, kind, cheery elf—." Kip added.

"An honest, hard-working, sincere, elf, then you must mate with one," Eldan finished. "It's the last step."

She collapsed on the bed, laughter bubbling up inside her.

"Oh my. *That is* the most original line any guy has ever used to get in my pants." She shook her head. "And you said *I* wasn't sincere."

Eldan's face fell; his heart plummeted too. "You think we're not?"

"Elves mate for life, Marni." Kip told her.

"He's right, lass. If you make love with us—"

"Then you're ours. Forever." Eldan's voice was deep and soft.

She folded her arms beneath her breasts. "Okay, prove to me that you all mean that. Show me that you're sincere, that it's just not about screwing me."

"You don't trust us." Kip and Noel said in unison.

"Why should I?"

Kip sighed. "There's only one way to show you, love, just how honest we are."

They walked toward the door.

"Wh-where are you going?'

Eldan turned to face her. "Elves never lie, and they never force anyone to do anything they don't want. That includes making love."

He opened the door. The three of them sailed through it, leaving Marni alone.

She sat there, her mouth hanging open.

Every time she thought she had them figured out, they turned the ornaments on her.

What in hell was happening?

She scrubbed her face with her hands. She was starting to think and say the 'elfiest' things, but she couldn't deny that her heart felt light.

Elves mate for life...

If that were the truth, then she'd be stuck here in Christmas Town forever. When she first arrived, that very idea seemed like a death sentence.

Now, it felt as if her life was just beginning.

She wanted a fresh start. She wanted her three elves.

Badly.

Chapter Seven

The sweet smell of warm, fresh cookies drew Eldan, Kip and Noel to the kitchen.

"When did Elise start baking at night?" Kip asked, furrowing his brow.

Noel shrugged. "Beats me. I thought she spent her nights with Santa."

Eldan sniffed the air. "Chocolate. It's melted chocolate."

"Maybe she made chocolate chip cookies!" Kip leaped into the air, tapping the curled ends of his boots together.

He collided with Noel.

"Calm down, man."

"It must be a special occasion." Eldan murmured. "Why else would she make chocolate chip cookies?"

They stopped at the entrance to the kitchen, their eyes wide. Table after table was strewn with racks of fresh-baked, chocolate chip cookies.

Missus Claus stood nearby, removing cookies from a pan, placing them on a rack, letting them slide slowly off her spatula. Then she turned, bending down to retrieve another pan from the oven, her rounded bottom on display. She didn't have a stitch on underneath her short, green dress, where a frilly, white crinoline peeked out from beneath the hem.

"Elise?" Eldan's mouth hung open and he covered his eyes.

He'd never seen her dressed like *that.*

She turned and gave them a jaunty wave.

Kip shook his head. "That's not Elise."

Noel grinned. "It's Marni."

Eldan's heart pounded. His cock did, too.

"Cookie?" She held one out on the end of the spatula. It's heady, sweet fragrance drifted by his nose.

Her smooth, naked thighs were visible just below the short hem of the dress. Shoes with six-inch red heels and shiny patent leather graced her slender feet.

The minx!

She bent to slide another cookie off the spatula, her deep cleavage beckoning.

Fresh baked cookies and sex...no elf could resist such a potent combination.

"We promised, man." Noel spoke from the corner of his mouth. "We're not going to touch her." He swallowed, his Adam's apple bobbing.

"I want you." Marni's stroked them through their haze of desire. "All three of you."

Kip took a bold step toward her. He snatched a cookie from the spatula, grinning, then chewed and swallowed the treat, licking his fingers.

A small bowl sat on the table. He dipped a finger into it, holding it up for all to see.

"Melted chocolate." He angled his head. "I'd like to try it."

He placed a dab between Marni's breasts. She tilted her had back, pushing her chest out. He bent his head and licked the melted candy, his long tongue delving into her cleavage.

"Kiiiiip." She moaned.

She clutched his head, her fingers threading through his thick, tawny hair.

"Tonight, you'll have more pleasure than you've ever dreamed, love." He kissed each breast then stepped away.

Noel approached. He lifted the hem of her dress, revealing her naked pussy. Placing a dab of the melted chocolate above her clit, he knelt before her and licked his way down.

"Ohhhhhhhhhhhhhhhhhh."

Marni wrapped her arms around his neck, pulling his head closer.

Her eyes locked with Eldan's. The sight of Kip and Noel pleasuring Marni made his already-stiff dick throb.

All he needed was a nod of her head, a final affirmation of her desire.

He held his breath, anticipation coursing through him.

"Eldan." She gasped. "Eldan, I want you. Do you want me?"

"More than you can ever imagine."

* * * *

Noel sucked her clit into his mouth. Kip moved behind her, dipping his hands into the front of her dress.

Tonight, you'll have more pleasure than you've ever dreamed...

Kip slid his hands around to unbutton her dress, his fingers brushing the skin on her back. It sent a pleasured shiver down her spine. He pushed the top of her dress down, revealing her breasts, their tender tips sliding against the heavy velvet of his tunic.

Her clit pulsed.

His lips trailed down the side of her throat, across her shoulder and the bony ridge just above her breasts. He bent his head and kissed her nipples, sucking them gently into his mouth. He kissed her long, hard and deep, the taste of chocolate on his lips.

Noel stood behind her, pushing her dress down around her hips. It landed at her feet, a green puddle against the red of her shiny patent leather heels.

Kip knelt before her. He grasped each of her ankles, encouraging her to lift her feet.

He tossed the dress aside.

Marni stood before them naked as the day she was born.

Except for her feet.

Noel bent to remove her shoes.

"No." Eldan held up a hand, his dark gaze penetrating. "Leave them."

Wearing just the shoes made her feel barer than without.

"You're beautiful." He whispered.

His eyes roamed over her nakedness.

She shivered.

Kip dropped to his knees. "Our gift to you."

He fastened his lips to her pussy, driving his tongue deep inside her. She clutched his shoulders, grinding against his mouth.

"Oh, my."

He licked her little bud, drawing his tongue upward. The tip kissed her clit. He lingered there, pushing gently against her swollen button of flesh until her thighs quivered.

Noel stood behind her and wrapped his arms around her waist, using one hand to knead the tender flesh of her breasts. He stroked his other hand across her bottom, sliding his index finger down the cleft. Kip's agile tongue and the sensual strokes of Noel's finger almost sent her over the edge. She shut her eyes, pushing her backside against Noel's hand.

She stood on the brink of orgasm.

"Surrender, Marni." Eldan whispered.

"I-I don't know what you mean."

"We're going to make love to you for the next three days."

She gasped.

"I want you ready." His dark eyes smoldered.

Sweeping his hand across the table, he pushed everything aside, including the sweet treats.

"Bend over."

His commanding tone made her little bud throb—it ached for release. Anticipation and desire mingled together. She bent over the table, not knowing what to expect. Kip and Noel moved so that they stood in front of her.

Her essence drenched her pussy.

Eldan ran his hands across her bottom.

"When I spanked you," he whispered in her ear. "I wanted to see your beautiful, naked bottom. Now, my holiday wish is granted."

She turned her head to see him dip his index finger into a small bowl.

It was the oil she'd used to grease the cookie pans!

She rose up on her hands, rearing back when he touched her bottom hole, pushing his finger inside. He kept his finger inside, reaching between her legs with his other hand, stroking her pussy.

Knowing that Kip and Noel watched heightened the excitement.

Tears of pleasure washed over her face, the exquisite, full feeling in her bottom, and the delicious throbbing of her clit sending her over the edge of oblivion.

Marni lay across the table, wondering if she'd ever be able to move again. Eldan wrapped Marni's dress around her body, lifting her like a rag doll. The three elves took her to a secluded room in a wing of Santa's castle.

A huge, canopied bed decorated in red and green sat in the center of the room. A fire burned in the hearth, filling the room with warmth. Through the windows, she could see that a light snow blanketed the ground outside.

Eldan eased her onto the bed.

Noel slid beside her, coaxing her into his arms.

Kip lay on her other side. He cuddled his long, sinewy body against her, running a hand over her hip and bottom.

"What is this room?" she murmured. "It's so pretty." She let go of a yawn.

"It's the 'elfing' room." Eldan replied. He tossed another log on the fire. "We'll be here for three days and nights."

Three days! And nights...

Just the elves and I.

She giggled.

Noel raised a brow. "What's so funny, lass?"

"Nothing." She stretched her arms high above her head and grinned. "Everything!"

Noel and Kip returned her grin, stripping while Eldan kissed her clit. Never had a kiss felt so wonderful! He lifted her legs, placing them over his shoulders, allowing him better access to her bud. He kissed and sucked until her pussy dripped.

Marni squirmed, bunching the covers in her fisted hands.

When he nipped her pussy with his teeth, she ground her bottom into the mattress, her orgasm just within reach...

He pulled back, removing his clothing while Kip and Noel joined her on the bed.

Kip massaged her breasts, rolling her nipples between his fingers. She felt the jolt of pleasure clear down to her toes. She wiggled them in response, sliding her leg up his shin. The hair on his leg felt wonderful: soft—silky and smooth.

She eased onto her side, rising up on one elbow. Noel slid behind her, his large cock poking her bottom.

Kip rolled onto his back.

From the other side of the room, Eldan watched, his dark eyes intense.

He opened his legs, his cock rising upwards.

She placed her knees astride each of his hips. He grasped her hands in his.

"Ride me."

Marni rose up so that his cock slid insider her.

Noel rose up on his knees to steady her body, grabbing her waist from behind.

She moved—up and then down—the slow steady rhythm filling her body with new sensations. She felt like one of those shooting stars she'd seen during her ride on Santa's sleigh—like she'd burst into a thousand little pieces of glittering light.

Noel moved aside while Kip stretched out his long legs. She wiggled her bottom, feeling Noel's hands on both of her cheeks.

He slipped his dick inside, quickly filling her backside.

"Noel!" She shouted when he grasped her around the waist. "Noel..." She sighed. "Kip."

While she rode Kip, Noel rode her.

Marni's need built once more, her clit throbbing in time with their mingled strokes.

Exquisite torture. Sublime pain.

Her orgasm rammed into her with such force that she could barely breathe.

Kip spilled his seed inside her, while Noel filled her with his.

She collapsed on top of Kip. He grasped her head between his hands, kissing her mouth, her cheeks, and finally her nose.

Noel eased out of her. He rolled onto his back. Marni settled between the two of them, letting her body—and her mind—come back to earth.

She couldn't move a muscle.

Eldan approached them, his stride wide and purposeful.

She bit her lower lip, wondering what he would do.

I can't move...I can't!

Kip and Noel rose up off the bed as Eldan sat down, stroking Marni's breasts and clit. Then he stretched his legs out wide.

"Wrap your legs around my waist." He told her. "Come towards me." He eased her closer.

The satin coverlet skimmed Marni's backside, igniting a fire of need all over again.

The tip of his big cock kissed her clit. While he wiggled his dick against her slick opening, he massaged her breasts.

He pressed down on her little bud with the pad of his thumb.

"Eldan!" She gasped. "More. *More.*"

He chuckled. "Delighted."

He pushed his cock inside her, while his thumb circled and rotated her clit. Eldan took his time, sliding in then out of her with slow, even strokes. Each time he pushed into her, he made sure the tip of his cock touched her clit. She matched him, stroke for stroke, her body's rhythm in time with his.

"Faster!" she begged.

He slowed the pace even more. "No. You'll enjoy it more this way."

"I want to come." She sucked in a breath, her body on the brink of release. "Now, Eldan. *Now.*"

"My little elfmate." He sighed. "When are you going to surrender totally? To me?" He pushed into her again, the slick, wet tip of his penis rubbing against her swollen bud of flesh.

Her body hummed, the crescendo of need rising up until she gripped his shoulders, her nails digging into his skin.

"Eldan!" She cried, her orgasm making her clit pulse.

She came with such force that her eyes rolled back.

"Eldan." She repeated, her voice just above a whisper.

Marni didn't think she could string an entire, coherent thought together. Her body and mind were spent.

Eldan lay beside her. She moved to his chest, her head pillowed against his heart.

She could hear its beat.

Lub dub...lub dub...lub dub.

Kip slid next to her. He kissed her temple, his lips moving across her skin like the satin coverlet on the bed. Noel stretched out by her head. He stroked her hair, massaging her scalp.

Eldan kissed her forehead. His lips stayed there while her body spooned against him.

His heartbeat was like a lullaby, the soothing sound making her eyelids heavy.

She gave in. To sleep...to him.

To all of them.

Her surrender was complete.

Chapter Eight

For three days, Eldan, Kip and Noel loved her body.

She could only leave the bed to munch cookies and sip hot chocolate, which they took turns feeding her.

Once, she rose from the bed while they all slept, padding quietly into the bathroom. She shut the door and went about her business.

At the sink, she splashed some water on her face.

The bathroom door opened. She glanced in the mirror to see Eldan stroll in, his tall, naked form behind her. His big cock lay flaccid along his thigh, but the minute he touched her, it nudged her bottom.

He pushed some of her hair aside, nipping her earlobe with his teeth.

One of his hands strayed to her breast.

She shut her eyes, shuddering with pleasure at his touch.

"Open your eyes." He commanded. "Watch us—in the mirror."

He dipped his index finger into her wet pussy then slid his middle finger in, too. He pushed in and out, eliciting a moan from her. She could see his actions reflected in the mirror, doubling her pleasure.

Eldan turned her around, positioning her arms against the wall.

"Stick your bottom out." He patted her butt.

She did what he asked, pushing her backside against him.

Marni glanced over her shoulder and saw Eldan in the mirror. He bent his knees, easing his cock inside her.

"Oh my...I-I."

"This is good for your G-spot." He chuckled low in her ear.

He knew just what to do to please her.

He allowed her release then he came, his cock pulsing inside her.

"Naughty girl." He whispered.

Her eyes widened. "Is this going on Santa's list?"

"No." He smiled, his grin wicked. "On mine."

* * * *

At the end of the three days and nights, Marni felt like a new person. She had the most urgent sensation to do something good—all the time.

She showed up for work in the Toy Shop after her time alone with Kip, Noel and Eldan, eager to help the other elves.

"I hear you've mated," Celyn announced upon Marni's arrival.

Marni's face grew hot.

"There are no secrets here in Christmas Town." Celyn smiled.

Some of the other female elves giggled.

Marni sighed. "I guess not."

"Have you decided?" Celyn swept up a doll's hair into a fancy up-do.

"Have I decided what?"

Celyn lowered her voice. "Whether it's Eldan, Kip or Noel?"

Wait—she had to choose just one? How could she make up her mind? She couldn't choose one over the other.

"Is this more elf folklore?" Marni's heart raced. "That I have to choose one elf over another? Why would you say something like that, Celyn?"

Celyn drew her pointy little brows together. "So you understand how we do things. Ask any of the female elves. They'll tell you." She lifted her chin. "Elves choose only one mate. Ask Elise, if you don't believe me." Celyn glanced away, resuming her work. "Besides, you know that elves never lie."

Marni left the toyshop, tears filling her eyes.

* * * *

That evening, Marni watched the sunset. It glowed, a huge orange ball of fire in the wintry night sky. She sat in her favorite spot—the window seat of the solarium.

Her heart plummeted with every inch the sun dipped below the horizon. Celyn's voice rang in her ears.

Have you decided?

She'd rather leave Christmas Town than have to choose.

The elves and I...

She loved the sound of it.

She loved them. Eldan, Kip and Noel.

"Marni?"

Eldan's deep voice cut through her thoughts.

"I've been looking all over for you." He snapped his dark brows together. Lifting her chin in the palm of his hand, he wiped away her tears with the pad of his thumb.

She grasped his hand, holding it tight.

"Want to tell me what's wrong?"

"Please don't make me, choose, Eldan. *Please.*" Her voice wobbled.

"Choose what?"

"You, Kip or...Noel."

He took both her hands in his. He ran his thumbs across the back of them. "Who told you that you would have to make a choice?"

"Celyn."

He shook his head and squeezed her hands. "You belong to all of us, and we belong to you."

Her heart pounded so loud, she could swear someone in China heard it.

"Celyn said that elves select only one mate, that it is part of elf lore, but I can't, Eldan, I just can't choose only one of you."

"When we spoke about you becoming ours—mine, Kip's and Noel's—Santa gave us his word that it would be so. And *his word* is law here in Christmas Town." He grabbed her face between his hands and kissed her mouth. "On Christmas Day, when your 'elfing time' is officially over, Santa will make his pronouncement—that you belong to us. We tried to keep it a secret." He gave her a sheepish grin. "We wanted to surprise you."

"Oh, Eldan!" She threw her arms around his neck, hugging him tight.

"My little elf-mate." He rested his forehead against hers. She played with the collar of his tunic, fingering the soft, chocolate brown velvet.

"The next time you're upset, just speak to one of us—to me, Kip or Eldan." He gave her waist a little squeeze with his hands. "Otherwise, I may just have to paddle you again."

She raised a brow. "Oh, really?"

"Actually, I'll let Kip and Noel spank you this time. I'll watch." He grinned sardonically, waggling his brows.

"Oh you!" She swatted his arm.

He kissed her. Hard.

"Now, I've got to get going before it snows again."

"Where?"

"The children's hospital. Your toy production idea has worked so well that we were able to make more toys for the children. Kip, Noel and I are going to deliver them."

"Could I go with you?"

"Are you sure you want to?"

"I-I'd like to see that little boy again, the one with leukemia."

Eldan smiled. "He's better, I'm told. Our last visit cheered him up."

"Will you wait for me?"

"Santa's sleigh doesn't leave for another hour yet."

"I made some extra special toys for the children."

He smiled. "Go get them. And dress warm. It's getting cold outside."

She turned to leave, then ran back to Eldan. "I have to wrap them." She glanced at her watch. "Will you promise to wait for me?"

"Always."

* * * *

Kip and Noel helped Eldan to load the sleigh, placing toy after toy into Santa's large, red sack nestled in the rear seat.

"Did you find out what Marni was upset about?" Noel hefted a large box into the sack.

"I was about to ask you that same question." Kip chimed in.

Eldan placed two more brightly wrapped packages in the back of the sleigh. It was filled to the brim with toys and treats.

"Celyn told Marni she had to choose only one of us."

Noel's auburn brows rose. "She didn't!"

"Celyn's been doing a lot of naughty things lately." Kip scowled.

"She used to be such a nice little elf." Eldan angled his head. "What's she been up to?"

"Yesterday, the lass took Santa's sleigh for a joy-ride without asking him."

Kip's frown deepened.

"Someone's got to take that girl in hand."

* * * *

An hour later, Marni rushed out of her room carrying a bag filled with brightly wrapped boxes, the red, silver and gold foil paper gleaming in the light. For the first time in her life, she wanted to make someone else's life a little brighter.

A little cheerier.

Anticipation grew when she realized she'd spend the entire day with Eldan, Kip, and Noel.

Just the elves and I.

She hummed along with a familiar Christmas carol, stopping when she smelled an acrid odor...

Smoke.

A haze formed and swirled in the air, heading straight for her.

"Marni!"

She turned around to see Noel barreling toward her.

"Come with me." He tugged her hand. "We've got to get out of here."

Smoke filled her nose. She coughed violently.

Noel's voice filled with despair.

"The Toy Shop is on fire."

* * * *

Outside, Marni watched Santa's Toy Shop blaze, the wooden timbers crumbling from the intense flame.

She wanted to collapse into a heap, too.

All the elves' hard work vanished in a puff of smoke.

A brigade of elves lead by Aardel and Pepper Minstix splashed buckets of water onto the flames. They worked for over an hour, bringing the fire down to a smolder.

The Toy Shop lay in ruins, a few plumes of smoke rising up in the air from the dying flames.

"How could this happen?"

Marni placed an arm around Elise's shoulders. Deep wrinkles lined her face. Only a heavy heart could cause such distress on Elise's smooth skin.

"For hundreds of years, children all over the world received toys from me and now?" Santa shook his head, his voice sad. "It looks like there will be no Christmas."

Some of the elves cried. Others stood off to the side, shock evident in their eyes.

"I-I can't believe this." Marni shook her head. "It isn't fair."

She choked back tears, wishing her father still lived. If he did, she'd swallow her pride and get him here with his stock of toys.

Noel placed an arm around her waist, kissing the top of her head. "Ah, lass. I'm just glad I found ya in the hallway by your room, and got ya out of there in time."

"I want to know what caused the fire." Eldan's hand clenched at his side.

"Maybe it was this."

All eyes turned to Pepper Minstix. He held up a package of cigarettes and matches.

A collective gasp went up from the crowd.

Pepper walked over to Marni. "Aren't these yours?"

"I saw her." Celyn pointed her index finger at Marni. "She was smoking near the Toy Shop."

"That's n-not true."

"When you first came here, you offered me a cigarette." Celyn lifted her pointy little nose in the air.

All eyes settled on Marni. "I-I didn't offer her a cigarette." Marni's lips trembled. She glanced at Celyn, but Celyn wouldn't look at her. "I told you what a bad, nasty habit smoking was and that's the truth!"

"I think it's best if we all go inside—into the great hall." Santa's voice rang out. "I'll decide this matter there."

"Eldan, please. You've got to believe me." Marni clutched his arm.

"Did you smoke when you first arrived at Christmas Town?"

"Yes, but—."

"And Celyn was in your room when you were smoking?" Kip shook his head.

Marni's heart sank. Her guts twisted inside. "Yes."

"She offered me vodka, too." Celyn pointed at Marni. "She hides it in a flask in her bag."

"Did you do that, lass? Did you give Celyn vodka?" Noel asked her.

Elves don't lie.

"Yes." Her voice shook. "But I didn't mean—"

"What makes you think we can believe you when you say you didn't offer Celyn a cigarette?" Eldan questioned her, his voice flat and devoid of emotion. "When you admit that you offered her liquor?"

Then they all turned away...

Looking anywhere except at her.

Chapter Nine

"Here ye! Here ye! Santa's court is in session. All rise for the great jolly man himself."

An elf page rapped a long, golden staff on the floor next to Marni.

Santa made his way to his throne, flanked by Eldan, Kip and Noel.

Marni wanted cry, only she didn't think she had any more tears left.

"Celyn, do you hereby attest that your words are the absolute truth?"

Celyn nodded, giving Marni a snide smile.

"It's not only me who saw her smoking." Celyn nodded toward a group of female elves. "*They* all saw Marni smoking by the Toy Shop, too."

Marni lashed out at Celyn. "I quit smoking." She lowered her head. "And drinking. I ditched all my bad habits."

"Ladies, do you confirm Celyn's story?"

Celyn elbowed one of the little female elves in the ribs. "Ow! Cut it out." She rubbed her side.

"Well?" Santa raised a bushy white brow. "I'm waiting."

Seconds went by. Quiet descended upon the great hall.

Then the little female elves spoke at once.

"We saw her smoking by the Toy Shop."

"Marni did it. She started that fire." One of them pointed at her.

"She was smoking cigarette after cigarette." Another murmured.

The look on Santa's face bespoke of great sadness...and disappointment.

"Marni." He shook his head. "You've done a very naughty thing. I expected better from you. If we didn't have so many witnesses, I wouldn't believe a word of it."

Tears flowed down her face. She looked over at Elise, who quickly turned her head, wiping her eyes with a handkerchief.

Eldan, Kip, and Noel stood ramrod straight.

There'd be no bending, no changing anyone's mind.

Damn them! Damn these fucking elves!

Marni glanced at Celyn. A smug, satisfied look twisted her features.

Her heart shriveled, she could feel a cold chill slice through her soul.

"Marni, as much as it pains me to do so," Santa continued. "I must banish you from Christmas Town."

"No!" She clapped a hand across her mouth. "Please...don't, I—"

Santa rose from his throne. He seemed tired and old— Eldan helped him to stand, his eyes locking with Marni's.

They were filled with sadness.

"You are to leave. Now."

She bit back a sob.

"Never to return."

* * * *

Noel wandered the snow-crusted grounds outside Christmas Town long after Marni departed.

He wouldn't come inside, even when Elise tempted him with cookies.

His heart was broken. No cookie, no matter how sweet, could mend that.

Only Marni could.

Tears clogged his throat. They stung his eyes. It had been some time since he'd wanted to bawl like a child.

Probably not since his parents died in a car crash.

He felt a similar sense of loss now.

Noel rounded a corner of Santa's castle, stopping dead in his tracks. The smell of smoke drifted by his nose. He saw the glow of something red, thinking it was Rudolph's bright, crimson nose. His eyes widened when he saw a cigarette butt go flying into the snow.

"Celyn, what are you doing?"

She turned around quickly, away from his prying eyes.

"Lass, I asked you a question!"

He approached her. "What're ya doin'?" His brogue deepened.

She didn't answer.

He grasped her shoulders between his hands and gave her a shake.

She coughed and sputtered. Smoke left her mouth in a great puff.

Kip rounded the bend and stopped.

"Eldan's looking for you, he..." He sniffed the air. "Is that smoke?"

Noel gripped Celyn's hand.

"She's been smoking!" His voice sliced through the wintry air.

Celyn shivered. She tried to pull away, but he held her fast.

"Let me go!" She continued to struggle within his hold.

Kip narrowed his eyes. "Celyn, I want the truth. Did *you* cause that fire in the Toy Shop?"

Her eyes filled with tears. "Yes," she whispered. "I did."

"But why?" He shook his head. "You've always been such a good girl, and now...smoking? Why, Celyn? Why draw all this bad attention to yourself?"

"Because I love you!" She wailed. "And you wouldn't pay any attention to *me!*"

"Oh, Celyn." He shook his head. "This is horrible."

"We have to tell Eldan," Noel urged. "We have to tell Santa and Missus Claus."

"Oh no, nooooooooooooooooo." Celyn pulled on Noel's hand.

He growled low in his throat and tossed her over his shoulder. ."Lass, you're not gettin' away."

Kip drew his usually happy face into tight, angry lines.

"I know one little elf who's got an awful lot of explaining to do."

* * * *

A few minutes later, the great hall filled to capacity with curious onlookers as Celyn stood before Santa.

"Celyn, I'm ashamed of you." Santa's voice boomed. He stroked his long white beard. "What's worse is that you encouraged others to go along with your story." He gazed out onto the crowded hall. "My shame extends to several of you today."

Many of the little female elves bowed their heads.

Elise wagged a finger at them. "You naughty elves. You *should* bow your heads."

"Elves don't lie." Eldan's voice rang out. He crossed his arms over his chest. "You've broken the golden rule."

Noel looked at all of them. "You've caused someone we have come to love a great deal of pain."

Kip's anger festered inside him. He longed to put Celyn over his knee and give her a spanking she wouldn't forget. He glanced out the window where the snow fell. It swirled through the air, falling to the ground, piling against Santa's castle in drifts.

Almost a foot had fallen since Marni left.

Worry filled his mind...and heart.

"Celyn, you are to be punished." Santa's voice rang out.

"No!" She cried. Her body shook. "No, please, don't!"

Santa nodded his head. "I always grant one elf a special holiday wish each Christmas. This year, I choose Kip."

Kip's eyes flew to Santa's.

"Kip, what is it you wish this holiday? Name it and it's yours."

A corner of his mouth lifted, his playful nature returning. "I choose to punish Celyn."

"Granted!" Santa sat down on his throne. "Proceed."

Kip walked over to Celyn. He dragged her by the hand, until she stood directly in front of Aardel. "You're going to punish her."

Aardel's eyes grew wide. "Me?"

"Yes, you. Good luck, Aardel." He gave her a little push. She collided with Aardel's wide chest. "You're going to need it."

Celyn's lovely mouth formed a wide 'O' of shocked surprise.

So did Aardel's.

Eldan stepped down from Santa's throne. He bowed before him.

"Sir, you banished Marni from Christmas Town. Kip, Noel and I are asking your permission to use your sleigh so we can go find her."

Santa nodded. "Permission granted." He rose to his feet, his black boots and red suit standing out like a beacon in the great hall. "Bring her back to us."

"We owe her an apology." Pepper Minstix removed his little felt hat, holding it in his hands.

"Yes, we do." Elise joined Santa on the steps, her checked skirt swirling around fishnet-clad legs. "And I know some naughty little elves who will be delivering that apology *personally*."

* * * *

A little while Pepper Mintstix helped Marni into the sleigh.

"Santa said to take you as far as the border of Christmas Town and River's End." Pepper told her. He moved to the front of the sleigh, where the reindeer stood waiting for him. For one crazy minute, Rudolf turned to look at her.

His nose didn't glow quite as bright, his eyes looked sad, too.

She hid *her* swollen eyes behind a pair of dark glasses. She hadn't cried this much since Trevor died.

Damned elves! They had gotten under her skin and into her heart, now they tore it to bits.

"We're ready, Miss Sands."

She looked at Pepper. "I'll bet you're real happy to see me leave."

"I don't know if you'll believe this, but I'm not."

"Right."

He climbed up onto the sleigh. She couldn't take it anymore. "Don't do me any favors." She pushed him off the sleigh, sliding one of her legs out onto the snow-crusted ground. "I'd rather walk all the way back to River's End."

"That's crazy! You'll freeze to death. It's colder than—"

"An elf's nose?" She replied, her voice dripping with sarcasm. "Is that more elf lore?"

"Look, Miss Sands, Santa ordered me to take you to River's End; I don't question Santa's orders."

"Obviously." She snorted. Marni pushed at Pepper. He slid backwards, falling into a pile of snow. "Just leave me alone...I don't need anyone." Her voice cracked.

Pepper rose from the snow. "But—"

"Go!" She shouted.

The reindeer lifted their heads and stomped their hooves. Before she could utter another word, she was thrown back against the seat, the reindeer tugging the sleigh until it rose high into the sky.

"Miss Sands!" She heard Pepper shout. "Come back! You should have said 'go!' – the reindeer thought you meant them!"

She didn't know what to do. The reindeer were out of control, each pulling the sleigh in a different direction. She rocked from side to side, desperately trying to hold on.

In the next minute, the sleigh pitched down. Before she knew what hit her, it landed on the ground with a jarring thud.

She spilled out of it, the snow covering every inch of her.

One snowflake fell, soon followed by another...and another.

They landed on her cheeks and nose.

She rose to her feet and started walking.

It was just too bad she didn't know where in hell she was going.

* * * *

Marni didn't know how long she trudged through the snow, her body shaking.

Her fur jacket was no match for the wind's icy fingers. They swirled around her head, tweaking her nose.

Her fingers felt numb. She placed them against her mouth—her lips were numb as well.

She was tired, so tired...

She drifted in and out of consciousness, wondering how she continued to walk in the bitter cold, her feet as numb as her hands and mouth.

Up ahead she saw lights. A great castle loomed before her...

She was back in Christmas Town!

Marni ran, tripping once, landing in the snow. When she looked up, several elves stood over her. One held a lantern in his hand.

"Who goes there?" He asked, shining the light on her.

"It's Marni!" She called out.

She rose to her feet, wiping the snow from her jacket.
A tall elf stepped forward. His dark eyes met hers.
"Eldan?" She whispered.
A corner of the dark elf's mouth lifted.
"Glint's the name, holiday gloom is my game."
She fainted dead away.

Chapter Ten

A little while later, one of Santa's other sleighs rode high in the sky, flying past the moon.

Eldan's hands guided the reindeer through the swirling snow. He glanced down to see Glint's fortress. As they neared, a familiar blonde head came into view...

His heart lodged in his throat.

"Land this blasted thing, Eldan." Kip shouted over the wind.

The closer they got, the more Eldan could see. Glint and his evil little band of elves had Marni in their clutches.

"We've got to save her, man. Before it's too late." Noel reached over to grab the reins from Eldan.

The sleigh careened to the side.

Noel tried to pull the sleigh to the left, but the fierce wind made it impossible.

The reindeer tugged the sleigh, bringing it closer to earth.

CRASH!

They sleigh landed in a group of holly bushes. Eldan shook his head, and rose to his feet, brushing the snow from his tunic. Noel followed suit.

"Where's Kip?" Eldan frowned.

They heard a muffled 'Here I am!'

Kip had landed in a snowdrift head first, his long legs sticking up in the air. He kicked them wildly, trying to dislodge his head and shoulders from the snow.

Noel pulled Kip free.

"Thanks." He rose to his feet and shook the snow from his head and shoulders.

"Look!" Eldan pointed towards Glint's castle.

A group of elves led Marni toward the main gate.

"Marni, lass!" Noel cried.

They ran after her, their long legs eating up the snow beneath their booted feet.

"Marni!"

She turned her head, a look of disbelief on her beautiful face, then her eyes widened. "Eldan! Kip! Noel! Help me."

Glint turned when he heard her call out.

"Get her inside! Now!" He ordered his elf guards.

She disappeared before their eyes, the huge castle door shutting behind her.

* * * *

Eldan held a snowball against his eye, the throbbing there matching the anxiety twisting his gut.

"Here, let me see that." Kip shook his head and sighed. "You're gonna have quite a shiner." He flopped down on a log next to Eldan. "Well, we certainly showed *them*."

He glanced at Glint's castle where the guards marched back and forth.

"We gave as good as we got." Eldan grunted.

Noel chimed in. "But not good enough."

Kip rested his chin in the palm of his hand. "How are we going to get Marni out of there?"

Eldan jumped up from the log. It tipped, dumping Kip into the snow.

"This is no time for your antics." Noel sighed.

Kip rolled his eyes. "Like I was playing." He brushed the snow from his legs.

"What's goin' on in that head of yours, man?" Noel glanced at Eldan.

"The answer's right in front of us. In fact," Eldan lifted one booted foot, "it's right below our feet."

"What's right below our feet?" Kip scrambled to his.

"Snow."

"Huh?" Noel scratched his head.

"We surprise them... with snow."

Kip looked around. "If only we had a catapult—something to toss snowballs with."

Eldan picked up a ball of snow in his hand and tossed it at Noel. It bounced off his chest. "*We're* going to be the catapults. We'll fill Santa's sleigh with the snowballs. The guards won't know what hit them."

Noel grinned. "Now you're talkin,' man."

* * * *

Glint shoved Marni into a chair. He pushed a box of cookies in front of her.

She read aloud, "Kleeber Elf Cookies." She rolled her eyes. "Is that your idea of a bad joke?"

"Eat." He nodded toward the box.

"Kiss my...cookie crumbs." She aimed her chin at him.

Glint sat in a high-backed chair. He dangled a leg over the arm. "Maybe you'd like a drink, instead? Or a smoke?"

"You're disgusting." She shook her head. "How did you become such a bad elf?"

She had to keep him talking, especially now that she knew Eldan, Kip and Noel were nearby.

Hope bloomed in her heart.

"I thrive on other people's despair, especially during the holidays." He glanced casually at his fingernails. "I do so love to see the suicide rate go up, especially at this time of year." He grinned sardonically. "Ah, the holidays. Such a nice, lonely time of year, isn't it? Especially for those who are susceptible to depression."

"Well, you're not going to make me sad. I won't let you."

Just then, the door flew open. Two guards pushed a kicking, screaming elf at Glint. She fell against him, her big green eyes wide...

"Celyn!" Marni gasped. "What are you doing here?"

"Marni!" She pushed away from Glint and ran to Marni.

Marni wrapped an arm around her shoulders.

"I'm so sorry. For everything." Celyn sniffed back tears. "I got you in so much trouble because I was jealous of all the attention Kip was giving you. Can you forgive me?"

Marni brushed some of Celyn's red-gold curls from her eyes. "I forgive you, Celyn." Beneath Celyn's contrite expression, Marni noticed a loving glow lined her pixie face. She wondered how it got there.

"You really do forgive me?" Celyn asked. She lowered her voice. "Aardel and I hooked up. You were right...Kip's not for me." She blushed to the roots of her auburn hair.

"Oh really?"

"Really." Celyn winced, touching her backside. "The ride here was a little...uncomfortable."

Marni smiled. "Well, I'm glad you and Aardel worked things out. And I understand, Celyn. I was young once, too. I did some very foolish things."

Glint rolled his eyes. "Holiday hogwash."

Marni lifted her chin. "Your cynicism can't hurt us. I've got too much holiday cheer."

He crashed his hand down on the table. "Enough! I'm throwing you both in my dungeon."

Celyn gasped, huddling against Marni.

"Your holidays are over."

Glint's evil laugh echoed through the castle.

* * * *

Eldan, Kip and Noel tossed snowball after tightly packed snowball into Santa's sleigh. The freezing temperature turned them into hard little weapons, capable of felling even the strongest elf.

Kip sighed. "If we run out of snowballs, we're sunk."

"The objective is to breach Glint's castle. You two will stay out here and bombard those elf guards with these snowballs, while I sneak inside and get Marni."

Noel frowned. "I don't like the idea of you goin' in there alone, man. It's too dangerous."

"What else can we do? There should be enough of these..." Eldan tossed a snowball into the air and caught it deftly in his hand. "To keep the guards distracted."

"I just wish we had reinforcements." Kip told Eldan. "A few more good elves would help. Then you, Noel and I could breach Glint's castle together.

"And just where are we going to get reinforcements?"

"Look!" Noel pointed at the night sky.

They all glanced up to see a sleigh driven by several reindeer head straight toward them. A few minutes later, it touched town on the icy ground.

"Aardel, Pepper...what are you doing here?"

Pepper Minstix helped a female elf down from the sleigh.

"Eldan." She curtsied. "Hi Kip. Hi Noel."

"Erlina..." Noel shook his head. "Why are you here?"

Her little face turned pink. She crooked her finger. Noel bent his head so he could hear what she had to say.

"Pepper didn't want me to come, he said it was dangerous, but I snuck into Santa's auxiliary sleigh and hid under a blanket. I felt so bad about what I, Celyn and the other female elves did to Marni."

Noel patted her hand. "It's good you want to help Marni, but Pepper's right, you should have stayed in Christmas Town. Glint's castle is no place for ya."

"Don't worry, Noel." Pepper folded his arms across his chest. "She'll get her punishment later."

Her pink face turned crimson.

Kip leaped into the air and clicked the curled toes of his boots together. "I got my wish! Reinforcements." He shook Aardel's hand. "I'm glad you're here."

"I don't want anything to happen to Celyn and Marni."

"Marni *and* Celyn? How did Celyn get inside Glint's castle?"

Aardel folded his arms across his chest. "Celyn and I have come to an understanding."

"Ah." Kip held up a finger. "So the punishment went well, I take it?"

Aardel's face fell. "Sort of. I told her that things wouldn't be right between us unless Celyn made it right between her and Marni. Celyn took it to heart and ran off to find Marni and apologize. Now, she's Glint's prisoner, too."

Kip clapped Aardel on the back. "Don't worry, we'll get them both out."

Eldan smiled. His first since Marni left Christmas Town.

"Reinforcements. Well, jingle my bells. Kip, it looks like all of your holiday wishes are being granted this season."

"I guess I'm just a lucky, little elf." Kip grinned.

* * * *

"Ohhhhhhhhhh, Marni, there's spiders down here in this dungeon." Celyn huddled close to Marni's side. "And I'm freezing."

Marni tossed her fur jacket across Celyn's shoulders, lifting the collar around her neck.

"But you'll be cold." Celyn's teeth chattered.

"I'll be fine."

Marni glanced at the windows lining the walls. They were too small for even Celyn to crawl through. The walls were too high to climb.

Despair washed over her.

She beat it back, knowing any bad feelings would provide Glint with the edge he needed.

"There has to be a way out of here."

She drummed her fingers against the wall, but pulled her hand away when she made contact with something slimy.

"I've got it!"

"What?" Celyn shivered, despite the fur jacket.

"Slimy walls...hmmmmmmm...slimy little male guard elves. They should be easy to trick, and I've got one heck of an idea."

"I-I'm w-willing to try anything at this point."

Marni walked over to the door. "Oh Guard! Mister Elf Guard." She batted her eyes. "We need to use the facilities."

A beady-eyed elf sentry peeked through the small opening on the door.

In the next instant, it opened.

Marni stuck out her size 'C' breasts, lowering the collar of her tunic.

The elf's eyes widened.

She poked him in the eyes with two fingers.

"Arghhhhhhhhhhhhhhhh!" He fell back against the wall.

"Come on Celyn!"

They took off at breakneck speed, running down the hall.

Only to collide with Glint and two other elves.

"Going somewhere?" He grasped her shoulders. "But you haven't tried my Kleeber chocolate mint elf cookies."

"Let me go!" She struggled in his grasp.

One of the other guards grabbed Celyn.

She screamed at the top of her lungs.

"Stop that infernal screeching!" Glint clapped his hands over his pointy ears.

She kept at it, stopping only to take a breath. Elbowing Marni in the ribs, she told her. "Join in anytime. Elves can't stand the sound of loud noises. It hurts their ears."

Marni rolled her eyes. "More elf folklore?"

Celyn grinned. "You bet."

They yelled together.

Suddenly, there was a commotion in the hall. Several guards fought off three tall elves and a short, muscular one...

"Eldan!" Marni cried. "Kip! Noel! We're here!"

Celyn called out when she saw one of Glint's evil elves take a swing at Aardel. "Aardel! Oh, Aardel, be careful."

Marni watched the four elves battle Glint's guards, feeling helpless. They dodged blows from the evil elves' clubs.

She hated feeling powerless.

While Eldan fought off one guard, another raised a club over his head.

"You leave him alone!"

She ran for the guard, leaping onto his back.

Celyn joined in the fracas when one of the guards punched Aardel.

Marni beat on the guard's head.

"Don't you dare hurt these elves! I love them."

Suddenly, they stopped fighting.

The guard tossed her from his back. She landed on the stone floor—on her butt.

"What did you say?"

She scrambled to her feet. "You heard me, I said I love them."

Glint's guards scratched their heads. "Love?"

"Idiots!" Glint strode over to them. "Lock them all in the dungeon."

Not one of his guards moved.

"I had no idea they loved each other." Glint's guard shook his head.

Glint rolled his eyes. "Love stinks."

Celyn lifted her chin. She hugged Aardel around the waist. "Love is beautiful."

Glint turned to the guards behind him. "Get them! Now," he growled.

They shook their heads. "They're way too cheery. Isn't there some kind of elf rule that says if you harm a cheery person during the holidays, you'll get coal in your stocking?"

Glint rolled his eyes. "Don't be ridiculous. That's elf nonsense."

"It's true!" Marni piped in. "If you get Santa mad, he'll do a lot more than put coal in your stockings.

"You work for Santa?" One of the guards asked.

"You bet." Kip stated.

The guards walked over and stood behind them.

"So do we!"

"You idiots!" Glint stomped his feet. "You work for me, not Santa!"

"Not anymore!" Eldan growled low in his throat.

He balled his hand into a fist and did a very un-elflike thing: he punched Glint right in the nose.

Hopefully, Santa would forgive him.

Epilogue

"...and so, the elves worked together to rebuild Santa's Toy Shop, each lending their own unique talents to the job. They finished in time for Christmas, enabling Santa to deliver toys to children all over the world."

Marni closed the book then cuddled against Eldan's chest. He wrapped an arm around her, pulling her close. She snuggled next to him, her clit pulsing each time he played with the tips of her breasts.

"Did you like the story?" She reached up to stroke his face.

"Yes. The children will like it, too."

"Maybe I can read it to them the next time we visit them in the hospital."

Noel lay next to her, his fingers threading through her hair, massaging her head. Beneath the covers, he stroked her pussy, his fingers teasing her little bud. Each pass of his hand made her wet—her need for release building.

"You've got quite a gift for the written word, lass."

She beamed with pleasure—and pride.

Kip stretched out at her feet. He massaged each one, lifting her big toe to suck it gently into his mouth. She gasped when his long tongue slipped between her big toe and the one next to it.

Her body ignited.

She shifted against Eldan, allowing Noel to stroke her back and butt. He slipped a finger inside her ass, giving her that wonderfully full feeling.

Playful Kip.

He dipped his head under the covers. She lifted the sheet to see the top of his head. When his lips teased her bud, her clit throbbed, begging for release.

"Ohhhhhhhhhhhhhhhh."

Noel removed his finger, filling her backside with his shaft.

Eldan rolled to his side, watching his friends work their holiday magic on Marni.

Then he took her, sliding his cock inside, bringing her, and him, to orgasm.

"You're a wonderful holiday present, lass." Noel grinned.

Kip winked. "A sweet holiday treat."

"I love you." Eldan said softly.

Her eyes filled with happy tears.

"We all love you, Marni." Kip and Noel said in unison.

"And I love the three of you."

She'd received the best Christmas gift of all: one simple wish, just...

The Elves and I.

About the Author

Catrina Calloway adores writing romance, and her motto is: 'Two, hot, hunky heroes are better than one.' Born in Alaska, the land of the midnight sun, and now currently residing in New York, Catrina was an avid reader of romance for many years before penning her first erotic ménage romance story, 'Eight Erotic Nights.' Catrina loves to hear from her readers and fans so please feel free to email her at: www.myspace.com/catrinacalloway

Red Garters, Snow and Mistletoe Tales

Available at Resplendence Publishing

Unwrap Me, I'm Yours by **Demi Alex**

Hope Verdetti lies to her mother about having a phenomenal fiancé who surprises her on a trip to Vegas. Now her family expects him to come home with her for the holidays. She needs a man that fits the bill—and fast!

After seven interviews with hired, handsome applicants in three days, she finds her solution in the neighborhood coffee shop. Sexy and irresistible Jon Edwards volunteers for the task, having an agenda of his own.

With their holiday agreement set, Jon turns up the heat and gives Hope the present of her life…himself.

Red Ribbons and Blue Balls by **Tia Fanning**

After Nicolas punishes her for being naughty, the usually nice but now sexually-frustrated Winter arrives at their secluded mountain cabin bearing gifts—special gifts that will ensure his submission and her revenge.

With only seven days left until Christmas, Nicolas expects to spend the night decorating the house for the approaching holiday, but Winter has other plans…

Christmas might be coming, but if Winter gets her way, Nicolas won't be.

Nice and Naughty by Mia Jae

Cassie Franklin has to prove herself. After all, she's the first female head of the English department at the university. But that doesn't mean she has to prove herself sexually to Eric Marsh, a fellow professor in the English department, does it?

Then there is Ryan. Strong and sexy, with hands that can ease away the tension of most any job, he almost makes her forget her risky escapades with Eric.

Until Cassie realizes that Ryan and Eric have a closer connection than she ever could have imagined, and they have very specific plans for her...

Eight Erotic Nights by Catrina Calloway

The holiday season is a time for joy, but Laney Taylor couldn't be more depressed. She's selling the last piece of her grandmother's exquisite antique china to feed the hordes of 'new' homeless living in their cars in an abandoned parking lot on the outskirts of town. But on the way to the shop, an accident lands her in the hospital—and into the arms of the two hot, hunky Samaritans who saved her life.

Josh Goldman and Zach Brenner share a successful construction business, and a secret longing. They can't believe their good fortune when they save Laney Taylor from a freezing to death. Both men have desired Laney since high school, and made a pact that if they ever had the chance to have a relationship with the sexy, full-figured woman of their dreams, they wouldn't mind sharing.

When a winter storm gives Josh and Zach an opportunity to share the pleasures of the 'festival of lights' with Laney, and a chance to fulfill their long-held erotic fantasies, they can hardly believe the good fortune the Hanukkah holiday has brought them. While fate and circumstance may require their eventual separation, all three are determined that they will not waste a moment of their...

Eight Erotic Nights.

Handcuffs and Lace

Resplendence Publishing's Erotic Romance Line of Law Enforcement Themed Stories

Ticket Me More by **Tia Fanning**

Hailed by the bridal flower world as an artistic genius, Meli works long nights making bouquets for women lucky enough to find love, while she herself lives a life of solitude. She yearns to share her heart and body with someone other than Bob, her *Battery Operated Boyfriend*, but acute shyness keeps her from engaging the "living" world.

However, Meli's quiet and predictable existence takes an unexpected turn when she is pulled over and ticketed by the most gorgeous cop she has ever encountered—Officer Michael Johnson. Though he doesn't seem to notice her as anything more than a traffic violation, Meli makes plans to overcome her timid nature and seize the police officer's attention…using any speed necessary.

Cuff Me Lacy by **Demi Alex**

Three months is way too long to wait for some simple, low-down, straight forward sex. It's not like Officer Chrissie Hansen is asking for prince charming to offer her the love of a lifetime. All she wants is a good orgasm that she doesn't have to work for alone.

At least with "The Bull" she knows what to expect. But when Patrick MacKlick returns to her life and tempts her with new options, she discovers that lace can imprison a heart better than handcuffs can.

Search Me Baby, One More Time by **Melinda Barron**

Wren Thornberry's life isn't going according to plan. She let her father talk her out of marrying Bryan Stockard, the man she loves, and moved halfway around the world. Now she's back home in Texas, babysitting her grandmother while grandma and her boy-toy work through their list of sexual exploits, making themselves the talk of the town.

But what Wren doesn't know is that things in her hometown are about to heat up even more, and it will have nothing to do with her grandmother. It seems that Bryan Stockard is still around, he wants to get back into Wren's life—by any means necessary, and now he has just the tools to do it: A police uniform, handcuffs, and the authority to make Wren *assume the position.*

What the Cuff? By **Celia Kyle**

God really should have reconsidered making werewolves. That, or Lyssa needed to get better taste in men and stay away from those with wandering eyes—and other things. Drunk as a wolf, she stumbles to her best friend's house to sleep off her whiskey induced haze and wakes to… *cuffs?*

Caleb sees his chance and takes it. His buddies on the force ribbed him but good for buying silver plated cuffs. But with a werewolf in his bed, the woman he's yearned for since they were teens, he wasn't taking any chances. Lyssa was his. She just didn't know it yet.

Going Commando by **Catherine Chernow**

Bounty hunter Shyra Lawrence listens to her favorite radio station one morning where the DJ's are discussing "going commando" —*a.k.a* wearing no undies. Captivated by their conversation, she decides to shed her panties in favor of the freedom that wearing no underwear brings.

Enthusiastic, Shyra sends an email to her best friend, Donna, detailing the delights of panty-freedom, but unbeknownst to Shyra, she's hit the send key...to the wrong email addy!

When Derek Grayson opens his emails that morning, he discovers that his #1 employee and top bounty hunter, Shyra Lawrence, has sent him an erotic, enticing message about going commando. Derek has always been polite, professional, and so damned attracted to Shyra that it's almost painful. Working day in and day out with voluptuous woman has sent Derek's hormones into overdrive on more than one occasion.

Now, Shyra's shed her panties and Derek's got all he can do to contain his lust when she announces that she's... GOING COMMANDO.

Handcuffs and Lies by **Bronwyn Green**

Sometimes promises to friends are the hardest to keep. Undercover police officer, Michael Tanner, promised his dying partner that he'd take care of the man's little sister.

Trouble is, after her brother's death, Doctor Tori Spinelli wants nothing to do with Michael—or any other cop for that matter.

Tori has always fought against overprotective men and deception. Forced into protective custody with Michael, she's now faced with both in the same package. Despite their differences, Tori falls in love with him, but how can she trust a man who lies for a living?

Find Resplendence titles at the following retailers:

Resplendence Publishing
www.ResplendencePublishing.com

Amazon
www.Amazon.com

Barnes and Noble
www.BarnesandNoble.com

Target
www.Target.com

Fictionwise
www.Fictionwise.com

All Romance E-Books
www.AllRomanceEbooks.com

Mobipocket
www.Mobipocket.com

Made in the USA
Lexington, KY
17 November 2013